OCEAN OF *Regret*

OCEAN OF *Regret*

Restored

Part 1

Mary E. Hanks

www.maryehanks.com

Suzanne D. Williams Cover Design
www.feelgoodromance.com

Cover photos: micromonkey @ Fotolia & satamedia @ iStock

Author photo: Ron Quinn

Visit Mary's website:

www.maryehanks.com

You can write Mary at
maryhanks@maryehanks.com.

For Brice,

A sweet brother, a man of God, and one of the good guys.

For Jason,

Always for you. My hero.

Restore me,

and I will return,

because you are

the Lord my God.

Jeremiah 31:18

Author's note:

I've taken many creative liberties in this story—all I can say is, "That's the way it happened in Basalt Bay!"

Basalt Bay Residents

Paisley Grant – Daughter of Paul and Penny Cedars

Judah Grant – Son of Edward and Bess Grant

Paige Cedars – Paisley's younger sister/mom to Piper

Peter Cedars – Paisley' older brother/fishing in Alaska

Paul Cedars – Paisley's dad/widower

Edward Grant – Mayor of Basalt Bay/Judah's dad

Bess Grant – Judah's mom/Edward's wife

Aunt Callie – Paisley's aunt/Paul's sister

Maggie Thomas – owner of Beachside Inn

Bert Jensen – owner of Bert's Fish Shack

Mia Till – receptionist at C-MER

Craig Masters – Judah's supervisor at C-MER

Mike Linfield – Judah's boss at C-MER

Lucy Carmichael – Paisley's high school friend

Brian Corbin – Sheriff's deputy

Kathleen Baker – newcomer to Basalt Bay

Bill Sagle – pastor

Geoffrey Carnegie – postmaster/local historian

Casey Clemons – floral shop owner

Patty Lawton – hardware store owner

Brad Keifer – fisherman/school chum of Peter's

James Weston – Paul's neighbor

Sal Donovan – souvenir shop owner

Penny Cedars – Paisley's mom/deceased

One

Paisley Grant steered her Honda Accord back into the right lane after passing a white pickup on Highway 12 that looked oddly familiar. Wait. Was that Judah's truck? She stared hard into the rearview mirror, focusing on the male driver in the vehicle behind her. No, the guy with the beard was probably in his fifties, not thirty-three and clean-shaven like Judah. What a relief. Besides, at this time of day he'd be working in Basalt Bay, Oregon. Right?

Her rapid heartbeat settled down, but the idea of spotting her ex-husband in the middle of Washington State, on the same day she was passing through, sent her brain into a tizzy. Especially considering three years ago, she wrote Judah a Dear John letter, then left town. In all these years she hadn't contacted him, either—that was selfish, she realized now. He didn't deserve such treatment. Neither did Dad.

She felt the weight of her mistakes all the way down to her toes. But at the time, fleeing from Basalt Bay was the only way to break free from her crushing grief. Other reasons too. But they all boiled down to one thing—her feelings for Judah Grant had turned stone cold.

After four years of marriage, the passion of love, dreams, and even conflicts, withered and dried up like kelp stranded on the beach after high tide. What good was fighting with her husband when nothing mattered? When she didn't care? And in not caring, in her empty dissatisfied existence, she sought out something—*anything*—to make her feel again.

She made her share of mistakes. Swore never to return to Basalt Bay, located twenty miles north of Florence, on the Oregon Coast. Yet, here she was driving toward the Pacific Ocean. Another blunder? Maybe. If only she'd had a clue that going back someday would be as painful as leaving in the first place, she might not have fled. Then again, she may have run away sooner.

On the fateful night of her exodus, nothing could have stopped her. No sage advice anchored her to a town of gossips who despised her, or to a husband who didn't understand her. No light in the window coaxed her to return to the house where the evidence of too many mistakes lined the walls. Oh, if walls could talk, they'd have a tale to tell.

The things she said and did in her haste to make her callous heart beat as it once had were irreversible. However, maybe, just maybe, in the days ahead she might be able to make amends with those she hurt—even if it killed her. And she thought it might.

She inhaled deeply, longing for the first scent of sea air she took for granted for twenty-five years and craved since leaving the ocean. Still a hundred miles inland, she didn't smell anything yet, but she would soon.

She'd already been on the road for four days—minus gas stops, a few daytime naps at rest areas, and three nights of less-than-satisfactory sleep at the cheapest motels—since emptying her studio apartment in Chicago and heading west. Three years ago, she chose the Windy City because it was far from home, and big enough for a woman on the run to get lost in. However, four days ago, she didn't feel the least bit sad leaving the 300-square-foot shoebox she lived in, or driving away from the place where, to make ends meet, she worked as a stocker in a grocery store by day and a server in a diner by night. She mostly kept to herself. Because if anyone asked questions or pried into her past, then she would have been forced to face things she didn't want to think about.

Like now, and for most of her solitary drive across seven states, especially the bazillion miles of flatland traversing Montana, her thoughts were as tumultuous as the breakers along Oregon's coastline. The closer she got to Basalt Bay, and its 1,150 residents, the more anxiety she felt. The more questions churned in her mind.

After all this time, how can I face Judah?

What will Dad say?

What have the town gossips concocted about me in my absence?

Will Paige even speak to me?

With each question her heart pounded harder in her chest, reminding her she *was* more alive now, no longer dead to her emotions like before she left Basalt. Still, passing milepost after milepost, she fought a primal instinct to turn her car around. To disappear again. To forget the past, with its truths and its lies, that ate at her conscience like a relentless seagull—even though she tried hard to bury it beneath two thousand miles, two jobs, and no one knowing where she was for three years.

Good thing she ditched her cell phone when she moved east. Her family hadn't been able to call and tell her they were ashamed of her. Or demand that she come home, grow up, and face her responsibilities. Which she wouldn't have done. Not for Dad. Nor for meddlesome Aunt Callie. And not for Judah—her ex in every sense of the word other than by law.

As her purple car gobbled up miles along Highway 12, the difficulties she fled from in Basalt weighed upon her. She had to remind herself not to dwell on past mistakes. Those thoughts were dangerous. Toxic. So she stuffed guilt and regret deep inside where all her other mistakes were stored.

Blasting country music on the radio, she sang along loudly, then recited the Pledge of Allegiance, the Twenty-Third Psalm, her wedding vows—more hazardous thoughts—to keep her mind occupied. Still, internal pictures of those she failed, and devastated, wouldn't stop flashing an endless slideshow.

If only she could start over. Do something differently. But what? Never marry? Follow her brother Peter to Alaska? Try harder to get along with Mom? Too late for any of that.

The image of two graves—one large, one small—twisted something tight in her chest. Stole the air right out of the car. Uh-oh. Why did she allow her thoughts to run amuck? Her breathing felt devoid of oxygen. Her hands shook. *Not now. Please!* She sucked in dry, unsatisfying air and hit the steering wheel, hating the precursors to an attack.

She scratched at the strangling sensation in her throat. Yanked at her t-shirt neckband, trying to make it bigger. She lowered the window and inhaled. A breeze scented with pines brushed her cheeks but didn't cool the rising temperature of her skin.

Apprehension roiled inside her, but she was determined to keep driving. If she focused on the road and clung to the steering wheel, this incident would pass the same way others had.

Then, like a victim stuck in a whirlpool, thrashing around in water to save her life, negative thoughts and fears dragged her down to a dark place where exercising normal respiration became almost impossible. Where her heart thundered in her temples. When this awful feeling came over her in Chicago, she couldn't look anyone in the eye—as if every stranger on the Red Line "L" knew things about her she didn't want anyone to know.

Hadn't she left Basalt to find privacy? To grieve alone? That, and a million other reasons, repressed her breathing now, made her feel like someone held a pillow over her mouth.

A familiar pile of bricks pressed down on her chest, constricting her lungs, and muddying her thoughts.

Ungrateful daughter—the last words her mother said to her.

You were a terrible wife—what she often told herself.

Even your unborn child knew you wouldn't be a good mother—that worst assessment of all came from her father-in-law. *Horrible, horrible man.*

"I would have been a great mom!" She shouted at the rearview mirror as if it were the man's face. Then she sobbed, and a cry wrenched itself from her heart.

Why was she going back to Basalt? To a place where people believed Mayor Grant's lies? Where locals held grudges that ran canyon deep? She should have stayed in Illinois.

She slammed on the brakes, bringing the car to a stop in the middle of her empty lane. She stared at her moist dark eyes in the mirror. Saw a foggy daze in her irises. She struggled to catch her breath and bring her emotions under control. When a car approached from behind, she engaged the gas pedal again. She'd pull over in a minute if this black cloud didn't pass.

After driving two thousand miles west, returning to Chicago wasn't an option. She couldn't stop here in the mountains. But did she want to face the people back home?

She shuddered. Her hands shook where she held them against the steering wheel. The muscles in her esophagus tightened, threatening to cut off her oxygen. "Oh, God, h-help me." She didn't pray much in the last four years, held onto a few grudges of her own, but lately she talked to Him a little. Especially when her throat clenched, making her think she might die. Although she didn't know if He listened to her desperate prayers.

The instant relief she wished for didn't come. Her heart hammered double-time against her ribs. Her breathing turned shallow and hoarse. Would she pass out like she did a couple of times before?

"One." *Inhale.* "T-two." *Exhale.* "Th-three." Sometimes counting helped sidetrack her long enough to catch a breath. Not happening this time.

She banked the vehicle right, almost oversteering into the ditch. Her car came to a thudding stop on the shoulder. Slumping against the door on the driver's side, she sought a momentary respite. Who would come to her rescue along this mountainous stretch of highway? She drew in a puny amount of air. Hot tears filled her eyes. Her heart throbbed in her ears. She clutched her chest. Was she having a heart attack? At twenty-eight years old?

Would she die alone? Without making things right with Dad? Or Judah? Her body trembled with cold, then burned with an internal fire.

Breathe.

I can't!

Why did she choose this inland route? Highway 84 along the Columbia River would have been faster. Emergency vehicles could reach her quicker—if she had a cell phone to use. She probably should have gotten a new one in Chicago, but she didn't want anyone to find her.

A truck blasted by. Had she even turned on her flashers? Her fingers fumbled to find the button that would turn on the hazard lights.

She took in short breaths. Coughed.

Someone might assume she was having an asthma attack, but the doctor at the last hospital said she wasn't. He labeled it a panic attack, probably due to a crisis or something she hadn't faced—a *lame* diagnosis. What did he know about her life, or whether she needed to face something?

What she needed now was to flag down a vehicle. Someone who'd call 911 for her. But for several long minutes no cars passed. Where were the trucks blasting exhaust when she needed one?

Then she remembered something she brought, just in case. She stretched out her hand toward the backseat and flailed around under some blankets. Her fingers clutched a folded lunch bag. She pulled the paper to her mouth, forcing herself to breathe into the balloon-shaped bag. With each in and out breath, the paper made a crinkling sound.

She shut her eyes, then opened them slowly.

Find five things of beauty—one of the tricks she practiced during other attacks. Five things seemed like too many items to list when she couldn't breathe. Maybe that was the point.

Inhaling and exhaling into the squashed bag, she peered out the windshield.

Ponderosa Pines.

Mt. Rainier.

Beautiful blue sky.

Inhale. Exhale.

An RV with a painting of a smiling cougar sped past her in the left lane—didn't stop.

Did she hear a bird calling?

There. Five things.

Her chest didn't burn as it did before. Cool air seeped back into her lungs, reminding her of a waterfall pouring into a dried-up creek bed. The terror lessened.

Sighing with relief and exhaustion, she tossed the bag into the back—near enough to grab again, if necessary. She switched off the hazard lights and stared at her blotchy face in the rearview mirror. Wiped mascara smudges from her cheeks.

That was close. Way too close.

For the last year, panic was the scary monster under her bed. The unconquerable thing no matter how many beautiful items she acknowledged. The psychologist she finally agreed to see last month said there were reasons for her episodes. *Obviously.* But contemplating unhappy details caused more attacks which made her more fearful. So pondering her past—Paige, Peter, Mom, Dad, Judah, Aunt Callie, and others in Basalt—was off-limits.

Right. Her self-imposed rule didn't help. The episodes got worse, forcing her decision to head home.

Yet, how could she talk to family members and townspeople, or heaven forbid, confront them, without experiencing the grand-daddy of all panic attacks? She'd end up in the hospital in Florence, south of Basalt. Or dead. Although, the doctor assured her that wouldn't happen. A lot he knew about how she felt during a panic attack.

She took a deep breath, then exhaled. To reach her home-town by dusk, when the tourist shops were closed and the beach empty, and still be able to see the ocean, she had to get back on the road. If all went well, she'd slip into town without any locals seeing her.

She steered her Accord onto the highway and lectured herself. For the next two hundred fifty miles, en route to the ocean and then down the Oregon Coast Highway, she was going to focus on driving. *No* dwelling on the past. *No* thinking of awkward conversations to come.

Instead, she would imagine her favorite place in all the world—Basalt Bay Peninsula. As soon as she arrived, she was going to jog out to the farthest point of land protruding into the Pacific, drop down on the boulder jutting into the water, and listen to the crashing waves. Feel the sea spray cascading over her. Breathe in all the damp salty air her lungs needed.

She'd be home.

Maybe that would be healing enough.

If only.

Two

Judah Grant clutched the steering wheel of the company's sixteen-foot open-air skiff as he maneuvered through hammering rain and robust currents off Basalt Bay. He could almost follow this route blindfolded—although his supervisor, Craig Masters, and their boss, Mike Linfield, wouldn't condone such unsafe practices. During his eleven years at Coastal Management and Emergency Responders, commonly called C-MER, he'd driven a skiff along the coastline hundreds of times. Although, today's boat ride was choppier than usual. At least his rain jacket and bib overalls beneath his life vest kept him dry.

Due to the current poor visibility, he was on the lookout for chunks of driftwood or one of the more peculiar items—ice chests, patio furniture, bicycle tires—he'd seen floating in the surf during other high winds. However, he couldn't worry about floating debris too much; he had an important job to perform.

For the last month, ever since hurricane winds barreled up the coastline from the waters of southern Mexico all the way to Portland, Oregon, shocking meteorologists and scientific agencies with its unprecedented strike on the western seaboard, Judah was tasked with measuring high and low tides and monitoring coastal erosion in the Basalt Bay vicinity. The violent storm known as "Hurricane Addy" slammed the seaside town with eight-foot tidal surges, combined with a super tide and heavy rains, and took out a house-sized chunk of land next to the public beach. Since then, C-MER was gathering information and watching for warnings of any other potential storms.

Even now, C-MER employees were paying close attention to a tropical storm developing in the same region that Addy did, just in case it made its way north. Hopefully, it would fizzle and disappear into the sea the same as a plethora of storms had in the past.

Judah's mission to keep the residents of Basalt Bay safe usually helped him stay focused on the job. Today, with the three-year anniversary of Paisley leaving him and the four-year anniversary of the birth of their stillborn daughter approaching, he might have a harder time keeping personal thoughts at bay.

Still, he forced himself to concentrate on last month's storm that caused substantial damage to some of the beachfront buildings. During the apex of Addy, beached logs floated with the high tide and, propelled by strong waves, rammed into shops built on pilings, broke through windows, crashed down doors, even walls. Hundreds of thousands of dollars in damages were reported in the touristy section near the waterfront. Casey Clemons's Floral, Basalt Bay's only flower shop, was forced to close.

Paige's Art Gallery and Coffee Shop, his wife's sister's business, sustained the worst damage of all the buildings that were victims of the storm. Almost irreparable. Such a shame. Paige had high hopes for restoring her investment, but at some point it wouldn't be worth her throwing more money into it. Not that he'd say that to her.

Although, he would be surprised if Callie Cedars, Paisley's aunt on her father Paul's side, hadn't already spoken to Paige about it. Callie, with her short-cropped salt-and-pepper hair and rotund physique, was known around town for dishing out unsolicited advice. Woe to the person who got in her headlights of criticism. Judah grimaced as he thought of a few of his own encounters with the woman's "words of wisdom."

He steered the skiff around a nearly submerged log, and his thoughts returned to his sister-in-law's plight. Paige was a strong, determined woman. Her mother's death, Paisley's desertion, and an unexpected pregnancy hadn't knocked her down. He doubted the aftermath of Addy would keep her down, either. But if rumors were true—although he tried not to listen to the gossipmongers at Bert's Fish Shack—Paige lost her financial battle thanks to the bank refusing to loan her the money she needed.

He hoped his father, Mayor Edward Grant, an investor in the locally-owned bank, didn't have anything to do with such a decision. Maybe he'd ask Dad. Not that the two of them were on chatty terms—not since Judah married Paisley Cedars against his father's wishes. Old history that still irked him.

Mercy and grace, he reminded himself. *Lord, help me.*

If Judah had the resources, he'd fund Paige's project himself. The town needed the art gallery for local artisans to display their work. Unfortunately, his beachfront cottage on the south side of town was also damaged during the storm, although not to the same degree as his sister-in-law's building. But still, at his slower-than-a-slug repair rate, he'd be remodeling for the next year. Unless he sold it "as is."

A knot twisted in his gut.

A wave surged up the shore on the portside of the skiff, then swirled back toward him as if eating up every shell and pebble on the narrow stretch of beach—similar to how discouragement had eaten him up lately. He groaned.

A child playing alone near the surf on the next small stretch of beach caught his attention. He slowed down the skiff's speed and scanned the area. A woman stepped out of a red car in the parking lot and yelled at the kid, motioning the boy toward her. Good. The currents were too unpredictable here for any child to play unattended.

Judah resumed his charted course paralleling the shoreline, his thoughts returning to his damaged home. Maybe he needed a fresh start. Ever since last month's powerful storm, he'd pondered selling the two-bedroom sea-level cottage. Without Paisley, he didn't have the heart to put the effort into rebuilding their dream house. But selling? Wouldn't that be driving the final nail in the coffin of their marriage?

He groaned again.

Hadn't his wife leaving him three years ago done just that?

No one in Basalt Bay would blame him for selling. Not after Paisley left him a Dear John letter and then never contacted him again. Terrible way to leave a man.

He wiped rain water, maybe a few tears, from his face. He knew better than to regurgitate past problems during work hours. Especially when he was in a skiff in lousy weather. He stared forward, focusing on the sea swells in front of him.

A couple of seconds passed before he realized in his mind's eye he was seeing that crumpled-up note at the bottom of his bedside drawer. *I don't love you. There's someone else. Always has been. You should get on with your life . . . without me. Paisley*

Lies. A man knew whether a woman loved him or not. His wife *had* loved him, at least in the beginning. Yeah, things soured. But he figured she said that garbage about another guy to keep Judah from following her.

It worked too. For a while. Until he got his head back on straight.

Before he married Paisley, he was certain he couldn't live without her. That they *had* to be together, no matter the cost to them or their families. Without parental support or approval, they disregarded the traditional route and eloped. Happy and free, they thought. And, man oh man, when she was finally his wife, to have and to hold, talk about heaven. Bittersweet memories.

The last three years proved his theory false. He was surviving without her—although a lonely existence.

He steered clear of Beachhead Point, a protrusion of boulders surrounded by wooden pilings to keep boats from ramming into the mass. As he passed the orange flag marking the farthest point of the bulk submerged beneath the water, for some reason he recalled Paisley's accusation that he had a cold shoulder toward her, that he didn't care about her—something he denied. But after much inner contemplation, and considering how things turned out, there was a chance she might have been right. He probably inherited from his father the character flaw of drawing into himself and shutting out the world. Not that he wanted to compare himself to his dad.

However, that same withdrawing into himself may have given him the strength to face life without Paisley. To cope on some level other than feeling sorry for himself and being angry with her all the time. Even so, after a thousand days to ponder all they went through, he'd do things differently, given the chance.

Even if the gossips' tales swirling around town were true?

Agitation gripped his gut every time he thought of the rumors. Of the possibility that Paisley left town with another man. Combined with her note, the stories caused him a lot of sleepless nights. He prayed harder than ever. Cried his share of tears.

But when folks accused her of criminal activity—starting a fire in the mayor's office, trashing the library, and stealing from Miss Patty's Hardware—he had enough. Paisley wouldn't do those things. And if she didn't commit those crimes, she probably didn't leave with a stranger, either. He even stood up for her during an ugly town meeting—which probably made his mayoral father resent him even more.

As Judah approached the peninsula jutting into the waves ahead, he slowed down the engine. Thoughts of the childish term Paisley had called the mostly-basalt, rocky outcropping—Peter's Land, after her brother—came to mind. What would Judah's father think of such a pseudonym for a segment of the town's defining coastline? Edward Grant didn't approve of topics he deemed foolish. Or of a son who didn't live up to his expectations.

Judah's sigh felt dredged from beneath his ribs. Enough thoughts of Dad. And Paisley. He had work to do.

As he rounded the tip of Basalt Bay Peninsula, a sputtering from the engine surprised him. Did he run over something? He listened to the hum of the motor. Steadier now. He peered around the exterior of the boat. Didn't see anything afloat. Must have been a fluke.

He grabbed his binoculars with his left hand, still steering with the fingers of his right hand curled around the steering wheel and peered through the lenses toward the shoreline. After Addy hit, he noted some deterioration of the soil on the north side of the peninsula. After that, he labeled five of the largest boulders on the outcropping of land—Sample A, Sample B, etc., starting on the ocean side—so he could keep accurate notations.

Wait a sec. He fixed his gaze upon the high rocks midway back from the point. Something was different. Had the five-foot boulder he labeled Sample D shifted? It couldn't have. Yet, today, it appeared angled in a northerly direction. Odd. Was movement of such a giant boulder possible? Due to the storm? Or because winds from the south had increased significantly this fall?

Maybe his eyes were playing tricks on him. He squeezed his eyelids shut, then opened them and peered through the binoculars. Same result. Sample D had moved! A possible danger. A disaster if the sand beneath the boulder was undercut and gave way. What if a kid climbed the rock—as he did many times as a child—and the stone shifted? Tragedy might follow.

Not on his watch. He'd go ashore after his rounds. If nothing else, he'd wrap yellow warning tape around the rock until a work crew from C-MER inspected it. He shifted gears to forward and made a lazy turn, then aligned the boat parallel with the shoreline, his gaze at attention with the possibility of seeing anything else amiss.

Up ahead, he saw Baker's Point, where the gazebo was smashed to pieces during Addy. For decades, that picnic area was a local favorite for marriage proposals, birth announcements, and other celebrations. Folks in Bert's Fish Shack were already bombarding him with questions about when the structure might be rebuilt, as if he had any say in the matter. Maybe they thought he had connections with the mayor. Fat chance.

He steered into the next wave, veering the skiff away from his favorite landmark—Mountain Peak Rock, a gigantic basalt monolith only accessible at low tide. For a moment, he pictured Paisley and him exploring the giant rock, holding hands, telling each other their dreams and secrets. Stealing kisses. Man, he'd missed the closeness and camaraderie with her for so long now. Ached with longing for it.

The skiff's engine sputtered. Then died.

Judah groaned and turned the key for the starter. Nothing but silence, except for the sounds of the wind and the waves smacking against the skiff.

Without power, the boat jarred into the next wave, rattling his teeth. He tensed as another swell crashed into the starboard side, rocking him crazily. A second wave hit the skiff broadside, sending water spraying over the helm and drenching him. *Oh, man.*

Standing, rocking, trying to remain centered and balanced, he grabbed the top edge of the seat so he wouldn't be knocked into the sea as he made his way to the outboard engine at the stern.

The next incoming wave plunged the skiff toward shore, sending sea-foam arcing over him. He spit out a mouthful of salty water. His heart racing triple-time, he tried anticipating the next wave strike. He hadn't been in a stalled skiff in years. As the rolling waves rushed out to sea, dragging the skiff with it, the boat careened straight toward Mountain Peak Rock. Dangerously close. Next time, he could be crushed against the massive monolith.

He yanked on the manual pull cord protruding from the engine cover. Nothing happened except an empty clattering of parts as he pulled, but no ignition. The engine couldn't be out of gas—he checked before leaving the dock.

Rain fell harder. Water pelted his face and rushed down his coat and rain pants. An incoming wave rammed the side of the skiff, almost lifting it out of the ocean, throwing him to the side.

"God, h-help." He coughed out the words that came to his mind.

He grabbed the oars. Powerful waves beat against the boat, pointing the bow east, then north. All it would take was one giant wave to sink him. He was a good swimmer, but fighting a raging current? That was another thing altogether. He wouldn't lose the boat if saving it were an option. He plunked the oars into the oarlocks as a three-foot wave sloshed over the side, partially filling the small craft.

Judah grabbed a plastic container attached to the bench with a cord and bailed water fast. His efforts seemed futile. Water was coming in faster than going out. Another wave. He didn't have time to brace for it. After it left him facing the wrong direction, he dropped the bucket, grabbed hold of the wet oars that were hard to hold onto, and rowed against the tidal force. Straining his muscles, he propelled the partially-filled skiff toward land, praying his efforts would get him to shore.

Just ahead, he had to find a way around Deadman's Reef—aptly named for dangers others faced when they got too close—but he was having a hard time seeing through the rain. Where was the safest route around the reef?

His hood had blown off, and his hair dripped water down into his eyes. No time to brush the moisture away.

A hundred yards south, he saw a sloping sandy place where picnickers sometimes spread blankets and ate meals—a good place to beach the boat.

Pull. Groan. Pull. Groan.

His shoulders ached. He growled with the effort to get the skiff past the reef and then the breakers. *God help me.*

With a final lunge, he plowed the boat through turbulent foaming white waves. But then, the front of the keel rammed into an underwater sandbar, and stuck. The abrupt stop nearly knocked him off his seat. When he saw how badly the stern plowed back and forth in the waves, almost like a pirate ship's mizzenmast caught in a hurricane, fear raced up his spine. What if the boat jerked free and flipped? If that happened, he didn't want to be in the craft.

He'd have to do the thing he never imagined doing in such rough seas, although he trained for it. He made sure his life jacket was secured, then he stepped onto the backseat of the skiff. Closing his eyes and plugging his nose with his hand, he leapt outward, tucking his legs like a cannonball jump, and landed hard in the roiling ocean. Water and sea-foam plowed over his head, submerging him, sucking him down to the ocean floor, maybe eight-feet deep. He kicked and came up sputtering and spitting.

The next wave smashed over his head and pressed his shoulders against the bobbing skiff. Part of him wanted to climb back into the boat for safety. But ignoring the cold water and the momentary terror of being thrown about by the sea, he gripped the left gunwale and kicked his boots hard in the water. With waves rolling up to his chin, he fought to stay upright and propel the skiff toward shore. Still determined to save it, he used the incoming wave's momentum and shoved with all his might.

The boat gave way and his head went under again. He came back up, spitting saltwater and kicking. Finally, his boots thudded against something solid. He pushed his soles off bottom soil, then tripped over a rock. Exhausted, and still fighting the gravitational pull of the sea toward open waters, he flailed his hands in the direction of the towrope. He missed the first time. Tried again. He grabbed hold of the rope, using his waning energy to drag the skiff toward shore. The heaving waves propelled the boat forward, but the pounding waves against his back and legs nearly took him down.

When he couldn't nudge the boat forward another inch, he struggled against the cement-like muck gluing his boots to the sea floor. Weary, and drenched beneath his raingear, he made it to shore and wrapped the towrope around a drift log. His double bowline knot would have to be sufficient. The stern bobbed back and forth in the bubbling surf. If the tide got much higher, despite his efforts, the craft might break free and be lost. Nothing more could be done now, other than calling for backup.

He unclipped his life jacket and tossed it in the skiff. His teeth chattered as water poured down his t-shirt. A blast of wind hit him, sending shivers racing over his shoulders and along his spine. He could use a blanket and a bucketful of hot coffee to fend off hypothermia.

He had to keep moving, stomping his feet, but walking in waterlogged boots was miserable. Should he hike toward town? Or head for his house in the opposite direction where he could change clothes? He should try calling the office first.

With stiff fingers he patted his coat, relieved to find his cell phone still in his pocket. Gingerly, he pulled it out and tapped the black screen with his index finger. Nothing. He pushed the fingerprint button. No blip, light, or anything.

Lord? A little help would be appreciated. He groaned at his impatience. He was alive. Thank God for that! And the boat wasn't lost—something else to be grateful for.

He'd noted his time and destination on the clipboard back at C-MER, so his coworkers knew where he went. But he wasn't expected back for another hour. He couldn't stand here, freezing, and wait for someone to come looking for him.

He gazed down the rocky beach toward the south. Mostly seasonal homes in that direction. And he didn't have a landline at his place. He'd do almost anything to get out of these wet boots, but he had a duty to perform. Two, actually. First, see to the company skiff. Then, post a warning on the rock at the peninsula.

Judah shuffled through slimy mud and wide tide pools en route to Bert's Fish Shack, the closest business from his location. His chilled legs felt like stilts. He gritted his teeth as he leaned forward, bracing into the wind and rain. At least, Bert's had coffee—a small consolation. Maybe the business owner would lend him dry clothes. He pictured Bert Jensen's response: "Playing in the water, Sonny?" Bert called him Sonny ever since Judah was a kid. It used to make his father furious. Maybe that's why Bert continued the habit. Judah almost snickered, but he was too cold.

When the peninsula came into view, he automatically perused the rocky protrusion of land and checked the unstable rock's position. *Wait.* Was someone—a woman?—sitting at the tip of the peninsula with waves splashing up on her? In such strong winds? "You've got to be kidding me."

Despite his fatigue, Judah veered away from Bert's, his boots bogging down in wet sand. If a tidal surge hit the foolish woman seated on the tip of the peninsula, he'd have to perform a rescue. "Tourists," he muttered.

The next time he glanced up, the woman's hands were extended toward the water, palms out as if welcoming the waves to hit her. He froze. Déjà vu. Only one person he knew would sit so close to the edge of Basalt Bay Peninsula in torrential rains—like she had no fear of the untamed current. As if she greeted the ocean like her dearest friend.

Paisley.

A chill that had absolutely nothing to do with his wretched condition sprinted up his spine.

Three

For about twenty minutes, Paisley had been sitting at the edge of *Peter's Land* with its swirling, foaming, crashing waves catapulting over the rocks and over her. Icy water shot up her shins, knees, and even as high as her thighs. She gasped at the shocking sensation of cold waves hitting her, but then as white spray exploded all about her, she laughed like she did as a child sitting in this exact spot.

Bigger waves imploded, and she didn't retreat. Wasn't afraid. The sea's dance mesmerized her. She tasted salt on her lips and licked it. When a more powerful wave splashed up to her stomach, she drew in a sharp breath, but didn't shuffle backwards. How had she stayed away from *her* ocean for three years?

But then, a memory from when she was young and played on the peninsula for too long crept into her thoughts. She could almost hear Mom yelling at her to get in the pantry, a dark scary place, and think about her rebellious behavior. Paisley begged Mom not to shut the door—that pondering her mistakes with the door open worked just as fine. Mom didn't listen.

Paisley shook herself. She was home now. Loved the sea. *Focus on that.*

Another wave crashed against the boulder, soaking her. She braced her feet against the basalt as water splattered up her chest and face. This time she didn't laugh. Her past was here like a living, breathing organism. Every beach and inlet held memories.

She and Judah had spent hundreds of hours walking hand in hand along these rocks, dreaming of a future together. She loved coming here with him, sharing their love of the sea. They often walked to the edge of the peninsula and kissed. Made promises. Some she'd broken.

Don't go there.

The pinched feeling twisted in her throat. Despite her icy wet condition, heat prickled up her neck. Her heart rate increased. No, no. She would not have another panic attack. She was home at Basalt Bay. She should feel amazing peace by the sea.

Except, didn't she sit on this same rock the day after her graduation debacle? Then, after the light went out of her life forever, didn't Judah find her here weeping inconsolably? She remembered how he lifted her tenderly in his arms and carried her to their car. Then, a year later, after being humiliated by her father-in-law, she sat here with guilt choking her. She thought it would be easier to disappear than to have to see the hateful man ever again, or to explain what happened to Judah. That night she wrote him the note and then drove out of town.

The good, the bad, and the ugly had been contemplated on this boulder. How could she ever let go of the past?

Four years ago, she sat here six months pregnant, whispering to her unborn daughter about the fun they were going to have running on the beach. After two previous miscarriages, Paisley prayed her third child would be born healthy and love the sea the same way her mommy and daddy and grandpa and Uncle Peter did. But Misty Gale's heart stopped beating in Paisley's womb.

31

Then her own heart broke like a clam shell dropped on stone. She couldn't fathom how a loving God allowed so many bad things to happen to her. That's when she stopped talking to Him. And drew into herself.

"The babe is in a better place," Aunt Callie told her.

What better place for a baby to be than in her mother's arms?

"It was God's will," Maggie Thomas, local innkeeper and Paisley's thorn in the flesh, said with a self-righteous sniff.

Why people said such ridiculous things to grieving mothers, she would never understand. Each time her heart hardened a little more.

Mom didn't say a word about Paisley's loss. She didn't express any grief over the death of her own grandchild. Paisley never understood that, either.

The waves rolled in and out, a perpetual motion, the sea and her past mixing together.

Her neck felt itchy. She didn't taste salt on her lips anymore. Her heart thudded an irregular beat.

Find five things of beauty.

I don't see beauty. I should leave.

She fought to breathe and swallow normally. But she stayed in the water's spray until she barely felt the cold. She gazed outward, searching for something. Anything.

A jack salmon leapt into the air, its sides glimmering in a ray of sunlight.

Whitecaps bobbed like sailboats in a tornado.

In the distance, a fishing boat.

A thin rainbow.

Mica glistened near her shoes.

She inhaled and exhaled. A wind gust blasted against her back, pressing her forward almost into the waves. She clenched her stomach muscles and planted her feet against the wet rock, resisting the pull.

She remembered how Mom wouldn't step foot in saltwater. How she said she didn't trust the currents or the creatures beneath. What did Mom think was under the water's surface? A Pacific Ocean Loch Ness Monster? How silly. Paisley and Peter didn't pay any attention to her fears, however, their sister Paige took her warnings seriously.

While Paisley and Peter spent their time running up and down the rocky beaches of Basalt Bay and swimming in the ocean every chance they got, Paige was content to sit at home and draw and paint with Mom. Paisley and Peter were the adventurous ones like Dad. Maybe that's why Peter and Mom argued so much, especially when he decided to head north to fish with Uncle Henry in Alaska, instead of going to college.

Peter didn't attend Mom's funeral, either; although, no one faulted him for his decision.

More grievances.

Another strong wind blasted against Paisley and she turned away, glanced toward the public beach. That's when she saw him— a man stomping across the sand, waving his arms. Was he yelling at her? She swept her wild-flying hair out of her eyes to see him better.

The man wore a dark green slicker drooped to his nose, and his rain pants shimmered with moisture. He kept trudging toward her. His heavy step made her think his boots must be filled with water. Had he been in a boating accident?

She stood, her legs trembling. A wave hit her at knee level, almost knocking her over. Her heart pounded as if it knew something she didn't.

The guy shoved his hood back, and startling blues pierced her gaze.

Judah.

A hitch caught in her throat.

He grimaced and waved his arms again. Yelled something.

How did he find out she was in Basalt? She didn't want to see him today. She needed to get her bearings first. Then figure out how to explain. Could she outrun him to her car?

Although, one glimpse of his sapphire eyes set her heart on fire with something she hadn't felt in four years. Not love . . . but something.

"I promise to love you 'til the end of time"—her wedding vow rushed through her thoughts.

Suddenly, she was desperate for air. She sucked in a long draw of unsatisfying oxygen. A searing pain burned up her chest. "I c-can't bre—" Judah turned blurry. The sea disappeared. From raspy breaths to no air in five seconds, this attack hit her swift and hard.

She dropped to her knees on the ocean-drenched rocks, clutching two stone protrusions as waves slammed against her, nearly forcing her into the water. She fought for her next breath. For life, it seemed.

"He—" She tried to say, "Help!" She reached out her hand toward Judah. Did he see she was in distress? Needed him?

Concern crisscrossed his face. Then he was running. Climbing rocks. Clutching hand over hand to get up the boulder pile. Did that warmth in his gaze mean he still cared for her? That he might forgive her?

She floundered to suck in air.

The beautiful eyes she adored in the past seemed to be speaking to her. Telling her that he'd save her. Before the water swallowed her whole?

"Paisley?" His voice. Had he called her *my love?*

A fog. Then blackness.

Four

Judah charged up the rocks, with water-filled boots and little regard for his own safety. When Paisley met his gaze even for that split second, it felt like an electric shock to his heart. Joy. Astonishment. Fear. A flood of emotions barreled through him. But then she fell, unconscious, dangerously close to churning water.

"Paisley!" He yelled, but his voice got drowned out by the roar of crashing waves. He had to reach her before she slid into the ocean. From this distance, it appeared the current tugged on her shoes. If a big wave hit—

God, save her!

Inwardly he pleaded with her to wake up and move back. He kept calling her name as he climbed the mound of basalt he clambered over a hundred times as a kid. He knew every indent for his boots to best maneuver the rocks. Even so, his foot slipped. Lousy boots. He dressed for riding in the skiff, not rock climbing. He had to hurry. Paisley needed him. Seeing her limp form, an emotional power surge hit him, fueling him with strength to climb the rest of the massive rock formation.

One powerful gust could topple her into the fomenting sea. If that happened, perish the thought, he'd do whatever he had to do to rescue her, including jumping in himself. *Hold on. I'm coming.* Then prayer again. *Lord, help me save her.*

Once he made it to the top of the rocks, he scuttled down the trail to the tip of the peninsula, some thirty feet from where he climbed up. As soon as he reached Paisley, he dropped to his knees and pulled her limp body into his arms. "Oh, sweetheart." Such a powerful need to protect her overcame him. He tried to be gentle with her in case she sustained injuries in her fall, but he still held her to him. "Come on, Paisley, wake up." He turned her cheek toward his chest, offering her his warmth, even though he didn't have much to give.

He pressed two icy fingers against her neck. A pulse. *Thank God.* He leaned his ear toward her lips, checking for air. A brush of warmth touched his cheek. Relieved, he rocked her. "Paisley? My love."

A wave splashed forcefully against them, snatching one of her loafers. He watched it churn in a circle, then disappear into the vortex. That could have been her. What if he'd gone home instead of heading for Bert's? What if he hadn't been close enough to see her or help her? God must have been directing his plans today. *Thank You!*

He nudged Paisley's legs away from the rocky ledge, farther from the water still breaking over them. What was she thinking, sitting here with waves bursting over her? Didn't she realize the danger?

He groaned. That was the Paisley he'd known for twelve years. Always doing chancy things. Exciting things. Wasn't that one of her charms?

He stroked her cheek. "What were you doing out here in the rain, so close to deep water?" He knew this was her special place.

He leaned his body over hers, sheltering her from the rain and incoming waves. "I've missed you so much, Pais." He didn't think she heard him.

Long eyelashes flickered. A glimmer of dark chocolaty eyes peeked out from nearly closed eyelids. A low moan. "J-Judah?"

"It's me, babe. I've got you." Relief spiked through him. His wife had finally come home. He'd do anything to keep her from wanting to run away again.

Paisley rotated her right shoulder and groaned. Why had she fainted? Was she sick? He wanted answers, but he wouldn't bombard her with questions, yet. Other than, "You okay?"

Her dark eyes opened to half-mast. She squinted at him, then glanced away. Was she uncomfortable with him being so close? Too bad. He wouldn't ease his hold on her until he knew she was all right. Maybe he'd carry her to the parking lot, unless he called for an ambulance first. Oh, right, his cell wasn't working.

"You scared me when you fell. How are you feeling?" He wanted to tell her how wonderful she looked to him. How her sparkling eyes made him long to kiss her like a man desperately in love with his wife. If he were so bold, would that scare her off?

Slow down, Grant. Give her space.

"I . . . couldn't . . . breathe."

His thoughts returned to the crisis. "And now?" He brushed wet hair off her forehead. He gazed into her eyes, checking to see if her pupils were dilated. Maybe he should scoop her up and transport her to the hospital in Florence. She might need medical attention.

"I'm b-better." She didn't sound better. Her inhalation seemed frantic. "I need to stand up." She pushed her right hand against his chest.

"Okay. Let me help." He stood and nudged his hand under her elbow, and with his other hand at her back he helped her stand. "You want to get checked at the ER?"

"No, I'm fine."

"But you passed out."

"I know." She drew in a long breath.

Another wave hit them. More water sloshed into his boots. He ignored the cold but couldn't stop his teeth from chattering.

"Thank you for rescuing me."

"Of course."

Waves continued breaking over the boulders, sending sea-foam bursting into the air. For a moment, they just stood there staring at each other. As if seeing each other for the first time. Or memorizing one another after their three-year separation. Either way, he loved gazing into her eyes and knowing she was finally home—that, maybe, she'd come back to him. Although, he saw a certain caution, or a desire to keep distance between them, in the way her gaze didn't quite hold his.

"I'm so glad you came back." Hadn't he prayed this morning for the chance to be a better husband to her? He dared to touch her cool cheek.

She stepped back. "It was time."

For him it was time thirty-six months ago, but he didn't say so.

When she swayed slightly, he put his arm around her and led her from the edge, focusing on getting her to safety. He avoided the path beside the boulder that might be in jeopardy. "If you walk out here again, beware of that rock." He pointed at Sample D. "It may have shuffled down the slope a bit."

"How?" Her eyes widened.

"Wind, probably."

"What's with the boarded-up buildings in town?" She limped without her right shoe.

"Hurricane Addy hit a month ago." He helped her step down from a large flat stone, wondering if she still felt weak.

"Really? Like the night—"

"Worse." He guessed what she was about to say. After they lost Misty Gale, he was out in the skiff in a tempest. Just released from the hospital, Paisley drove straight to the peninsula. He found her huddled on the edge, soaking wet, trembling, weeping. That night he took her in his arms also.

"Were you out there when it happened?" She nodded toward the sea.

He linked her hand in the crook of his arm and walked her slowly toward the parking lot. "I was." His skiff nearly capsized— no need to tell her that. "The house took a hit."

"That's sad. I know how much you love it."

She said, "how much *you* love it"—not how much she loved it. Something for him to ponder later.

"Where are you staying?" Thinking better of that, he quickly rephrased. "Did you want to stay with m-me?" Now, why was he tongue-tied?

"I don't think so." A blush crossed her wet cheeks. "I mean—" She shook her hair and saltwater droplets splattered his face. "I'm going to stay at the Beachside Inn if Maggie has room."

The Beachside Inn? That she didn't want to stay with him wasn't a surprise. Not after what she said in her letter to him three years ago. Staying at Maggie Thomas's? That shocked him down to his soaking wet socks.

"You could, you know"—he took a risk—"stay with me. In the guest room, not in our room. I wouldn't expect, I mean—"

"Things have changed between us, Judah."

"I know that." Of course, he did. Still, he hadn't given up hope that their love could be restored, even though three years had passed. "You can come home whenever you want." He kept his voice soft. "The cottage is yours too."

She inhaled what seemed like a fifteen-second breath. "I need time to figure stuff out."

After all these months, she *still* needed time to think? Inwardly, he groaned. Then he remembered about her fainting and determined to focus on her needs. "Are you sick, Pais?" A knot formed in his middle at her possible response.

"You could say that."

"Oh, no. What's wrong?" Cancer? Her mom died from that disease.

"I'm not sick in the way you might think." She touched his arm as if offering him comfort.

She was sick, but not in the way he thought? Confusing. And cryptic.

Her footfall increased in speed, creating space between them. Obviously, she didn't want to talk about whatever illness she had. He subdued his need to press for answers. Getting her to her car and out of the rain was the most important thing right now.

He trudged closer, reducing the space between them. "Are you here to stay, Pais?" He needed to at least know that.

"Can we talk about it later?"

"Sure." For her benefit, not his own peace of mind, he changed the topic as they approached her Accord. "How's the car running?"

"Good." She patted the wet hood. "Other than two flats. Can you believe it? Two."

"God was watching out for you." *And me.*

She withdrew a key and unlocked the car. "Thanks for helping me, Judah."

"You're welcome." He blocked her entry into the driver's seat. "You probably shouldn't drive." He held out his hand as a request for the key.

"I'm fine." She nudged his arm away. "Really."

Her coloring seemed more normal now, so he stepped back. "If you need anything, call." He thought better of that. "Actually, my cell phone's dead. Got soaked."

She slipped into the front seat and wiped strands of wet hair off her cheeks. Shivering, she nodded toward him. "You must be as miserable as I feel."

"It's a long story." He thought about his need to call the office. "You don't have a cell phone, do you?" He should have thought to ask her before, but he'd been preoccupied.

"No."

He stared at her for several moments. When she first left him, he tried calling her cell a hundred times. Left dozens of messages. Eventually, he deduced she must have gotten rid of it. Didn't want him contacting her. A tough thing for a husband to accept that his wife severed all communication with him.

"I haven't had one since I left."

Just like he thought.

So, she stayed in that rundown apartment building, riding the "L" to work, wandering around the south side of Chicago alone, then traveling cross-country without a cell phone? Who did that in the twenty-first century?

His wife, apparently.

His chest suddenly burned. That Paisley wouldn't appreciate his knowing her whereabouts for the last two of their three years apart made him avoid meeting her gaze. Not that he did anything wrong in searching for her. But what would she say when she discovered that, thanks to modern technology and his hiring a detective, he had photographs of her entering and leaving her dilapidated apartment? At some future time, he'd come clean. Not today.

He coughed. "The engine on my skiff died. I had to jump in the bay. Now, I have to find a phone to call work."

"Oh, wow." She pointed toward her passenger seat piled with packages of snacks and empty wrappers. "Get in. I can drive you to Miss Patty's." She grabbed food containers and tossed them on the floor in front of the backseat.

"Thanks." He dashed around the car and dropped onto the mostly-clean seat, happy to prolong his time with her. "I'm getting your car wet." He shifted on the seat.

"Me too." She brushed off her sleeve and chuckled, the sound reminding him of a perfectly played chord on Mom's piano.

He'd missed her laugh. Her nearness.

He let out a long sigh, realizing for the first time in ages, and even though it might be a temporary high, his world felt righted. As if he was living in a fog for thirty-six painful months and could suddenly see clearly.

She started the engine he tinkered with plenty of times in the past, and out of habit he listened to the hum. He heard a slight rattling. Might need a tune-up. Spark plugs. Oil change. Especially after the extensive drive. But he wouldn't mention anything that might reveal he knew how far she traveled.

As warm air from the heater reached his fingers, a sharp tingling dueled with relief in his nerves. He sat quietly as Paisley drove through town. He didn't even comment on her missing shoe. The silence wasn't as uncomfortable as the shivering taking over his body. His teeth chattered almost uncontrollably.

Paisley giggled, apparently at the sound he made. She held out her hand. It was shaking too. She turned up the lever on the heater.

"We both better get out of these wet clothes." A red flush skittered over her face. "Oh. I. Didn't mean—"

He clamped his lips shut to keep from laughing, but inwardly smiled. Getting out of their wet clothes was an innocent comment for a wife to say to her husband, but she was obviously embarrassed by it.

"Yeah, we're pretty soaked." He wrung out the edge of his shirt sleeve and glanced out the window to avoid her gaze or cause any further awkwardness.

After he called C-MER, would Paisley drive him home? If so, would she come in and talk? Any chance he might convince her to stay?

Five

Maggie Thomas opened and closed her mouth five times before acknowledging Paisley's question. Paisley had never seen the woman speechless before.

"Do you have any rooms available?" She asked again. Her icy fingers gripped the edge of the well-worn counter at the Beachside Inn. She wouldn't have come to Maggie's except it was the only overnight accommodations within the city limits. She shuddered as a chill rustled up her back. If she didn't get out of her damp clothes, she'd be sick by tomorrow.

"No one told me *you* were in town." Maggie sniffed and made a face as if something in the room smelled rotten. "You should have made reservations online."

"So, no rooms?" Fine. Paisley would drive to Florence, or farther south to Coos Bay. Might be better to put some miles between her and Judah anyway. What was he thinking asking her to stay with him like there wasn't a sea of hurts swirling between them? Even though he said she could stay in the guest room at the cottage, how awkward would that be sharing the rest of the house? And the heated way he gazed at her before he exited the car? She hadn't expected that. She didn't think of him as anything other than her *ex*-husband, right? "I'll go somewhere else." She strode toward the door.

"I didn't say there were no vacancies."

Paisley paused and glanced back at the woman she avoided for most of her life. "What then?"

Maggie peered over her maroon reading glasses at Paisley as if checking her for bugs or lice. Did she look that bad? She was dripping water on the floor.

Could she sleep under the roof of this judgmental woman who would probably send out a citywide text about her arrival the instant Paisley walked out the door? Thanks to her past story-swapping with Aunt Callie, another gossip queen in Basalt, Maggie had done her share of harm. A bitter taste filled Paisley's mouth.

"A room?" A sharpness she meant to subdue cut through her words.

Maggie squinted. Then frowned. "This *is* an inn." She pointed at the window. "The vacancy sign is up. Although, I can refuse service to anyone I want."

Of course. "May I have a room?" Paisley forced her voice to a sweeter tone.

"How many days will you be staying?"

"I don't know."

Maggie glared, tapping a rhythm on the countertop with her squared purple nails.

"Three nights." Paisley tossed out a number as she tried not to roll her eyes. By then she'd know whether she could stay in Basalt, or if she needed to find another coastal town to live in. Maybe Yachats, although the smaller neighboring town to the north was probably a little too close.

Mrs. Thomas harrumphed and clicked keys on the keyboard, staring at the computer screen. She quoted a tremendously steep price for it being the off-season.

Paisley cringed, thinking of her limited funds.

"Due in advance." The innkeeper eyed Paisley like she expected her to rip her off. "I take credit cards with proper ID, but I prefer cash."

"No problem." Paisley wouldn't give Maggie the satisfaction of hearing her complain about the cost. She pulled a stack of twenties from her wallet and slid them across the dented counter.

"Hmm." Maggie held up one bill, then another, to the light as if they might be counterfeit. Without glancing at Paisley, the older woman finished the transaction, then dropped an old-fashioned key in her hand. Apparently, Maggie still hadn't modernized the Beachside Inn.

Paisley almost reached the door before Mrs. Thomas cleared her throat loudly.

"I remember what you did."

Paisley stilled. Had Maggie found out she pelted the inn with mud balls when she was a teenager? "What did I do?" She didn't turn around, but she imagined Maggie's squinty gaze aimed at her. If Paisley wasn't desperate for a room and a place to sleep, she'd get back in her car and head south on Highway 101.

"I won't soon forget, either."

Her and half the town, it seemed.

"You must have a good memory." *And a wicked tongue.* Paisley gritted her teeth. Irritation steamed up her pores, heating her core in opposition to her chilled frame. Slowly, she faced the innkeeper. "I don't know what you're implying. You might as well spit it out, Mrs. Thomas, since you seem bursting at the seams to do so."

"I'm talking about the night you crept through my inn."
Maggie pulsed a purple fingernail.

"To use your bathroom, that's all." Paisley bristled. What did
the woman think she'd done?

"Next morning, my pearls were missing." Maggie's eyelids
scrunched to thin slits. "Mama gave me those for my sixteenth
birthday. Same ones Gran wore on her wedding day."

"You've got to be kidding." Did every act of thievery and
mischief in Basalt fall at Paisley's feet? Would she never outgrow
the locals' disdain?

"Everyone knows you're a thief." Maggie's chin lifted.

"Thanks to your lies." Paisley's backpack banged against the
doorframe as she exited the office. She pictured herself throwing
fistfuls of mud at the windows of the inn, again. However, she was
a mature adult now. She paid Maggie for a bed for three nights—
in cash. She'd use that room or else curl up against a chunk of
driftwood on the beach right in front of the Beachside Inn. Then,
what would Maggie Thomas have to say?

Stuffing her anger deep inside, Paisley tromped around the
first of three narrow, archaic-looking buildings with cedar shakes
flanking the outer walls, then strode down the walkway. Stopping
at the red door that matched the number on her key, she paused,
her limbs shaking. She'd anticipated the return to her hometown
might be fraught with struggles, but to think after all these years,
Mrs. Thomas condemned her for stealing some family heirloom
Paisley had never even seen. What else might she be blamed for?

Edward Grant's face flashed through her mind. Did he still
blame her for ruining his son's life?

She groaned.

Inside the tiny motel room, she removed her wet clothes, dug
leggings out of her pack and slid into them, used the facilities,

hung the "Do Not Disturb" sign on the outside doorknob, then collapsed onto the double-sized bed, curling up in the blankets. After all the hours she spent on the road, then that exhausting episode at the peninsula, she succumbed to sleep in seconds. However, her last thoughts before drifting off were of her opening her eyes after she fell on the rocks, and finding Judah holding her tenderly. Of his deep blue eyes gazing into hers.

Then long-forgotten love songs filled her dreams, and she slow danced with someone.

Hours later, a loud banging at the door awakened her. When she opened one eye, filtered sunlight glinted through the narrow window.

She pulled the pillow over her head. If she ignored whoever was at the door, would they go away? What time was it anyway? She peeked out from under the pillow and peered around the room. On the wall, an anchor-shaped clock with a set of oars for hands pointed at twelve and three. Three o'clock in the afternoon?

Goodness, she slept a long time. And she was still tired enough to keep sleeping. She closed her eyes.

The banging came again. Didn't they read the sign?

"I don't want the room cleaned!"

After another round of knocking, she hurled a pillow at the door. "Go away!" Had the "Do Not Disturb" sign blown off the door handle? She wouldn't put it past Mrs. Thomas to remove the sign on purpose.

"It's me, Pais." Judah's voice. "I took a chance on this room being yours, since it's the only one with the sign on the door handle."

She didn't want to see him again so soon.

"You okay?"

"I'm still sleeping." She yawned. "Come back tomorrow, okay?"

His chuckle reached her. Why were the walls of the inn so thin? She heard something shuffle against the door.

"I brought food." He must not have heard her comment. "You're probably hungry."

Her stomach growled. Perfect timing. She hadn't eaten in twenty-four hours. "Okay. Just a sec." Grumbling, she stood and pulled on a sweatshirt. She ran her fingers over what had to be messy bed hair in need of a washing. In three steps, she was at the door. Opening it, she saw Judah leaning against the doorframe, smiling at her. She'd always loved his masculine grin. What was that song she was thinking about last night? Something about a man loving a woman. Not what she should be contemplating right now.

"Hey."

"Hi."

He clutched a white bag with a Bert's Fish Shack logo. Just seeing the bag, smelling something wonderful, made her mouth water. Would he hand it over? Or did he expect to come in? If so, she had to set clear boundaries. No admiring his smile. No staring into his shiny blues. Meeting his gaze, that seemed to be staring straight into her heart, was totally unacceptable. And no talking about them getting back together, either.

She was hungry, that's all.

"Bert's best." He held up the bag. "Want to go down to the beach and eat with me?"

No. "Uh, maybe."

"I have an idea I want to run by you." His eyes seemed moist like he might be near tears, and she wondered why. Was her being back in town emotionally difficult for him, too? "What do you say?" His dark hair blew slightly in the wind. "Come eat and chat with me?"

Eating and having a conversation seemed harmless. "Why not? I'll use the bathroom, then be right out." She shut the door before he entered the room or had the chance to say anything else.

Was she making a mistake in thinking they could hang out and talk, as if a mighty storm hadn't wrecked their marriage? What did Judah want to discuss? She said okay about meeting him for lunch. Maybe she could still do that and then draw those lines she already decided on.

After washing up and putting on a thin layer of gloss—due to dry lips, not because she was having a picnic with the man she loved for three years, then despised for four—she pulled on a knitted hat.

Would Judah go along with making their separation more permanent? Surely, he suspected that outcome after three years without communication. But he was so nice to her yesterday on the peninsula, then again on their drive out to the cottage, making her remember some good things about their life together. She had loved him. But then, they fell out of love and away from each other in the aftermath of overwhelming loss.

Time to move on.

Yet, seeing him again sparked something undeniable in her. Something gentle and endearing about him surprised her. After all this time apart, was there possibly a smidgeon of romance, or love, still lingering between them?

Ugh, no.

Hadn't she called it quits the day she left him? And every day since? All that remained was signing papers, right?

Unless her fickle heart discovered he still loved her.

Not even then. She was in Basalt to face her past and then start a new future—independently and alone.

Judah's concern about her passing out was the reason for his kindnesses. As her husband, he'd acted coldhearted. Didn't understand her. She told herself that over and over for a year before she left him. Now, as she stared at herself in the antique mirror, she wondered. Was he indifferent and judgmental toward her, or was that her perception of him based on her own indifference?

She groaned. Too deep of thoughts.

One thing she knew, she couldn't encourage an attraction between them that might linger like fumes, then combust and evaporate. Maybe she should feign illness. Renege on lunch. Although, she *was* famished.

Phooey. She slammed the motel room door behind her on her way out—not caring that Mrs. Thomas probably didn't approve of guests slamming doors—then she trotted toward the beach below the inn.

Judah wanted to talk? Fine. Let him get whatever he needed to say off his chest. Then she was making one thing clear—she no longer planned on being his wife.

Six

Had Judah taken a risk by inviting Paisley to meet him at the beach and then not sticking around to wait for her? She needed time to get ready, right? Besides, if Mrs. Thomas saw him lingering around a woman's room, she might call the cops. Better for him to stay clear of Mrs. Thomas. He had enough trouble with her in the past.

But what if Paisley took off? Distress danced a jig over his heart—a familiar reaction. She wouldn't put him through that again, would she? She drove two thousand miles to get here. She must plan on staying for a while. Longer, if he convinced her to move in.

Slow down, chump. She left you. Period.

Yeah, yeah. Had he ever been able to sweet-talk Paisley into doing anything she didn't want to do? If she came back to him—and he doubted she was ready to do that—it had to be on her terms. Still, he wished for the outcome he daydreamed about for two years.

He sighed.

Earlier at work, he was so distracted. His thoughts kept replaying the moment he saw Paisley fall on the peninsula, his wild trek across the sand, trying to reach her before something worse happened, and then how amazing she felt in his arms again.

In between contemplating yesterday's events, he went with Craig to retrieve the beached skiff. Fortunately, they found it anchored to the log where he tied it. After they bailed it out, they dragged the boat back to the C-MER dock where mechanics could work on it. Then they backtracked to the peninsula to check on Sample D. Scrapings against a companion basalt rock bore chalk-like markings, confirming the rock had moved. Why, was the question. There were no recent earthquakes. No superstorms other than Addy.

After taking pictures with the new cell phone he was issued, he wrapped yellow tape around the rock to warn tourists and hikers of possible danger. Then Craig steered the skiff back to C-MER. The whole way, Judah lined up excuses for taking off a few hours early. Normally, he was committed to his research and duties. Today, thoughts of Paisley held his thoughts captive. Did she go see her dad? Was she feeling okay?

Back at the office, he was useless. After staring at one screen of storm data for an hour without assimilating anything he read, it was time to leave.

He uncurled the top of the bag, snagged a french fry between his fingers, and stuffed it in his mouth. He stared at the waves rolling up the sand.

Maybe he should sprint back to the inn and check on Paisley. Make sure she didn't leave. He groaned at the recurring thought. What if in the future things got rough in their marriage—if they got back together—would she run at the first sign of conflict? When he disagreed with her about something, would he fret she'd be out the door by morning? Man, he had to stifle those relentless, nagging thoughts that ate away at his peace of mind.

He devoured a couple more fries. Sighed.

He chose this chunk of driftwood to sit on, midway between the inn and the ocean, so Paisley could find him. Unfortunately, it was within Maggie's binocular range. Was she watching him now? If he did anything out of line—not that he planned to—the innkeeper would probably chase him with her broom. She did that when he was ten and built a sand castle on her property. That day, she shot out of her office, yelling like the world was on fire, swinging her broom. Nearly hit him, except he was a fast runner.

Mrs. Thomas called his parents too. Dad grabbed Judah by the arm and chewed him out all the way to the Beachside Inn. His father demanded that he apologize to the woman of "upstanding character"—if she was ever an honorable person in the community, Judah hadn't figured out when. All that fuss and embarrassment over a sand castle? A bad memory still.

To make matters worse, after Paisley left three years ago, Maggie showed up at C-MER claiming Paisley stole some priceless necklace. She demanded he reimburse her loss. Without proof, he refused. Ever since, he avoided the cranky innkeeper.

His stomach growled. He hadn't eaten breakfast. Barely slept last night. Around three a.m., he got up and trudged down to the strip of sand below his cottage. Sometimes he walked to the seashore when he woke up worrying about Paisley and their separation. Now she stayed a mile away from him, and he longed to be near her. If only she wanted that too.

A brush of sand pelted his lower back. He swiveled on the aged log to see Paisley, dressed in a long Chicago Mets sweatshirt, navy leggings, and a knitted hat on her head, wearing a slight smile. "I heard there was free food around here." She sniffed the air.

Was she keeping things light? If so, he'd go along with that.

He lifted the bag and pointed at Bert's logo of a salmon with a crown on its head. "Best burgers on the West Coast."

"Can't wait." She dropped down on the log, leaving a defining space between them.

He ignored the distance she created and dug out the wrapped sandwiches. He handed her one.

"Oh, um, about the cheese?" She quirked an eyebrow.

As if he'd forget. "No cheese. I remembered."

"Thanks."

Her sweet smile left his gaze lingering a little too long on her rosy lips. Lips that used to taste of cotton candy on a summer night. Lips he kissed so many times before. Inwardly, he groaned. *Tone it down, Romeo.*

He bit into his burger. At least he could count on a hamburger from Bert's remaining the same.

Next to him, well, not quite next to him, Paisley sighed. "Mmm. I've missed these."

But not him? Man, why did he have to jump to that conclusion? He groaned, then covered it by clearing his throat.

"You okay?" Her voice came softly.

"Yeah, fine." A small mistruth. He chomped into his cheesy bacon burger and focused on the salty flavor of Bert's finest.

"What did you want to talk with me about?" Paisley's wrapper rustled in her hands.

Judah's mind went blank. He just wanted to be near her. He didn't plan on blurting out something that might cause her walls to go up. But he wouldn't tiptoe around her as if he had to avoid Mom's freshly mopped floor, either.

He stuffed a fry into his mouth. After he swallowed, he nodded toward the water. "How does it feel to be back at the beach? You always loved that." So did he.

"I'm glad to be home."

Home? A 220-jolt zinged through him. Home to him? Her dad? The sea?

With effort, he tamped down his internal overreaction to her words. "I'm glad you came home, too."

Her dark eyes turned almost black. One eye squinted at him as if she were trying to figure out something about him.

His hunger abated, he set the remainder of his burger on the wrapper. Time to tell her what he was thinking. "Look, I realize it may seem too soon for me to be saying this, but I'd like you to move back in with me."

Her jaw clenched. She shook her head.

His nerve almost vanished, but he promised himself to tell her the truth if he got the chance. He clasped her smaller hand and noticed her ring wasn't on her finger like his wedding band was still on his left hand. That was a bad sign. He peered into her eyes that had often reminded him of dark chocolate. If only she weren't so aloof now.

"Judah—" Paisley pulled her hand free and stood.

He tugged on the sleeve of her sweatshirt. "Please hear me out? Then you can go, if you want."

She stared toward the ocean as if debating his request. Then she sat down stiffly on the white faded log and nodded once, but didn't look his way.

He needed to clarify something. "What I meant was, I'd like for you to move into the guest room."

Her shoulders lifted and fell. "Still won't work."

"Why? I said the guest room. Not my bed." Man, too much hurt blasted out in those words.

"I'll never sleep in your bed again." She bristled. Arms crossed. Her eyes squinted at him.

"Never, huh?"

"I want a divorce."

Sharp arrows plunged into his heart. Although, he should have known she'd want to end things with him. Hadn't he pictured them getting a divorce in the first year of their separation when he was so angry at her? But then, his heart changed. God was changing him. "Not me. I do *not* want a divorce." He had a right to his opinion, too. "Please, come back to the cottage. Stay until you've seen your family. That will give us time to talk things over."

"There's nothing to discuss." She leaped to her feet and moved a few steps away from him, obviously putting distance between them.

"I doubt you believe that." He stood and walked through the sand to stand beside her. "Three years and a world of hurts, and you think there's nothing to discuss?" He didn't believe her, wouldn't let himself believe her.

"I've m-made my d-decision." She hiccupped or coughed. Her breathing sounded irregular.

"There's two of us in this marriage." He felt determination rush through him. He let her walk away before. He wouldn't make the same mistake again. "There always has been two of us."

"Funny you should say that now." Paisley glanced at him, tears and pain evident in her gaze.

In that second, he saw her as the broken young wife who begged him to stay with her in the hospital after they lost their baby, and his frustration melted into nothingness. He saw her as the wife who he should have held close to him all that night, supporting her through the toughest time of their lives. Instead, after she fell asleep, he went home and returned to work the next day, finding a measure of solace in his job. A sword of regret pierced him. So many mistakes.

He had to say what was on his heart now. "Paisley, I'm so sorry I wasn't there for you like I should have been when we lost Misty Gale."

She drew in a sharp breath.

"You're still my wife." He needed to say this. "And I . . . I still love you."

Even though they hadn't talked things out, God was working in his heart, bringing healing and love, teaching him about forgiveness and grace. He wanted to offer her the same mercy he experienced. Maybe someday she could forgive him too.

She met his gaze, shook her head as if telling him to stop talking.

He wouldn't be the person who reverted into silence during an uncomfortable topic ever again. "We're still a family, you and me."

"No, we're not." She turned away from him. "Not anymore."

Her words felt cruel, but the remembrance of the vulnerability he saw in her gaze moments ago made him want to take her in his arms and hold her. He didn't have that right, but he wished he did.

"Three years ago, you left me. You said you didn't love me anymore." He touched her shoulder gently, wanting her to turn around. When she didn't, he watched her in profile. "Paisley, I've changed. I know I wasn't there for you like you needed me to be. And I'm so, so sorry you felt abandoned. I never wanted you to feel that way."

Her breathing turned loud and raspy. Did she have pneumonia or something? She didn't say anything. Just put her hand on her chest and seemed almost in a trance. Had she even heard him?

The only sign that she may have been touched by his apology were a couple of tears dripping down her cheeks. Her face crumpled. Then a sob.

"Oh, sweetheart." He moved closer until he faced her, then pulled her into his arms, and she didn't resist. "If you'll give me another chance, give us another chance, I promise to be a good husband to you." He stroked her back. Felt her shudder. "I want you with me as my wife."

She shoved her hands against his chest and glared at him, although tears still ran down her cheeks. "It's too l-late for that. Don't you s-see?"

"Come stay with me for a few days." He was being persistent, but this was his one and only shot. He had to take it. "It'd be better than staying at Maggie's."

"Anything would be." She wiped her cheeks, then scuffed the toe of her shoe in the sand. "But I can't."

"Can't. Or won't?" Uh, that might have been too pushy.

"What do you want from me?" She asked such a loaded question, but she was still avoiding his gaze.

A couple of answers came to mind. A real marriage. A wife who loved him. Instead, he said, "I want you to come home." The simple truth.

"I left you, Judah."

"I know." Hurt sizzled through every fiber in his body. "But I want you back." If only she could see inside his heart, she'd know he was sincere.

She huffed. "As what?"

"My wife. Friend. Lover." He threw down his cards. Hadn't she asked him to be more open with her three years ago?

"You've got to be kidding me."

"I'm not. I'm asking you to come home. Separate rooms are

fine." He'd take what he could get. Having her close enough to talk with, to try to work things out, would be a miracle.

"How can you even ask that?" She inhaled and exhaled loudly, seemingly unable to catch her breath. "H-how can you say 'm-marriage, friend, *lover*' after my being gone for three years? After all I've done? How do you know I haven't been with . . . with someone else?" She kept her head down, and her shoulders sagged.

His litmus test of grace. Acid burned through his gut. He didn't trust himself to say anything for a few seconds. "I don't. But that doesn't change anything." He already battled his decision on his knees and in prayer during his skiff rides.

She faced him then, thrusting out her hands as if exasperated. "We're finished, Judah. I don't love you!"

It was hard to have a comeback for an absence of love.

She trudged through the sand toward the inn, leaving a gaping trail through the tall beach grasses.

His emotions felt wrung out and raw. If he were a drinking man, he'd head for Hardy's Gill and Grill for something to dull his senses. Yet, he couldn't let Paisley go off alone. Even if she didn't love him. Even if she'd been with—

He didn't finish the thought.

He scooped up the trash they left on the log, then he tromped after his wife, stepping into the footprints her rubber boots made in the sand—two footprints becoming one. The old Judah would accept her terms and leave her alone. She wanted a divorce? Fine. He'd been alone longer than he would counsel any friend to hang onto a dream of reconciliation. All these years, he waited faithfully for his absentee wife to return. He was true to her in mind and body. Now she was back and still didn't want him? Why should he push for her to come home?

Other than mercy, grace, and forgiveness, he didn't have an answer. He stomped after her, his footfalls heavy in the sand.

Something didn't add up. Her words didn't ring true. If she went astray like she implied, why did her eyes light up like sparklers when she opened her eyelids to find him holding her on the peninsula yesterday? As if she missed him too.

Paisley kept a steady pace, heading straight toward her motel room. Judah's legs could easily outdistance her, but he stayed about ten feet behind. However, if this was his last chance to speak up, he had to say what was on his mind and heart. What he would have said before she left, if he'd been wiser.

"We need to talk, Paisley." He had to yell over the breeze billowing from the sea.

"Leave me alone!" The wind snatched the words and threw them over her shoulder. "We're done talking."

"I don't think so."

She whirled around and jabbed an index finger toward him. "You are *not* setting the rules!"

His temper ignited, bursting into flame, matching the fire in her gaze. He reduced the space between them in a few steps. "Why not?" He parked one hand on his hip, the other hand clinging to the food bag. "You ran off. Left me to face everyone alone. I'm the one who had to explain your absence to your own family. Why can't I make a few rules?" Paisley flinched, but he kept going, fueled by her previous rejection and the injustices between them. "You've been running the show for three years. Camped out in some low-income studio apartment in South Chicago, while I—" Oh, man, he didn't mean to say that out loud today.

Her mouth dropped open. "What? How do you—?"

"That's right." He gritted his teeth. "I've known where you were for the last two years."

"How . . . how did you—?" Her eyes widened. She breathed loudly.

"Didn't you wonder why your landlord suddenly reduced the rent two years ago?" His voice rose.

"N-no-o." The one syllable word came out as three. She pressed her fingers against her temples.

"How do you think it made me feel to know my wife had to put two thousand miles between us to get far enough away from me? That she hated me so much she wanted to disappear from everything and everyone she ever knew?" He breathed harder now too.

"How did you find me?" The wind blew her long dark hair across her face. She fingered it away, making her look younger, more like the woman he fell in love with. The one who still filled his dreams. And the one who said she didn't love him anymore. "I thought you might follow me. Come looking. But you d-didn't." She inhaled and exhaled noisily.

"You thought—" In an instant, his anger melted into a puddle of wounded pride. She wanted him to come after her? A slug in the stomach wouldn't surprise him nearly as much. "Paisley, I, uh, I didn't know. If I knew you wanted me to find you—"

"It doesn't matter."

Obviously, it did. She sounded defeated, looked defeated, and he didn't feel like the victor. He reached out to her, but she impatiently brushed his hand away.

"I didn't mean to tell you that I knew where you were yet." He ran his hand through his hair, frustrated. "Being without you has been hard on me. Now that you're here, I just want to make things right, to try to fix things, but I don't know how."

"You can't fix it. Or m-me." Her uneven breathing reminded

him of someone with asthma he knew in high school. "I have to know. H-how did you f-find me?"

"I hired someone. A detective." He didn't want to explain this now, especially when he could see she was getting more upset.

"So, what? You saw p-pictures of m-my wretched cracker-box apartment? P-pitied me?" She seemed to be breathless, then she ran the rest of the way to her motel room door, hacking all the way.

He followed her, determined to stay right with her until she slammed the door, locking him out. As she shoved her key into the doorknob, he clasped her shoulders and turned her around. "Paisley, what's wrong with you?"

She didn't answer him. Her cheeks were pasty white, her breathing scattered.

What could he do to help her? He dug in the wrinkled food bag and yanked out the leftover iced tea cup that had a bit of liquid left in it. He pulled off the lid and thrust the container into her hands. "Drink this."

She clasped the cup to her mouth and swallowed a couple of gulps. Then she laid her hand over her upper chest, breathing with wheezing sounds. He didn't know what else to do.

When she dropped the empty cup and fell to her knees, drawing in great breaths of air, he sank to the ground beside her. "Should I call 911?" He yanked his new cell phone out of his slicker.

She grabbed his hand. "It w-will p-pass. Just h-hold m-me." She sank into him, wilting like a flower left out in the hot sun too long.

He gladly wrapped his arms around her, holding her against his chest, rocking her, and praying.

After a few moments, she pushed him away and lunged for the bag their lunch came in. Dumping the contents on the sidewalk, she bunched the bag to her mouth. She inhaled and exhaled rapidly as if hyperventilating.

"Breathe slowly. Not so fast." He rubbed her shoulder.

She nodded, her eyes filling with tears. She pointed toward the ocean. Then at something else. She stared straight at him, breathing into the bag, her dark eyes going from fudge color to black then brown again. Finally, she lowered the bag, let out a long sigh. "Panic." She picked up the food wrappers and the cup she dropped on the ground.

Compassion for her gripped him in the center of his chest. "How long has this been happening?"

She shrugged. "A while."

"On the peninsula yesterday, when you fainted, was this why?" He gulped over the hardships she must have endured in the last three years. Had she suffered with these attacks all by herself? "Panic, huh?"

She nodded. "This time . . . about what you said."

"About coming home with me?"

"And your knowing where I've been." She swallowed. "I thought no one did. I made sure no one did—even if I may have secretly wished you would find me."

He'd have to be more careful about what he said. Except, now he wanted to be with her through whatever she was dealing with. Protecting her. Caring for her. Loving her as the husband he still was. "I wish you'd reconsider. Come live with me."

"No." Paisley stood and opened the door. Before she slipped inside, she paused. "But thanks for helping me. That was kind of you." She closed the door.

Kind? An ache started in the pit of his stomach and ended in his brain. What could he do to show her that he loved her with an undying, unconditional love that went far above kindness, no matter what she said about them getting a divorce?

He wouldn't forget the devastated look on her face during the panic attack. What if that happened again? He didn't want her to be alone. Not tonight. Not ever. He'd go home and grab a sleeping bag. Then he was coming back and staying at the foot of her door. He wanted to be close in case she needed him.

The only thing that gave him a moment's pause was the thought of Mrs. Thomas finding him sleeping in front of a guest's door. But even if she beat him with her broom and called the police, he'd willingly face the consequences to protect Paisley. His Paisley. His love. His wife.

Seven

The next morning, Paisley riffled through the remaining bills in her wallet. She already used up a lion's share of her traveling fund. Gas expenses crossing half the continent were more than she planned and spending three nights at the Beachside Inn was highway robbery. She had to figure out what to do next. Stay with Dad? Paige? A heavy weight settled in the pit of her stomach. She couldn't accept Judah's offer.

They needed to settle things, but she didn't even have enough money for a divorce. Maybe looking for a job should be her first step.

Sometime in the night she heard Mrs. Thomas yelling at someone in the walkway between the buildings. Paisley crept to the peephole and tried to see out, but she couldn't tell who Maggie was speaking to in such a demeaning tone. Was a vagrant sleeping near Paisley's room? She shuddered. Maggie threatened to call the police. And she may have even hit the guy with a broom.

When no sirens sounded, Paisley figured Mrs. Thomas was satisfied that the drifter left. Still, she had a hard time getting back to sleep after the ruckus.

Now her mind churned with indecision. Should she talk with Dad this morning? Did he know she was in town? Maggie must have alerted Aunt Callie who would have gone straight to Dad. When did his sister ever keep a secret? In fact, Paisley was surprised Aunt Callie didn't already show up at the Beachside Inn demanding to see her.

Paisley needed to talk with Dad, but the thought of entering the house where she had the last argument with Mom, seeing the closed pantry door, staring into the peculiar eyes of paintings she hated as a kid, shattered something within her. It made her never want to visit her childhood home again. Yet, she'd promised herself she would.

Maybe she should walk down to the peninsula first. Fortify herself before seeing anyone.

The phone rang. Who would be calling her? Judah? Aunt Callie? Warily, she picked up the old-fashioned white receiver. "Hello?"

"Maggie Thomas, here." The woman's voice came through the line clipped. "You tell that ex-husband of yours to stay off my property!"

"Why?" What did he do now?

"The pervert loitered outside your door last night, probably trying to peek through the peephole." Maggie harrumphed.

"What? No way." Judah wouldn't do that. *Ohhh.* Was he the one Mrs. Thomas yelled at? Had she hit him with a broom, again?

"He slept in a sleeping bag right there, in front of your door. Without paying for the privilege." Maggie snorted. "He took off when I threatened to call his dad. I'll have you know Mayor Grant won't put up with such shenanigans. I've called him about the reprobate before."

Reprobate? Judah? What a joke. But then, Paisley had to tamp down the burn of anger her father-in-law's name caused.

"If you plan on spending another night here—"

"I do." Paisley cut into the woman's tirade. "I already paid—"

"Then Judah Grant cannot be on my property, you hear me?" Something about the woman's snippy tone reminded Paisley of her mom yelling at her to leave and never come back.

"Well?" Maggie demanded. "Do you promise to keep the scoundrel away from my inn?"

Her words cranked up Paisley's irritation. "Unless he pays, right?" That probably sounded like the flippant girl she used to be, but she didn't care.

Maggie gasped. "I'll have you know I can refuse service to anyone I wish."

So she told Paisley before. "No wonder no one wants to stay at your rundown inn. Your rooms are archaic. The toilet barely flushes. The shower's cold. Even though it's off-season, your prices are outrageous!" As soon as she uttered the heated review, she wished she hadn't.

"Get out!" Maggie shrieked. "Now. Get off my property!"

"Mrs. Thomas—"

"I don't need your tainted money. I want you off my premises immediately." An object clattered in the background as if something dropped and broke. "Now, you've done it!"

More blame cast at her feet. "Maggie—"

"Mrs. Thomas."

"Mrs. Thomas, I'm"—she forced out the words—"I'm sorry."

"I don't want you in my 'rundown' establishment for another night." Maggie huffed. "Vacate by noon or I'll call the authorities. Brian Corbin is deputy now, you know."

Brian Corbin? High school troublemaker, Paisley's prom date, and a co-conspirator in a few of her mischief-making schemes? She could picture him in jail. Not the one tossing criminals into the slammer.

"I paid for another night." She gritted her teeth, old angst toward this woman steaming up her pipes. She had a few choice words she'd like to say, maybe some mud balls to fling.

"I guess you paid for Judah's stay last night, after all." The woman had no mercy.

"Fine."

"Fine."

The receiver clicked loudly in Paisley's ear.

Fire simmered in her gut. She wanted to march over to the motel office and give Maggie Thomas a piece of her mind, a blaze that had been smoldering for years. Here she planned to make up for past mistakes. Now, she wanted to do something notable on her exodus from the tiny rental—like stuffing the toilet full of beach sand.

She whirled around and grabbed the few items she unpacked and put them into her backpack. She wouldn't stay in this shoebox another minute. She collected her toiletries from the ridiculously small bathroom. How Maggie charged top dollar when the facilities hadn't been updated since the sixties, Paisley would never know. Someone should report her to the Better Business Bureau. Blast her name all over the front page of the Basalt Bay *Journal*.

Settle down. No use going nuts-o on a woman who wasn't worth it. She was better off getting out of this dump.

What did Maggie say? Judah slept by her door in a sleeping bag? That didn't make sense. Surely, he knew such an action would incite the innkeeper's anger toward both of them. Was he worried she'd disappear again? Concerned for her health?

Before she left town, she accused him of being heartless and uncaring. Perhaps he was showing her he had changed, like he said.

Not that it mattered. Only, in some way she didn't quite understand, maybe because she'd been alone for so long, it did matter. The idea of him watching over her, wanting to be close, for whatever reason, pleased her.

She scooped up her backpack, raincoat, and boots, tossed her room key on the TV tray near the door, then left with a firm door slam. Hopefully, Maggie heard that. Staying at this inn was a lousy idea. Didn't something bad always happen when Paisley came within twenty-five feet of the innkeeper?

No doubt, Mrs. Thomas already informed Aunt Callie about kicking Paisley out. Dad would hear about it too.

"Basalt Bay's gossips are back at it," she grumbled.

Before she went to see Dad, if she went to see him today, she had another stop to make. She was going to find out for herself why Judah slept by her door.

Eight

Paisley drove her Honda Accord through town, avoiding eye contact with anyone on the sidewalks along Front Street, and pondering the dilemma of where she should stay. On the north side, she swerved into the parking lot of the C-MER building—Judah's second home. In the past, she came here to bring him lunch or deliver a vanilla latte or to discuss some aspect of their lives. Today, she felt weird crashing into his turf. Not really his wife. Not exactly his ex-wife, although she planned to change that. She stared at the "Visitors Only" sign in front of where she parked. Was visiting him at work okay?

They had things to discuss. Although, she didn't want to move back in with him, right? Too much emotional baggage. But Maggie *had* given her the boot. Paisley could ask Dad about staying in her old room, but she hadn't gotten up the nerve to see him yet. Was she crazy to consider moving in with Judah, even temporarily?

She leaned her forearm against the steering wheel and rested her forehead against her wrist. What was she doing? What woman planning a divorce—who put two thousand miles between her and her husband for thirty-six months—would entertain the idea of sharing the same space with him again?

Perhaps, one whose spouse slept outside her motel room door? Ugh. She had to get the heroic image of him curled up outside, watching over her, out of her mind. And what about him knowing where she was for two years? Even paying a portion of her rent? She still couldn't believe he did that. What about the way he held her when she fainted two days ago? How his sparkling blues shined down on her with something akin to adoration. Hadn't he called her "sweetheart" and "my love"? Kindnesses she was starved to hear. Mercies she couldn't ignore. Although they changed nothing. Or did they change everything?

Talk about confusing.

She got out of the car and strode toward the steps of the main entrance, her shoes scuffing through a layer of sand on the footpath. Around the ocean side, and thanks to strong incessant winds, sand got everywhere and into everything. On the first step of the single-story building, she paused and stomped grit off her sneakers.

What if the possibility of her staying at the cottage made Judah expect something more than she wanted, like romance or getting back together? She turned around and gazed at the parking lot filled with about twenty-five cars.

She could head to one of the other coastal towns. Look for a cheap motel and a serving job. Her wallet was thinner than when she left Chicago, but she had some money. If she ate skimpily, or not at all, she had enough for a couple nights' stay. Sleeping on the beach was a possibility, if it weren't for the threat of unexpected storms.

She sighed. She came this far. Why not at least talk with him?

She stared at a slanted tree growing through a tall mound of sand. Such determination and endurance it demonstrated by having pressed through the resistance. Was that like Judah pushing through every argument she hurled at him against their marriage and them staying under the same roof? She caused him enough grief, why did he even wish to be around her? He said he didn't want a divorce. Why wouldn't he choose that after the way she deserted him and told him she loved someone else? Something twisted inside of her at the lies she piled up.

He was better off without her.

Stiffening her back, Paisley jogged up the steps, then entered the glass entryway of the C-MER building.

A woman dressed in bright pink stood behind the receptionist's desk, gaping at her. Mia Till? How did the young woman advance from being a mailroom assistant to the receptionist of this prestigious company? Shock blared from the short-skirt-wearing woman's owlish eyes. Her hand covered her mouth.

"Mia," Paisley offered first.

"Paisley, is that really you?" As if she didn't know. Mia shook her variegated blond locks.

Discomfort bristled inside Paisley. Maybe she should have changed into something a little more feminine before coming here. "It's me. In the flesh."

Her mind flipped through times in past years when she wondered if something might be going on between Judah and Mia. Even before she left, the young assistant seemed flirty with him at office Christmas parties Paisley attended. Then Aunt Callie caught wind of rumors in town and demanded answers. *Why are you permitting that hussy to fawn over your husband?* Paisley hadn't "permitted" any such thing.

Judah wasn't the only recipient of the woman's flirtations,

either. Rumors spread that she'd been friendly with a few of the C-MER men—many of them husbands and fathers whose heads were momentarily turned by the leggy blond coworker.

But considering Paisley's past actions, she didn't have any right to judge the other woman. However, her first instincts toward Mia weren't polite, either.

"Did you just waltz back into town?" Mia smirked.

"Something like that." Paisley ignored the "waltz" bit. "I'm definitely back."

Mia's red lips surrounded glistening white teeth that appeared over whitened. "It's . . . so fab . . . to see you again." Mia cleared her throat awkwardly as if distracting Paisley from her insincere words.

"Yeah, you too." *Cough, cough.* "Is Judah around?"

"Of course."

Paisley turned toward the door at the back where she visited Judah at his cubicle in the past.

Mia dodged in front of her, palms outward, like a security guard keeping a child from a priceless sculpture. "You can't just go in there." Her hands lowered, and she straightened her short skirt.

The woman's apparel didn't seem very professional.

"Why not?" Paisley crossed her arms, her resentment rising. The model-wannabee thought she could stop her from speaking to Judah? She could walk through that doorway any time she wanted.

"There are procedures we follow now." Mia's voice turned crisp.

The company's previous receptionist, Mildred Mackey, always let Paisley go into the work area. No problem. No questions asked.

"Judah is in a meeting." Had Mia whispered his name on purpose? As if she had a claim on him?

I think I'm going to be sick. Paisley didn't plan on stirring up anything with Judah, but she didn't want him dating this makeup junky. He deserved someone good for a second wife. Someone better than Mia Till. *Someone better than me.* Her gut tightened.

"I can wait in his cubicle." She took a couple of steps toward the door again.

"No, you can't." Mia waved her hands in front of her. "Things have changed since you've been gone."

Apparently.

A haughty expression crossed the office worker's face, as if she were peering down on Paisley. Which was accurate since Mia wore four-inch heels. Oh, were those *So Kates?* Paisley stared at the sparkly red shoes while trying not to gawk. Those beauties had to be five hundred bucks! What kind of salary did Mia make?

"If you'll just have a seat—"

"No, thanks." Should she remind the pink-clad foyer police that she was still married to Judah, and therefore had access to him?

But then, didn't she give up her wifely rights when she wrote him that note and disappeared? Not that Mia needed to know their personal information. Or maybe she already did. Had Judah explained their marital status to her? Was he lonely and—?

Ugh. She didn't want to think about that. The mental image of Judah pressing his lips anywhere near this woman's red mouth made Paisley's stomach turn. She should have grabbed a bagel or coffee before charging into such a volatile situation.

"Wait here"—the receptionist pointed toward the lobby—"and I'll call Judah. He may not have time for you today." One of her sleek eyebrows arched.

He might not have time for this surprise visit, but eventually he'd exit that door and head for his truck. When he did, she'd be waiting. For her to leave now would be a point on Mia's scoreboard. Paisley wasn't having any of that.

She strode to the giant window with its southerly view of the dunes and ignored Mia. Did she think Paisley might make a run for the forbidden door? Her impish nature made her want to do that very thing just to see how the other woman might react.

Instead, she feigned disinterest and stared out the window. Outside, the dunes topped with long beach grasses weren't far from the building. If they were open to the public, it would be a fun place to tromp around and explore.

"Paisley."

She turned at Judah's soft voice, in time to catch him smiling at Mia. Gratitude? Or something else?

That twist in Paisley's stomach wrenched tighter.

Mia's toothy grin had a suspiciously more-than-friendship quality.

A growl started somewhere in the pit of Paisley's stomach and emerged from her mouth. She met Judah's surprised gaze. *Mia? Really?*

Maybe he was more eager for things to be finalized in their marriage than he admitted. But if that were the case, why did he sleep outside her door? And tell her he loved her.

Judah's brow furrowed. "You okay?" He stroked his hand down her arm, and she didn't back away from his touch. Not with Mia watching them from behind her desk.

"I'm fine." *Not really*. While things could never go back to how they were between them four years ago, if Judah took up with Mia, Paisley was getting out of town. "What's going on here?" She bobbed her head toward the receptionist, then glared at him.

A blush she'd rarely seen on him hued his cheeks. "Nothing at all." His Adam's apple bobbed, revealing his discomfort over the question.

She stared at him more fully. His black hair stuck out in a few places like he'd dragged his fingers through the strands in frustration. Dark shadows beneath his eyes made him look fatigued. Probably exhausted after a restless sleep. Which reminded her of Mrs. Thomas's accusation.

"What were you doing sleeping outside my motel room?" Her fists landed on her hips.

A huff came from the other side of the room. Paisley should have lowered her voice. However, Mia hearing that detail might be perfect. The receptionist needed a reminder that Judah had a wife—for now.

"You heard about that, huh?" He sighed.

"I don't have a place to stay, thanks to you. Maggie kicked me out." She stared into his eyes that resembled tide pools on a clear blue-sky day.

"Oh, man." He stroked his hands down both of her arms, something he did in the past when he tried comforting her.

She should have stepped back from his touch, but she didn't. Not for Mia's benefit this time. Although, she didn't want to analyze why.

"I'm sorry, Pais. I didn't mean for that to happen. I just"—he linked their pinkie fingers, something else he used to do—"wanted to be near you. Listening, in case, you know—"

In case of a panic attack? In case she ran? When he drew her to him, for the slightest breath of time, she allowed a hug. She leaned her forehead against his chest, seeking comfort or a bit of human kindness. He laid his palm on the back of her head and kissed the top of her hair. She inhaled deeply of his Old Spice scent, remembering how she used to joke with him about smelling like her dad. He still did.

What happened to us?

She almost got choked up. Until she recalled where they were and who was watching. Besides, she didn't want to be close to Judah physically. Only, in that moment she did. She wanted him to wrap his arms around her and—what? Kiss her? No, no. That's not what she wanted. She stumbled back a couple of steps. Crossed her arms—a protective measure. Yet her traitorous gaze glanced at his lips a couple of times. Bad idea.

"What will you do now? How can I help?" He swayed his hand toward the couch as if to ask her to sit down.

She ignored the gesture. "About your offer." She spoke quietly now, not wanting Mia to hear this part.

He smiled, and there was something lovely and inviting in his expression that gnawed at a tired, lonely place in her spirit. They were such good friends before. Could they find a way back to that, without the complications of marriage and romance?

"You mean it?" His eyes lit up. "You want to come back and live with me?" He spoke loudly. As if he wanted Mia, the only other person in the room, to hear.

That didn't make sense if he'd dated her.

Paisley glanced over her shoulder and saw the receptionist talking on the phone. Mia's gaze darted toward Judah, then Paisley, like she was watching them. Hopefully, she wasn't speaking with Aunt Callie. Did she have connections to Basalt's gossip ring?

"I thought we could talk about it, you know, since I've been kicked out. Unless you meant for that to happen." She peered into his gaze, seeking ulterior motives.

"Of course, I didn't." He huffed. "I never meant for Maggie to see me. You know me better than that."

She knew each of them avoided the woman for their own reasons.

He glanced over his shoulder as if checking on Mia also. "I'm in meetings all day. Do you want to head out to the cottage and get settled before I arrive?"

"Okay." There was something he had to know. "Look, I need a room, and that's it." She lowered her voice. "There's no hope for us. You've got to understand that."

"There's always hope." His eyes flooded with moisture.

She blinked back a tug of emotion that surprised her. "I just need somewhere to hang out while I figure out a job and my life. Your place would only be a temporary stop in the road."

He jerked like she slapped him, and she hated his reaction. But then, as if she didn't say something that might destroy his hopes, a soft smile replaced his momentary grimace. Apparently, whatever bitterness she caused him in the past didn't affect his ability to offer her a genuine smile. She stared at his soft mouth a tad too long.

If she were going to share space with him, she had to remember her own strict rules. No staring at his inviting lips. No gazing into his blue eyes. And stay fifty feet from his bedroom. By then she'd be outside. Maybe sleeping in the hammock on the porch would be safer. For whom? Judah? Or herself?

"The key's still under the crab shell on the porch." He grinned. "I made up the guest bed yesterday, just in case."

Even when she adamantly said she wouldn't stay with him?

"You did? Thanks." Although, the thought of staying at his place again made her feel unsettled, maybe afraid. Like she was embarking on a journey in a rowboat without oars.

"Judah, Mr. Linfield wants you to rejoin them in the conference room." The receptionist held up the phone as if she just took a call.

"Okay. Thanks." He lifted a hand.

Paisley didn't see any guile or attraction toward Mia on his face. In fact, his eyes seemed to be glowing toward Paisley. But that meant she was gazing into his blues again.

"Now?" Mia's nails tapped a steady, annoying rhythm on her desk.

Judah touched Paisley's little finger. "We'll talk later, huh?"

"Sure." Warmth spread through her. "Oh, sorry to have bothered you," she called after him.

"I'm glad you came by. Stop in any time." He winked at her before sauntering back through the door he exited a few minutes ago.

Any time? She bet Mia wouldn't approve of that.

Paisley made a beeline for the main entrance, avoiding further contact with the office help.

"When did you get back, anyway?" Mia sure moved fast in those heels.

With one sneaker out the door, Paisley paused, surprised by Mia following her. "Two days ago."

"Funny your aunt hasn't seen you."

So, Mia *had* talked to her. "How would you know whether I've seen Aunt Callie?"

"Oh, we talk." Mia's laugh tinkled like a windchime. "I met her when I first moved to town. She's the one who introduced me to Judah, and he helped me get my job." She swayed her hands toward her desk.

He did? "Well, uh, I've got to run." Before she said something she'd regret. She rushed down the steps to the path.

"Goodbye, Miss Cedars."

Hearing her maiden name, Paisley didn't turn back to dispute it. She might even reclaim it if she and Judah went their separate ways. Now, why didn't that sound as appealing as it had before?

Nine

Paisley climbed the three broken-down wooden steps at Dad's house, each board creaking with old age. She stood there for at least ten minutes, staring at the glass square in the wooden front door, trying to get up the nerve to knock, debating whether to turn around and go back down the stairs. She didn't see any movement inside, which was good. She needed a few minutes to collect herself.

She scratched at a tightness in her neck. Swallowed.

God, if You're there, please help me breathe normally through this visit.

She quickly searched for five things. There—a child's half-chewed tennis shoe. Mom's rhododendron bush in need of a trimming. A brown dog collar draped over the railing. Four rocks near the screen door. An upside-down empty soup can. She breathed in and out, controlling any overreaction to being here.

The house she pretended was a pirate's ship when she was a kid could almost be called a beach house. If it weren't for the row of houses on the ocean side of the street, she would have had the perfect view of the sea while growing up. However, that didn't stop her and Peter from running through the neighbors' yards to reach their beloved beach and finding treasures left after high tides.

Thinking of Peter, her childhood friend and confidant, had the calming effect she needed. If only he were here. Had Dad or Paige heard from him while she was away?

She lifted her fist to knock on the door, then paused. Would Dad understand why she left three years ago? Why she didn't call? Was he still upset about her not attending Mom's funeral?

Something thumped on the steps behind her. She whirled around.

"Why, if it isn't Paisley Rose." Aunt Callie's voice bellowed like she was hard of hearing.

"Aunt Callie, hello." Paisley subdued her groan, frustrated that her aunt found her before she got to speak privately with Dad.

"I heard . . . you . . . were . . . home." The plump woman huffed up the stairs as if there were fifty steps instead of three. "It's about time you came home and faced the music, Missy." The older woman pressed Paisley into a hug, squashing her against her ample body.

Face the music, indeed! "Nice to see you too, Auntie." She used the endearing term half-heartedly.

The screen door screeched open. By the noise, her dad hadn't oiled the hinges in years.

"What's the r-racket out h-here?" Dad's voice broke, making him sound much older than sixty. His gaze met Paisley's, then flitted away. He didn't extend his arms in a hug. Didn't invite her in.

The muscles in her throat bunched up. *You can do this.* She came back to Basalt to see him, didn't she? "Hi, Dad."

He stared off in the distance. Didn't respond. He looked so tired. Were his eyes bloodshot? Maybe he wasn't sleeping well. Or sick?

"See who's here, Pauly?" Aunt Callie nudged Paisley. "About time she showed up, wouldn't you say?" She stomped her foot on the porch as if demanding Dad's attention. "We don't blame her one bit for leaving that no-good son of Edward Grant, do we?"

At her aunt's harsh assessment, a rock slammed into Paisley's heart. While she didn't think kindly of Mayor Grant—she pretty much despised him for the way he treated her—Judah didn't deserve the same branding. Had Aunt Callie told people around town that her leaving was all his fault? Inwardly, she groaned. She *had* left him to deal with why she left, just like he said.

Dad's reticence in moving toward her made Paisley shuffle back to the cracked post on the porch. She leaned against the wood, taking a casual stance she didn't feel, and forced herself to breathe calmly. "How are you, Dad?" She looked at him even though he didn't return her gaze.

"Oh, so-so." He seemed to be staring at the broken slats on the porch floor. His eyes were more gray than blue now, and liquid flooded his orbs as if he were suppressing tears. Although, she couldn't be sure. His hair was grayer. Thinner. More wrinkles lined his eyes and mouth. A scar of some sort creased his chin. A shaving accident? He still didn't take a step toward her. Should she drop down on one knee and beg for his forgiveness? That seemed overly dramatic, especially with Aunt Callie watching her every move.

"Hamburger's on sale down at Lewis's Super." Aunt Callie chatted, filling in the awkwardness. "Did you see the blockbuster price on chicken, Pauly? My, my, haven't seen such low prices in a decade, have you?" She went on about picnic supplies being useless in late September.

Dad stared at something in the yard, maybe the old apple tree, or else he was trying to glimpse the ocean. Obviously, he was avoiding eye contact with his daughter. Did he wish she hadn't shown up at all?

Paisley forced herself to swallow. To breathe in and out lest she fall apart and make a complete mess of this first visit.

"You just going to stand there like a zombie, Pauly?" Aunt Callie huffed. "I need some sweet tea. Got any?"

"Nah. Haven't made any in a week." Dad ran his fingers through the strands of gray hair sticking up vertically.

"Figures." Aunt Callie snorted. "Guess I have to do everything." The older woman plodded into the house with heavy footsteps. The screen door slammed shut.

Then silence.

Maybe Paisley should go in and help. The icy chill left in her aunt's wake was hard to bear.

Did Aunt Callie depart to give Paisley and Dad some time alone? Strange, considering she usually wanted to hear all the details about everyone in Basalt. Was she standing inside the living room, listening? Collecting gossip to distribute later? The notion irked Paisley. She didn't appreciate people talking about her.

Inside, the oven drawer squawked open and closed, reminding her of old times. Sounded like Aunt Callie was using the pot they always used to make sweet tea in.

"Where you been all this time?" Dad's unexpected question made Paisley jump.

"Oh." She met his gaze for a moment before he glanced away. "Chicago."

"That far, huh?" He fiddled with his thumbnail.

Had he ever been concerned about her? Missed her? Or with the embarrassment she caused, was her absence a relief?

More silence. Anxiety twisted and turned in her stomach. But what did she expect? So this talk wasn't progressing as she hoped.

At least, they were both still standing here. She should say something. "You're right, I went far enough to get away from everything and everyone."

A wounded look crossed Dad's face, which made her feel terrible. He gnawed on his lower lip. "Seems you and Peter had the same idea—run as fast and as far as possible."

"Yeah, I suppose." No use lying to him.

A crash came from inside.

"Lousy pitcher!" Aunt Callie shouted. "Pauly, I've done it. Broke the only decent thing you got in this house to make tea in." She said something derogatory.

"I better see what she's done now." Dad shuffled toward the door.

He didn't ask Paisley to come in, so she didn't follow him. The door scraped against the edge of the doorframe, then clattered shut. Lots of things seemed wrong with the place. Didn't Dad do repair work anymore? Judah could fix the door. Good night, with the right tools she could fix it. Living alone taught her how to do a lot of stuff she never did before.

She leaned against the porch railing—the one she and Peter draped a blanket over and hid behind to throw mud balls at the neighbor's house—and noticed the peeling paint on the porch walls, the gaps in the floorboards, and the broken window by the side of the door held together with duct tape. Had it been damaged in the storm that hit other buildings in town? Or was age and neglect catching up with it? The ancient house had seen better days, that was for sure.

"Can't you buy anything?" Aunt Callie's voice rose from inside. "Penny would be shocked to know you haven't purchased a thing since she's been gone. How am I supposed to make tea?"

"Go home, woman!" Dad shouting? "Make tea at your own place and stop meddling in my affairs."

Even when dealing with Peter's and Paisley's shenanigans, Dad rarely raised his voice. He was more the brooding type. An internalist. His glare spoke buckets more than she ever wanted to hear him say out loud.

Aunt Callie harrumphed, then made a bunch of rattling sounds. Apparently, she was determined not to leave the kitchen without her beverage. She probably didn't want to take off as long as Paisley and Dad hadn't talked things out. She'd hunt for something to make tea in, even a bread pan, just for an excuse to eavesdrop.

"For your information"—Dad's voice got louder and forceful, surprising Paisley even more—"I've bought my own groceries for years. Even before Penny passed on." He cleared his throat as if it wasn't used much. "Paisley isn't the only one who's been gone for a long time." Hurt seeped through every word like blood through a bandage.

Paisley dropped to the edge of the porch, her shoes on the next step down, as an awful silence engulfed the house behind her.

Aunt Callie's voice came softly then. "Your daughter's here now, Pauly." Aunt Callie sticking up for her? Big surprise. "Aren't you going to speak with her?"

Paisley held her breath, waiting.

Dad muttered something about too many burned bridges.

Aunt Callie burst through the doorway, letting the screen door slam, and handed her a chipped glass filled to the brim with tea. A couple of ice cubes clinked against the sides. "Here you go, Paisley Rose."

"Thank you." She sipped the still-warm tea, then swished the ice cubes around. Wasn't Dad coming back out? Now might be a good time to talk about those burned bridges.

Aunt Callie took a long chug of tea, then sighed like it was the best thing she ever tasted. "Nothing like tea to calm the nerves."

She dropped onto the rocker that looked ready to topple over or disintegrate in the next windstorm. She scooted her backside deep into the seat as if she planned to spend the night there.

Paisley toyed with condensation on the outside of her glass, feeling insignificant next to her aunt.

"Chicago, huh?" On each back-and-forth motion, the rocker thudded.

"Uh, yes."

"Too far from the ocean for me." The woman made a tsk-tsk sound like no one should live in such a dry climate.

"There's a large lake. Waves and everything." Paisley shrugged. "But not the sea."

"Not by a long shot."

If Dad planned to hunker down and avoid her, Paisley should leave. Give him time to adjust to her being back in town. Maybe he was more shocked than angry. She shouldn't take his reaction personally. But, boy, oh boy, did she. Leaving town became more tempting in this minute of rejection than two days ago when she first arrived. But maybe that's what Dad, and Judah, feared. That she'd run again as soon as she got the chance.

How could she prove them wrong?

"Seen Paige?" Aunt Callie's blackish gaze pierced Paisley's.

"No."

"Going to?"

She hated the grilling. "Eventually." Paige was her sister. Not that they were ever close. Or that Paisley felt she owed her sibling any explanation.

"I heard that no-good husband of yours bedded down in front of your door at Maggie's." Aunt Callie had to bring that up. "Disgusting, if you ask me. As if you'd stoop to taking him back. Word on the street is—"

Paisley blocked out her aunt's rambling for a moment. Judah may have been foolish to sleep by her door, but his actions were far from disgusting. Honorable and sweet, perhaps. She tuned back in.

"Serves Edward Grant right to have his lowdown son dragged through the mire of a divorce. The mayor is far too pompous." Aunt Callie drained her tea glass in a noisy guzzle. "That you married into that self-righteous family on the cliff riles me to the bone."

Indignation burned through Paisley's veins. "Auntie"—this time she said the word crisply—"I haven't decided if I'm going to divorce Judah." Now, why did she say that? Of course, she'd made up her mind. But she didn't want Aunt Callie going on and on about the Grant family, and Judah as if he were the worst person in Basalt. Besides, Paisley's last name was still Grant. Her aunt should respect that.

"What do y-you mean you h-haven't d-decided?" Aunt Callie coughed like she was choking on her tea. "I thought that's why you left. To get away from the scum of the sea."

"Yes, I had to get away from him"—she came back to Basalt to be honest—"and a few others." She gave her aunt a pointed glare. "However, Judah's a decent guy. He doesn't deserve your scorn."

Aunt Callie scoffed. "He put you, and therefore this family, through a world of hurt." If glares could burn something, Paisley's skin would be on fire. "It's time you end this farce of a marriage and start living like a Cedars." Her lips bunched up in a scowl.

Did Aunt Callie presume that all she had to do was point her finger and Paisley would jump to do her bidding?

"I have to go." She set down her tea glass on the porch railing, then rushed down the stairs. If she said anything else, she'd say too much. Which would mean more apologies.

"Hold on, young lady!" Aunt Callie shouted.

Paisley didn't pause. She got into her car, started the engine, and backed up. Speeding might get her into trouble with Deputy Brian Corbin—that's all she needed—so she drove slowly away from Aunt Callie who still sat in the rocker on the porch.

It hurt that her father hadn't come back outside. Like he didn't want to speak with her at all. If her own dad didn't want her, who did?

I have loved you with an everlasting love.

Oh. At the beautiful sentiment she hadn't thought of in such a long time, warmth spread through her. Did God still care for her even after the way she'd acted toward Him?

She sighed, not daring to answer that question. However, the inspiring words soothed some of her pain over Dad's cold reaction. But not completely. Not when the man who could have opened his arms wide in forgiveness and welcomed her home didn't.

Ten

Judah knew he'd been in too many meetings when he couldn't stay focused on anything the speakers said. But when Mike Linfield, a man he considered to be a temperamental boss, stood up and shouted at attendees sitting around the conference table as if they purposefully neglected the coastline and left it unprotected, Judah bristled at the lambasting. He and his coworkers were conscientious about their jobs and public safety. Why else would they put in such long hours and contribute so much effort to protecting the citizens of Basalt Bay? However, while part of him wanted to say something contradictory about Mike's accusations, since Paisley came by a couple of hours ago, his mind *had* been preoccupied.

He forced himself to concentrate on Craig's introduction of safety measures for future evacuations. That worked for about a minute. His heart wasn't in today's sessions, no matter how important they were. Especially when a memory of Paisley and how things used to be in their relationship danced through his mind. Then his attention to policy details faded lightning fast as he remembered how she would snuggle up with him on the couch, like she never wanted to be far from him, and they watched a show next to each other, or sat close and talked. He could almost smell her rose-scented perfume, feel her hand clasped in his as if their palms were glued together—at least in the early days of marriage. Was it possible for them to recover those warm emotions and the sweet love they lost?

God could do anything. But what if Paisley didn't want to be his wife anymore? If she pursued a divorce regardless of what he wanted? There was nothing he could do to stop her then. He suppressed a groan that would have given away that he'd again tuned out what Craig was saying.

What about the things Judah previously decided? Hadn't he spent hours and hours praying about what he'd do if Paisley came back? And if she ever cracked open the door to reconciliation, hadn't he determined to do everything in his power to love her like the husband he should have been before?

During the last twenty-four months of knowing her location, so many times, he wrestled with the impulse to go to her apartment and beg her to come home. But, other than the one time he bought the plane ticket, he knew if he flew to Chicago and insisted she return with him, she'd dig her heels in even more. She had to find her way back to him in her own time.

And now she was here. Hallelujah!

Please help her remember our love, before it's too late.

But it was never too late for him to show her forgiveness and grace, right? Hadn't God called him to be a good husband, no matter what? To love Paisley even though she made it clear that a relationship with him was impossible. That the only way she'd move back into the beach cottage was if things remained platonic between them. *Platonic*, seriously? Not his choice, but he agreed.

He covered a disgruntled moan with a cough, then took a sip from his water bottle. Time to listen in to Craig again. A few slides displaying north and south routes out of town flipped through the PowerPoint rotation. Things Judah had seen before. Still, determined to pay attention, he leaned his elbows on the table and faced his supervisor. Craig described the congestion the duo corridor exits encountered during Addy. He expounded on details of damage to the southern arterial during the flooding stage and how the repair work wasn't finished yet.

If another disaster hit, and Judah hoped it never happened, keeping Paisley safe would be his priority. In the next second, Craig's monotone voice got whisked away by thoughts of her. Maybe Judah should tell his wife what he was thinking—that she was the most important person in his life, that he'd do anything for her, including risking his life to save hers. If he told her that, would she realize how much he cared? How much he still loved her? That he'd never again put his job above her?

His thoughts flitted back to when their relationship altered forever. Four years ago, a day after their baby was born without life—even the thought of holding Misty Gale, so tiny and still in his arms, squeezed something tight in him, choked him up—Paisley got out of the hospital earlier in the afternoon than he realized. If he knew, he would have been there. But he was on patrol during a threatening storm, and unbeknownst to him, she drove back to town in a deluge of rain and wind, alone. After work, he went straight to the hospital in Florence where he found out she'd been discharged. He drove by the cottage, but she wasn't there. Crazy with worry, he feared she might have had an accident along Highway 101.

But then, he thought about the peninsula, the place she loved most. There, he found her slumped over at the edge of the point, devastated, broken, sobbing her heart out. He felt so helpless. A failure as a husband. He should have stayed at the hospital with her. Skipped work. Shared more in their grief. If he did, they might still be a real couple. Truth was, he didn't know how to deal with such overwhelming heartache, then. Still didn't.

He blinked fast to rid his eyes of moisture. No use falling apart in front of his coworkers about something that happened four years ago. Yet, if the loss still affected him, it had to be tough for Paisley too, especially with the anniversary of their child's death approaching.

"Right, Judah?" Craig's dark eyes stared him down, one eyebrow lifted. Did he know Judah wasn't listening?

"Yep. Absolutely." He nodded. Gulped. What did he just agree to?

It seemed he deserved his superior's wrath for inattentiveness. When Craig continued his presentation, Judah sighed, relieved the speaker hadn't pressed for an answer about whatever topic he wasn't listening to.

What was wrong with him? Usually he was passionate about how storms could harm his community and how C-MER would assist their neighbors during a disaster. In an earlier session about the possibility of ocean plates scraping each other, getting stuck, and then shifting, sending out a powerful wave surge toward Basalt Bay and other cities along the Oregon Coast, he was completely engaged. But then, that was before Paisley showed up, demanding to know why he slept outside her motel door.

Now Craig was speaking about how to safely evacuate all the citizens in town—which seemed an impossibility given the narrow road system and the city only having two junctions with the main highway. "Whether it's a tsunami or a Category 3 hurricane"—he pointed at a photo of a tsunami illuminated on the wall—"residents will be aware of imminent danger faster thanks to our recent purchase of a new early warning system. In the future, evacuations will be more efficient and swifter."

"Here, here," someone in the back affirmed.

Others clapped.

The words about "imminent danger" made Judah shudder. Hopefully, the town would never have to face a storm like Addy again. The men and women seated around the perimeter of the table had to be prepared in case it did happen.

Someone asked Craig a question, and Judah zoned out again. He'd have to warn Dad to keep his big mouth shut about his grievances toward Paisley. His father seemed incapable of silencing his opinions. In his official capacity as mayor, he usually acted civil. However, since Paisley left, Dad took every opportunity to inform Judah of what he thought of the woman his son chose for a wife. He called her names that riled Judah every time, widening the emotional gap between them.

Finally, the training session ended. A few coworkers stuck around to ask questions, but Judah shot through the door, grabbed his jacket from his cubicle, then hustled out to his truck. He was eager to get to the cottage to see if Paisley arrived yet. On the way home, he'd pick up salmon sandwiches at Bert's. Even though they had burgers from there yesterday, he didn't want either of them cooking tonight, giving them plenty of opportunity to talk.

At the beach house, seeing Paisley's car parked in the narrow driveway again gave him a surge of hope. "All things are possible," he reminded himself. As he walked up the path toward the front door, he listened to the gentle roar of the surf coming from below the house. Man, he loved the smells and sounds of the ocean. He opened the unlocked door. "I'm home!" It felt amazing to say that to his wife again. He set the food bag on the counter. "Paisley?"

When she didn't answer, concern slashed through him. What if she collapsed? Ran? No, her car was outside. She loved the sea and was probably at the beach. He'd take their dinner down there. She'd like that.

He threw on his Oregon Ducks sweatshirt and grabbed the food bag on his way out. He didn't have far to go. As soon as he tromped over the slight rise, he spotted her dark hair blowing in the wind. She sat on the sand, her face lifted to the partially sunny sky, and her eyes were closed.

What a beauty. He grinned. Couldn't help himself. His life had meaning again. His wife was home! Now, how could he convince her to stay?

She left you once; she'll leave again. A negative voice that sounded like his dad's whispered in his thoughts.

Not if I can help it.

Judah stopped in the middle of the wind-brushed trail and stared up to the heavens. He took a second to collect his thoughts and pray. God could heal and restore them. His wife was here now, and he'd rejoice in that blessing.

With a lighter step he approached her. "There you are!"

She opened her eyes and waved at him. Her smile made him weak in the knees. Forget butterflies. Being in Paisley Grant's presence caused a tidal wave of emotions to barrel through his core.

"I see you stopped at our favorite diner." She pointed at the bag.

He loved that she used the term "our favorite," as if she still thought of them as a couple with favorite things to share.

"I couldn't resist." He couldn't resist her, either. If he thought she wouldn't mind, he'd plant a doozy of a welcome-home kiss on those rosy lips. Too soon. He'd respect the safe distance she asked for. He dropped onto the sand beside her, the sides of their hands touching. Too imposing?

She scooted her backside about a foot away in the sand, giving him an answer. He wouldn't be discouraged. God was working. Judah was depending on Him.

He checked the contents of the bag. Two fish burgers. Fries. Two plastic containers filled with iced tea. He handed her a cup, a package of fries, and a paper-wrapped sandwich. "House special. Your favorite."

"Salmon burger with avocado?" She sipped her tea and her gaze met his. "Thanks for remembering."

"Of course." *I remember everything about you.* He nudged her arm playfully. "Besides, Bert's special hasn't changed in years."

She unwrapped her sandwich and took a bite. Her quietness made him wonder what she was thinking.

He thanked God silently for the food, then bit into his meal. Suddenly, he felt famished. Sitting through all those meetings gave him an appetite. Or maybe eating a meal with his wife made him feel normal, finally. He inhaled the salty air, felt the wind brush against his face. Life was good. So good.

"Thanks for this." She held up the wheat bun oozing in green guacamole sauce. "And for letting me stay at the cottage."

He swallowed down a fry. "No problem." Didn't she see how happy he was that she sat here with him? Should he say so? No, the look of caution in her eyes kept him still.

"It'll just be for a few days, you know."

A pain searing his throat had nothing to do with the hot sauce Bert added to his sandwich. Time to shed a lifetime of confrontational resistance. "Look, Paisley"—he faced her—"I want you here with me more than anything."

"But—"

"No buts." He took a chance and laid his hand over hers in the sand. "I get it. You were unhappy in our marriage. And you left."

Her eyes widened as if she were shocked to hear him speaking so forthrightly. She pulled her hand out from under his, like he figured she would.

He took a deep breath. "You're here wanting to end things with us. But so we're clear, I don't want that. I never did."

Her mouth opened and closed, but she didn't say anything.

"I've had three years to consider what I'd say to you when I got the chance, so I plan to speak my mind. I want to hear what you have to say also." His heart hammering in his chest, he bit into the sandwich he'd lost his appetite for and set it aside.

Paisley's lip trembled. "If you feel that strongly, maybe I shouldn't stay with you." She crinkled up the sandwich wrapping paper.

The wall that rose swiftly and effortlessly between them blasted away his confidence. If she'd said that to him in the past, he would have taken off for a beach walk by himself. Never again. He told her things would be different. He meant it. If being honest caused embarrassment or made him look foolish in her eyes, so be it. A rotting bandage of hurts and past mistakes needed to be ripped off. Even if yanking off that bandage might tear apart his chance to have her in his house, or in his arms, again. They both needed healing, although their mutual scars might remain.

"Do you remember the day you promised me forever?" He stroked her knuckles, needing some contact between them, and gazed into her eyes. "I do." He kept his voice soft.

She swallowed and pulled her hand away. "It didn't work, Judah."

Her unfinished sandwich was on her lap. Apparently, neither of them were hungry now.

He sighed. "I believe things can still work between us."

"I don't see how."

"We'd have to focus on fixing the things that went wrong before." He wished for a magical phrase or a romantic line that would touch her heart and bridge the chasm. None came. Honesty might be better. "Pais, I know I messed up. I let you down in a hundred ways. I've relived those last arguments we had before you left until I can't bear to think about them."

"Me too." Her admission surprised him. She cleared her throat. "Not that it changes anything. But since you were being honest—"

"Why can't it change everything?" He was laying his heart on the line.

"Judah—"

"I mean it. I still love you, Pais. I care for you as a person and as my wife." Her silence tore at him. "Is it because . . . you love . . . someone else?" The words wrenched from his mouth, but he had to know if what she said in that note was true. If what the town assumed was true. Not that it changed whether he wanted to stay married to her. Even if she fell for someone else in the past, Judah planned to try winning her back. He promised her forever in his wedding vows. He promised himself too, and God.

"It isn't that."

"Really?" His heart skipped a beat. "I'm so glad." He wanted to throw his arms around her and hug her.

"Don't be."

Dread replaced his relief. "Uh, why not?"

She groaned. "Don't you see? If I were in love with someone else, this would be simpler." *If?* So she *had* lied. "Then you'd accept my reason for divorcing you."

"No, I wouldn't." His heart would be broken again, but he would still try reconciling with her. A commitment was a commitment to the end, no matter how difficult, terrifying, or rocky the journey might be.

"Yes, you would." Her eyes filled with unshed tears. "I know you, Judah."

Something about the way she said she knew him pricked his heart. "You know who I was before we lost Misty Gale. You don't know the man I've become since you've been gone." He picked up a handful of sand and tossed it into a pile.

"Maybe not." She fingered a pebble, picked it up and threw it onto his sand mound.

"Guess you'll have to stick around and find out for yourself." Was he flirting with her so soon after his feelings were pummeled by her threat of divorce? He sighed. "I prefer to think I've matured, but that might be pushing the truth a little." He tossed a few small rocks on the pile, just like old times. "I hope I've become a better man."

A tear trickled down her cheek and she swiped it away. Seeing her even a little emotionally broken sent a fierce protectiveness through him. If only he could wrap his arms around her and hold her against his chest as he did during that panic attack of hers.

"Thing is, while you may have changed, I'm the same ol' me." She sipped her tea. "There's no hope of change for us."

Judah disagreed. God's love could change everything. Of course, so could bitterness. Best not to go there. Instead, he sought a lighter turn in the conversation. "You know when I first fell in love with you? Twelve years ago when I saw you pelting mud balls at the Beachside Inn." He snickered, then flipped a rock on to the pile.

"All this time and you never told Mrs. Thomas?" Her eyes squinted at him.

"Not on your life." He linked their pinkies, knowing she'd probably pull away. She did. "The best part is . . . I still love you."

She snorted like she didn't believe him.

An impish thought came to mind, something that might make her smile. He pointed offshore to where a fishing boat plodded through the surf. Cupping his hands to his mouth, he yelled toward it, "I love Paisley Rose Grant!"

"Stop that!" She sounded indignant and threw a handful of sand at him. "What's gotten into you?"

He laughed, enjoying the more carefree interaction. "I told you I've changed. I said I love you, and you, Mrs. Grant, didn't believe me." He jumped to his feet and, barely containing his laughter, yelled at the top of his voice, "I love my wife!"

She leaped up. "Judah, stop already!" But she was chuckling too.

He'd missed having fun with her, teasing her, spending time together. He gazed into her eyes, stroked a strand of dark hair back over her ear, then he almost did something that would have made her mad. He leaned in and nearly kissed her on the mouth. When he realized how close he came, how much he wanted to touch his lips to hers, he let his mouth briefly caress her forehead instead.

"Want to walk?" He reached out his hand toward her.

She glanced at him but didn't accept his offer of hand-holding.

"Stubborn. Same as always." He teased.

"I told you I'm the same. I bet at heart you are too." She took off running down the sandy beach toward the dunes.

He left the food where it was, knowing they'd be back to clean up in a while. Then he ran after his wife, hoping her perception of him might change, and for love to find its way back into both of their hearts.

Eleven

Paisley awoke to sunshine splashing across the twin bed in the guest room where she slept, and to the unfortunate clatter of banging pots in the kitchen. Why was Judah making all that racket? She checked the alarm clock on the nightstand. Seven o'clock? Too early for a Saturday morning.

A firm knock sounded on the closed door. "Paisley? I'm making scrambled eggs."

If she didn't answer, would he assume she was still sleeping? Or, maybe, that she escaped through the window? "Yeah. Uh-huh." She grumbled.

"Pleasant this morning, are we?"

She'd show him pleasant by swinging open the door and chucking her pillow at him. But then he might think she was flirting. She didn't want that.

She remembered how she ran down the beach last night with him chasing her. How he yelled that he loved her at a fishing boat going through the bay. What was with him? When did he become so open and honest? And affectionate? Things deteriorated in their relationship long before she left. Why was he flirting with her now? He told her that he'd changed. That God was working in his life over the years they were apart. Maybe she'd ask him about that sometime.

"We can eat on the veranda. It's a lovely morning." His footsteps moved down the hall.

The veranda? So, he didn't forget what they used to call the six-foot by six-foot section of broken cement pavers. They'd planned on redoing the outdoor space, making it large enough to have friends over for dinners, but never got around to it.

She might as well get moving. Judah made enough noise to wake the whole south-side community, except most of the neighbors were summer dwellers who already left for warmer parts.

After she washed up in the bathroom, she shuffled outside into the brisk September ocean-side air. Judah had placed a two-foot circular café-style table with two wrought iron chairs in the middle of the "veranda." He even set a little fall greenery in a vase between two turquoise plates filled with scrambled eggs and canned peaches. He bowed slightly and swayed his right hand toward the spread. Why was he being so charming this morning?

She reached for her coffee cup and dropped onto the chair with a sigh. The sweet steaming brew made waking up early not quite so painful. It was nice of Judah to add a dash of coconut creamer too. She smelled it immediately. One of the chair legs wobbled on the broken paver beneath her. "Oops." Some coffee spilled on her sweatshirt.

"You okay?" Judah eyed her from across the table where he sat down.

"The chair—" She groaned. No use pointing out his flawed patio furniture.

He jiggled his chair. "They both need work." He winked. "Kind of like us."

"Yeah, yeah." She rolled her eyes. If he didn't let up on pushing for a marriage makeover, she'd be out the door before she finished the toast he added to the table. She eyed him coolly.

He shrugged and smiled, then seemed to focus on his food.

She slid her fork under a bit of egg and took a cautious bite. Not bad. "When did you learn to cook?" Her grumpy tone came out before she filtered it. Judah had been pleasant to her ever since he found her unconscious on the peninsula. Why not attempt to be polite herself?

"Practice."

She appreciated his honest answer when he could have said something mean—*Otherwise I'd have starved after you left me.*

She sighed, then ate her breakfast in silence, glad Judah seemed to realize she needed quiet. Or maybe he required some time to ponder this situation they were in as much as she did.

After they finished eating and he refilled their cups with coffee and more coconut creamer, Paisley turned in her chair in the direction of the sea. A seagull traipsed across the dune to the left of the trail. A rustling in the trees made her think it might be a squirrel.

"I was hoping you'd help me with something today." Judah smiled at her.

"Like what?"

His blue gaze sparkled with playfulness or mischief.

"What do you have up your sleeve?"

"Other than the sand you threw at me last night?" He chortled. "Hard to get that out of my armpits."

That made her laugh. "Seriously, what's up?" She had her own agenda. People to see. A job to find. Hopefully somewhere else to stay.

One of his eyes squinted, then he gazed toward the ocean. Was he nervous about telling her something? He'd been generous about letting her stay here without strings attached. She could probably help him for a couple of hours, but then she needed to go see Dad again. "Got a window to replace, or something?"

"Sort of."

"Sure, I can help."

He seemed about to say something, then he stood and scooped up their plates, silverware, and glasses. "Meet me at my truck in twenty minutes."

"Wait. I thought you needed help here." She grabbed their cups. "Where are we going?"

"To town. Someone else needs assistance."

"Who?"

Judah stopped mid-step, the plates wobbling precariously. The turquoise pottery shimmered in the morning sun, but he obviously collected too many items. As the plates careened from his grasp, she lunged forward.

"Judah!" She caught the plates, but one crystal water glass—a wedding gift—toppled and smashed into a bazillion pieces against the pavers. "Oh, no."

"I can't believe I did that." He groaned and dropped to his knees, picking up shards of glass. "You okay?" He glanced up, his cheeks aflame with obvious embarrassment.

"I'm fine." She set the cups and plates on the table, then knelt next to him. Did he even know the glass's sentimental value?

"Sorry." He stood and placed chunks of broken crystal on a plate.

"Accidents happen." She stood and did the same with the shards she picked up, feeling a little sad about the glassware. In the years she was away, she never thought of the glass's unique

"G" design. However, this one breaking now seemed symbolic. Like everything she ever hoped for about marriage and relationships eventually broke or died.

Sigh.

Judah piled dishes back in his arms.

"Let me help this time." She took the other glass from him, protecting it without saying so.

He gave her a sheepish grin. "I wanted to make you a nice breakfast and clean the dishes on your first morning back."

"You did make a nice breakfast. Thank you." She took a few more items out of his hands. For a second, she experienced déjà vu. Eating together and then cleaning up the kitchen side by side felt so familiar. Hadn't they helped each other with after-meal chores hundreds of times?

Inside the narrow kitchen, she bumped into him on her way to the sink. "Oh, sorry."

He leaned back to open the fridge and ran into her and didn't apologize. His twinkling eyes made her think he might have meant for that to happen.

This housing arrangement was already putting them in an awkward proximity with each other when she was wanting to keep her distance. She still wanted that, right?

"I can finish up here while you get ready." He nodded toward the guest room.

"Oh, sure." She was glad for his offer to do the chores, but why wasn't he telling her who needed their help? Why the secrecy? What about the stuff he said about honesty and speaking his mind? Time to test that theory. She walked to the sink, then gazing up at him—he was four inches taller than her five foot eight—she saw his eyes widen as if he were surprised to see her standing so close. "Who did you say we're going to help?"

He didn't break their gaze, but by the loud gulp he made, his swallowing seemed impaired. Stalling? Finally, he said, "Paige." He set the plate he was holding in soapy water.

She didn't expect that answer. "Why?"

He wiped his hands on a towel. His gaze met hers, as if begging her to understand. "If you could just trust me, Pais. Please come with me and you'll see why."

"Not good enough." Yesterday's meeting with Dad and Aunt Callie was difficult enough. Today she had to go back and try again. She didn't need the stress of talking with Paige too.

"You've seen Addy's destruction around town." He rocked his thumb toward the plywood spanning the living room window.

She shrugged. "Hard to miss."

"Paige's business was—"

"Business? Since when does Paige own something?" News to her. "What kind of business?"

"An art gallery."

That sort of made sense. When they were kids, while Paisley and Peter were out fighting imaginary ocean dragons, Paige was at home, sketching them.

"She put in a coffee shop last year." His shoulders rose, then dropped. "The whole thing was damaged."

"Huh."

Judah frowned, probably at her apathetic tone.

Despite being sisters, she and Paige were never close. "Was it a souvenir shop?" She had a hard time wrapping her mind around Paige being a businesswoman.

"An art consignment shop." He washed a couple of plates. "She provided a spotlight for local artists' work."

"And it's ruined?"

"Pretty much. She needs a helping hand, that's all." He grabbed a few more dishes off the counter and slid them into the soapy water.

"Maybe you can help her while I sort things out with my dad." Paisley smoothed her palms over her face. She needed a shower. Another cup of coffee. "Yesterday's attempt was a bust."

"I'm sorry to hear that." Judah wiped his hands on the dish towel again. "Here's the thing. I know things have been off between you two for a while."

"Try our whole lives." Old frustrations simmered up her breastbone. She glared at him, annoyed that he was trying to fix things in her family.

"Reaching out to her might—"

"I don't need you stirring the pot." She groaned. "Don't you have enough dysfunction in your family without messing with mine?" Time to end this conversation. "I'm going to take a shower."

"Paisley—"

She stomped out of the room, entered the bathroom and slammed the door. Staying with her ex was a bad idea.

Why did he think she'd consider working at Paige's art gallery as if a fortified wall wasn't erected between them as kids? Mom's favorite child versus the worst kid in Basalt. The two sisters were doomed from the beginning.

And since when did Paige want to own an art gallery? Mom was the painter in the family. Although she was no Picasso, anyone who stepped inside the Cedars's house could see the abstract paintings that brought fear and awe into Paisley's girlish heart. Especially when she was locked in the pantry with a ghoulish eye staring at her from a partially finished canvas.

Now, she'd have to face some of those paintings later today—if Dad allowed her inside the house.

Twelve

Judah hesitated outside Paige's gallery, toolbox in hand. Showing up to assist his sister-in-law was the right thing to do. To say he wasn't frustrated with Paisley for leaving without saying anything to him would be a lie. Maybe he had pushed her about meeting up with her sister. But he didn't see any harm in asking her to help out. Might break the ice between the siblings who hadn't spoken in years. If he were blessed with a brother or sister, he wouldn't want an iceberg of hurt feelings caught between them. An image of Dad came to mind. Well, maybe he was a tad hypocritical. He groaned.

Mercy and grace.

Apparently, Paisley felt it wasn't any of his business to meddle. But Paige was her sister, and Paisley was still his wife, which made it sort of his business. Besides, he and Paige had become friends in the last couple of years. Her building sustained serious damage during Addy. Wasn't that reason enough for him to pitch in?

He also hoped Paisley might meet her adorable niece, Piper. He didn't think she even knew about the toddler yet. Something he thought the two sisters should share in person. Now he didn't know when that might happen.

He knocked on the plywood-covered door. It budged open beneath his knuckles. "Hello! Paige? It's Judah."

"We're back here!" A feminine voice that had to be Paige's called from somewhere in the cavernous building. "Edward and I are trying to open up a window."

Edward? Judah's footstep froze to the swollen laminate beneath his shoe. His dad was here?

"Grab some tools and join us, if you dare."

If you dare? As in, if you dare to face the work? Or, if you dare to face Mayor Grant? His good feelings about helping Paige dissolved.

His gaze fell to the aged metal toolbox he clung to that had belonged to his granddad. His father wasn't a handyman. Did he even own a hammer or a tool box? The always-well-groomed mayor getting his hands scuffed and dirty seemed like an oxymoron. What was Dad doing here? Had he anticipated Paisley might show up? Was he here to cause trouble? A knot twisted tighter in Judah's gut.

Maybe it was a good thing Paisley didn't come with him. Was Paige even aware that her sister was in town? Maybe Dad told her. Was that why he was here? To stir up problems between the two families? As if he hadn't already done enough.

Good grief, his thinking was getting paranoid. Judah should have gone with Paisley to face her dad. She probably needed his moral support. Of course, her leaving without speaking to him was a clue she didn't want him tagging along with her.

His scrambled eggs churned in his belly. If he slipped away now, would Paige be offended?

Just then, with a red bandana wrapped around her dark hair

that matched Paisley's, Paige Cedars bolted through the damaged back doorway, a huge smile on her face. "Howdy, brother-in-law. Am I ever glad to see you!" She pranced into his arms and gave him a fierce brotherly hug.

Hard to un-volunteer now. "Hi, yourself." He patted her shoulder. "How's it going?"

"I was afraid you'd take off." Nodding toward the back of the building, she made a face. She guessed right. "Where's that brat sister of mine?" So she had heard. Her eyes sparkled as she gazed past him as if Paisley might be hiding somewhere in the room.

"She didn't join me. Sorry." He hated disappointing her. "Never know, she might show up later." Although, he doubted that.

Paige's sad expression let him know she doubted it, too.

"Oh, well." Her grimace transformed into a smile." "You're here. The world's a better place already."

He chuckled, feeling unworthy of such praise. Especially since he'd been contemplating hightailing it out of here, thanks to his father's presence. Still, Paige's sentiment lightened his mood. "Where's Piper?"

Paige got a proud-mama smile on her face. "She's at a play date with a neighbor."

"Sorry to miss seeing her."

"She'll be sad to miss "Unca Dzuda" too." She nudged his elbow. "Enough stalling. Let's head into the back of the gallery where the worst damage is." She waved for him to follow.

How about if he fixed the front door? Kept a building's length between him and his father? "Sure." He nodded, but his feet scuffed the floor, moving slower than a crab at low tide. He stepped over a pile of damaged boards and dawdled over them.

Paige seemed to understand and waited on the other side of the dark space.

After a minute, he followed her through the chaos that was previously a beautiful foyer and coffee bar to get to the ocean side of the structure where the work of Oregon's artists was no longer on display. As soon as he entered the empty gallery, he smelled the damaged wood. Rot? Mold? Man, he hoped not.

"Nice to see you, Son." Edward Grant's gravelly voice reached Judah before he saw the man. How long had it been since he heard his dad call him "Son"?

"Dad." Judah peered through the semi-lit room that had been boarded up for weeks.

His dad wore a tie and held a pry bar. The tool looked out of place in his smooth hands. "Glad you squeezed in time for a little civic duty." Leave it to Dad to hammer some guilt into Judah.

"I'm glad to help Paige any time I can." He nodded at his sister-in-law who must be feeling awkward in the middle of the father/son barbs. Paisley was right. His family did have its share of dysfunctional quirks. He shouldn't have pointed out hers.

"Thanks, Judah." Paige approached the partially exposed window. "Your help means a lot to me."

Dad chuckled in Judah's direction. "Too bad you didn't marry *her*."

"Dad!"

"Mr. Grant!" Judah and Paige both spoke at the same time.

"Just teasing." Edward coughed.

Judah glanced in Paige's direction. What did she think of his father's rudeness? She probably understood the dynamics of family difficulties better than most.

"Where do you need my help?" He'd have to jump right in, or Dad's comments would fester under his skin. Dad knew that too. That's probably why he said such irritating things.

"Edward offered to help take down this window covering." She pointed toward a section of the wall where a sheet of plywood let a smidgeon of light in around it. Looked like Dad had it about half off.

Judah grabbed a hammer from his toolbox, then inserted the metal claw under the bowing wood and tugged. The window frame would need repair. The whole thing might have to be redone.

The two of them worked, prying and yanking on the board, without speaking until the plywood came down in a flurry of dust and clambered to the floor. Paige coughed from behind him. Judah covered his mouth in case any of it was moldy.

When the dust settled, Paige groaned. "Looks worse than I imagined."

The window frame was busted. The wall beneath it had caved in.

"Have you had it inspected for mold?" Judah hated to ask.

She frowned, then sighed. "The insurance company did an inspection four weeks ago after Addy."

Something smelled off when he first came in. "You might want to have someone check it again."

"Seriously?"

"He's paranoid, that's all." Edward waved both hands at Judah like he didn't value anything his son said. "A worry wart. Same as his mother."

What? He wasn't a big worrier.

"What you've got to do is get everything uncorked. Let the boards breathe." Edward guzzled water from a plastic bottle. A splash of liquid dripped down his chin and made a streak on his button-up shirt.

"I'd hate to go through mold removal." Paige paced in front of the gaping window overlooking the bay. "I'm still waiting on the insurance settlement."

"But you had good insurance, right?" Dad's voice sounded superior, which irked Judah.

"Yes, of course." She nodded. "The usual. Property, liability, flood."

"That's good." Judah attempted a reassuring smile, hoping she didn't feel thrown under the spotlight by him and Dad. "You've done everything right. I'd just have someone check for mold again, if you can swing it." He knew she didn't have much capital, but ignoring a bad situation might make it worse. "If it turns out to be nothing, that'll be a good thing."

"But expensive."

"I know a guy," Edward offered. "I'll give him a buzz."

"Really?" Paige stepped closer to Dad. "Why would you do that for me?"

Exactly what Judah wondered.

Dad dropped the empty bottle on the floor instead of asking where a trash can or recycling bin was. "What's a mayor for if not to help a fellow citizen in need?" His voice rose dramatically like he was giving a stump speech. "We have to work together in desperate times such as these."

Yada yada. Since when did Dad help citizens in low income conundrums? A political scheme? Desperate for votes? Something didn't add up.

"Thank you so much." Paige rocked her thumb toward the foyer. "I brought chocolate chip cookies, if either of you are hungry."

Judah eyed his dad. What was he up to?

"Thank you. I love chocolate chip cookies." Dad nodded once at Judah, as if to ease his mind, then tromped into the entryway.

Judah didn't follow, although he might have a better clue about his dad's motives if he eavesdropped on Dad's and Paige's conversation. Instead, he continued working on the window frame.

It looked like it needed more help than he or Edward—neither of them being carpenters—could give.

He used a planer to scrape ragged edges from the ledge. "Do you have any spare lumber around?" he called toward the foyer. Maybe he could try repairing the broken section.

Paige stuck her head around the corner and rocked her thumb toward the opposite side of the room. "Salvaged wood in that pile."

"Thanks." He trudged over and picked up a couple of decent looking two-by-fours that might work.

Dad made a disgruntled sound from behind him. "You going to tell your old man what's going on?"

Judah turned, board in hand. "Going on? You tell me."

"What's your ex-wife doing back in town?" Dad squinted and bit into a cookie. Chocolate lined the creases of his lips.

Oh, that. Judah kicked his booted toes against a damp board, his miffed level rising. "She's staying at my place, so I'd appreciate it if you didn't call her my 'ex.'" Why did his father always have to push him off the cliff of frustration?

Dad gulped down his cookie. "You're kidding me, right?" He crossed his arms, and Judah figured a lecture was forthcoming. Just what he needed. "You've got to wear the pants, son. Who does Paisley think she is crashing back into town after what she did to you? What she did to all of us?"

"Dad, let it go, will you?" Judah stacked as many boards as would fit in his arms, his rough treatment of the wood inviting a few slivers.

"I won't let it go. You know how much her vandalism cost me?" Dad thundered. "What the town says about her? How can I forget that? How can anyone?"

Judah groaned. Everything came down to money, or appearances, with Edward Grant. "I don't want to talk about it."

He let the pile of boards drop to the floor. The clatter echoed in the empty room. He crossed his arms, imitating his dad's stance. "If you're so determined to pry and push your nose in where it doesn't belong, we've got a problem."

Dad took a step closer, his eyes bugged, a look Judah saw numerous times growing up. "Since when is a dad asking his son a question considered prying?"

"Oh, now you're going to pull the dad card?" He didn't want to be disrespectful. He felt a tug inside to settle down. Was that the Holy Spirit cautioning him to not say something he'd regret? If only he listened.

Judah glared at his dad. Dad glared back, fire in his gaze.

Paige rushed to the midpoint between the two men, her hands outstretched. "Whoa. What's going on in here?" Did she think they were about to come to blows?

With the forgiveness Judah was working on almost forgotten, he thought that too. "Nothing." He gritted his teeth. Only one way to end such awkwardness and keep himself from yelling at his father. "Sorry. I have to go."

"But—"

He grabbed his tools. Marched through the foyer. Couldn't get out of there fast enough. "I'll be back another time, Paige."

"Okay, I understand." Her voice sounded small and distant.

That he wasn't keeping his word about helping her today throttled something deep inside him. But while the proverbial smoke billowed from his ears, he couldn't stay in the same room as Dad. He didn't trust himself. And he didn't trust his father to not say something aggravating. How dare Dad discuss Paisley as if Judah wanted her gone as much as he did? Dad knew nothing about how he coped for the last three years. Not once did the man ask how he was doing in the absence of his wife. Instead, he spread his rotten negativity about her around town.

Judah still didn't get why a man of wealth and authority in Basalt Bay would suddenly be interested in Paige's gallery. He stomped in the direction of his truck. He needed coffee and answers. Only one place where he could get both. Bert's Fish Shack usually churned with gossip. It was about time he had a chat with the diner's owner. If anyone knew some dirt on the mayor, it would be a long-time resident of Basalt Bay like him.

Thirteen

Paisley had been sitting on the irregular floorboards of Dad's front porch for over an hour with the wind blowing against her and a light rain falling. Seeing the old rocking chair where she spent countless childhood hours reading and daydreaming, the apple tree she climbed hundreds of times, and the steps she skipped up and down as a kid, made her feel nostalgic. Observing the rundown parts made her sad.

The apple tree in front of the living room window had been here for as long as she was alive, probably for as long as Dad lived here. Now, boards were propped under its bent limbs. How much longer before the whole thing fell over? The grass was overgrown and sickly looking. Weeds were knee-high. Most of the plants Mom had tended were dried up. The whole house needed a paint job. Why wasn't Dad keeping things groomed? Did he need help?

And when did the yard shrink? She remembered how she and Peter and some of the neighbor kids played Annie Over, tossing a ball over the roof of the simple two-story house. Whoever caught it would run around to the other side like a tsunami wave was chasing them and throw the ball at someone. The property didn't seem small then. A matter of perspective, she supposed. As a kid, Oregon felt ginormous, and Basalt was the center of her universe.

Dad's 1968 Volkswagen Beetle finally pulled into the driveway and came to a rattling stop. Dad didn't wave. Didn't acknowledge her. He just sat in his burnt-sienna antique for a long while. Did he wish his eldest daughter would take the hint and leave him alone?

Not this time, Dad.

Although, she wouldn't pressure him, either. Their reunion had to come naturally. Slowly, like a simmering stew that couldn't be rushed. Mom used to yell at them not to taste the stew until she added her secret ingredient, whatever that was. If only Paisley had a secret component to making everything okay between her and Dad again. Was he pondering the years when he didn't hear from her, or the misunderstandings between Mom and him and her, or his disappointment over her marrying Judah on the sly? She groaned at the list of grievances.

When the rusty '68 driver's door creaked open, an eternity seemed to pass before she saw movement inside. Dad sat there not making eye contact. Frowning. Staring forward as if ignoring her long enough would make her go away. Any childlike wish for a happy welcoming from her father crumbled for a second day in a row.

If it came down to one of them outwaiting the other, it would be him. She never won a staring contest or a stand-on-one-leg competition in her life. She was the impatient one. Her personality didn't do well at the waiting game.

Dad still didn't move.

Anxiety rushed up her middle, a brain freeze in her gut. She sat stiffly on the porch, her toes tapping the only part of her that moved.

What if something was physically wrong with him? Or he was having a heart attack?

She stood and tried to see him without staring.

Enough wondering and waiting. She marched to the parked vehicle. Three feet from the open door, she stopped. "You okay?" When he didn't answer, she covered the distance. "Dad?" She leaned down and peered at him.

His hands clutched the steering wheel as if adhered, flesh to torn leather, and he didn't meet her gaze.

"Dad?" She spoke louder.

No smile. No nod. Just a tic in his jaw. The rejection scraped her insides. Watching him in profile, seeing moisture puddling in the eyes of the man she admired for all her childhood, dug a well of pain inside her wider than the Pacific. If there was one person in the world she never wanted to disappoint, it was this man. Her hero. Her protector—until the pantry lockups. She never understood why he didn't intervene on her behalf. Now, he wouldn't look at her? Like she was poisonous. Or repulsive. Was he ashamed of her?

Knots formed in her stomach. A bitter lump in her throat nearly choked her. "C-can't you s-say something?"

Silence, then, "Why are you h-here?" His voice, and his hands on the steering wheel, shook.

"To talk with you." She dug her fists deep inside her coat pockets, chilled from the hour of sitting on the porch. A scattering of leaves hit the car and brushed her legs. "Can we go inside? Looks like a storm is coming." She glanced up at the gray clouds overhead.

"I meant, why are you back in Basalt Bay?"

"It was time to come home. I wanted to see you. And Judah." What else could she say that would bridge the chasm?

"Time." He snorted and wiped the back of his big hand across his lips. "Three and a half years ago, before you snuck off and left town, that's when it was time to come home. Before your mother died."

So that's what his cold shoulder was about? He was bitter toward her about the funeral? "I know. I-I couldn't." Nothing would compensate for such a grave transgression.

"Wouldn't, you mean." He cut her a cross look.

"True. Not then. I'm here now, Dad. We need to talk." Although, this conversation wasn't going well either.

"Too late." He crossed his arms. His chin jutted out, reminding her of Peter.

Too late. Too late. Dad's words repeated in her mind. Did he mean their relationship was over? That he wouldn't ever talk with her about the past? If so, why put herself through standing in this blustery wind, and through the humiliation of begging Dad to forgive her? She should get in her car, turn the heater on high, and head to the cottage.

She couldn't cave so easily. A strong breeze off the ocean pressed her forward. She stiffened her knees to keep from falling against the VW. "Some coffee would be nice." Was that too much to ask? She rubbed the toe of her shoe against the threshold of the car opening.

Why didn't he get out of the vehicle? He couldn't sit here all day.

"Fine," she grumbled as a possible solution came to mind. She charged around the Volkswagen, then yanked on the passenger door handle. It didn't budge. "Come on." Had he secured the lock to keep her from getting in? "Dad, please open the door."

Silence.

Pulling again on the handle didn't help. She groaned, imagining herself kicking the door until Dad gave in and unlocked it. But a temperamental display would probably remind him of the teenager she'd been, not the woman she was. Although, standing near her father, and him not speaking to her, made her feel like that young, confused girl.

"Okay, so you don't want to talk with me!" Her voice was loud enough for their elderly neighbors, Mr. and Mrs. Anderson, to hear, but she didn't care. "Sitting in the car to avoid me is ridiculous. We're both adults. Yes, I made some terrible life decisions. I admit that." She stomped around to Dad's open door again. "Are you going to stay in the car until I get on my knees and grovel? If that's what you need me to do, I will." He barely blinked. She was out of ideas. "Will you *please* come in the house? I'm freezing. I'll even make the coffee." She tried softening her tone.

No response.

"Oh, for the love of Pete." As soon as she said the phrase, she thought of her brother Peter. Dad sniffed, wiped his nose. Perhaps his thoughts ran in the same direction.

"Every night I pray for you and Peter," he said quietly. "Every night my heart breaks for what I lost."

Tears she didn't want any part of filled her eyes. She tried ignoring the rivulets as they dripped down her cheeks. She knelt on the gravel and overgrown weeds next to Dad's car. Tentatively, taking a chance on another rejection, she laid her hand over his on the steering wheel. "I've missed you, Dad."

Tears streamed down his cheeks too. Shoulders hunched, he sobbed out loud, his body quaking. For a moment, she felt frozen as the man she'd never seen weeping before leaned his forehead over her hand on his, crying like a brokenhearted child.

She did this to him. Guilt pierced her. Was her arrival too great of a shock? Should she leave?

No, she came too far to run now. She was here to make amends where she could. She patted his shoulder. Leaned her cheek against his arm. "I'm so sorry, Dad." She didn't know if he heard her whispered words.

Then, taking her by surprise, he leaned slightly out of the car and his arms dragged her against his chest. He held her close, her cheek pressed against his soft flannel shirt that smelled of Old Spice and him, rocking her, and they both cried. No words were spoken. None were needed. He patted her back, and she did the same to him. He kissed the top of her head as he did many times throughout her childhood. Then he released her and wiped his face with the palms of both hands.

She wiped tears from her cheeks too, chuckling over the two of them crying and sniffling. It was a healing embrace, one she was thankful for. A fresh start, she hoped. Maybe he'd take her up on that coffee now.

"You should go." He lifted his chin in the direction of the ocean.

She hadn't expected that. "Why?" Didn't they just share a loving father/daughter moment of significance? Why was he sending her away?

He shook his head and bit his lower lip like he couldn't explain.

"Can't we try to talk?" She gazed into his grayish eyes.

"Will talking erase what's happened?"

"No, but—" A lead weight landed in the pit of her stomach. "Not erase exactly."

"Then what?"

Communicating with him was so much harder than she thought it would be. "I want to help you understand why I left." Could he fathom her grief? Or forgive her wrongs? "I want you to tell me what you're feeling too."

"Your mom wanted to see you—at the end." Both of his

shoes landed in the weeds. He stood shakily in increments, as if doing so hurt.

"I'm sorry I disappointed you." She swallowed. "And her." Not that she would have done anything differently at the time. Now, with three years of regret built up? Maybe.

Dad shut the car door, then shuffled toward the house, his gait unsteady. Was something wrong with him?

She scooted under his arm, offering support he didn't shrug off. They walked beside each other the way they did when she was a girl and they were on their way to the beach, or to get ice cream at Bert's, only much slower. She glanced up at the apple tree, thinking of times when he let her jump from a limb into his arms. *"I'll catch you,"* he'd said. She trusted him completely then.

When did that perfect trust in another human being cease? Something squeezed tightly in her chest.

A picture of herself sitting on the pantry floor in the dark, wishing her daddy would rescue her, came to mind. Old thoughts better stuffed away. But if she never took a glance at her past, how could she hope to live at peace in her future?

When they got to the porch, Dad stopped leaning on her and reached for the handrailing. It wobbled beneath his grip—something else that needed mending. He hobbled up the worn steps. The old place was as broken down as Dad appeared to be. He paused at the screen door, his hand on the brown rusty knob.

She held her breath, wishing he would invite her in. She'd convinced herself she didn't want to go inside and see Mom's paintings. But in this moment, her dad inviting her to come home was the greatest hope imaginable.

"Come back tomorrow?" His question was not what she anticipated, but perhaps he was offering her a white flag.

"I will." And the next day. And the next. She'd keep returning, trying to get him to talk, telling him again how sorry she was, until he forgave her and asked her to come inside.

"Paisley?" This time he sounded more like her dad, more like the man who shared her love of the sea. For a second, she wished he'd call her *Paisley-bug*, his nickname for her when she was a kid. Too bad she ordered him to stop calling her that when she turned eleven.

"Don't expect too much from me."

Ice particles re-formed around the perimeter of her heart. Was she expecting too much? Was forgiveness and love from a father to a daughter too lavish a gift?

She blinked fast. *Don't cry. Don't cave in.* "See you t-tomorrow, Dad." She tried her best not to be emotional, but she had only so much tolerance for rejection.

The screen door clattered shut.

Just then, the gray clouds let loose with a heavy rain. Paisley ran to her Accord parked on the narrow street. When she got in and turned the key, the engine hiccupped and rattled. Strange sounds. But when the car went into gear normally, she turned on the windshield wipers and the heater, then accelerated down Front Street. Maybe she'd look for Judah and ask him to check the engine.

Despite her recent emotional turmoil with Dad, when her stomach growled, grabbing some lunch sounded appealing. Maybe some comfort food. Hot coffee with lots of creamer. If she located Judah, maybe they could go to the Fish Shack together. Talk. At least *he* hadn't rejected her. In fact, he had opened his arms and his heart to her, even though she stomped his hopes of reconciliation into the ground.

How could she keep ignoring such a kindhearted man who said he still loved her?

Fourteen

Just as Judah stepped inside Bert's diner, his cell phone chirped a sound that made his heart race. The sharp clang meant one thing—an emergency. He yanked the phone from his back pocket and pressed it to his ear. "Hello." He plugged his other ear with his finger to stifle the café's rumble of voices. "What's happened?"

"That storm we've been watching?" Mia spoke quickly. "It's moving up the coastline fast—like Addy did. Possible hurricane force winds. May strike landfall by midnight, if it continues on its current trajectory."

"Oh, man." A second storm hitting Basalt Bay—unlike any that previously hit their shores with such ferocity in fifty years?

"Craig said get to C-MER pronto." She paused. "Please hurry, Judah."

Adrenaline ignited faster than he could answer. "Ten minutes."

"Make it five." Their connection ended. Mia probably had a slew of workers to call.

Clouds had been rolling in all day, although nothing unusual about that over the ocean. If C-MER thought this storm was a real threat, would they initiate the new early warning system? As far as he knew, it hadn't been tested yet. Bad timing. But did a storm ever hit in good timing?

If the winds lashed the coast like the previous storm, combined with high tides and flooding, they'd have to evacuate everyone. Daylight hours would be less complicated for initiating exit strategies. At night some citizens might refuse to budge from their homes, he knew this from previous experience.

Since he was already at the diner, should he give Bert a heads-up? The Fish Shack was located next to the old cannery near the end of Front Street where some of the worst damage happened last month. The business owner had been forced to close for ten days while he and a crew rebuilt an entire wall. The outer portion of the building still wasn't finished, and the dock remained upended. Bert wouldn't take news of another storm well, but Judah felt compelled to warn him.

However, he didn't want to start a panic, and he wasn't authorized to make any announcements yet. The winds might still die down or change course. Over the years, he was called into work many times, only to discover the anticipated storm veered away. Hopefully, that would be the case today.

He marched over to the register where Bert was explaining serving etiquette to a teenage boy. In a hurry, Judah rapped his knuckles on the counter. "Can I talk with you for a second?"

Bert stroked his grayish handlebar mustache and squinted. Apparently, he didn't appreciate anyone interrupting him, Judah included. However, he grunted in acquiescence.

Judah waved him toward a window facing south.

"What's up, Sonny?" Bert's thick brows quirked.

Judah rocked his thumb toward the window. "Take a gander at that."

Bert leaned over and squinted in the southerly direction where a bank of clouds was building steam over the ocean. He whistled. "Another doozy?"

"May hit landfall tonight."

Bert thumped his palm against his forehead. "I can't win. The whole weather system is out to get me." A little dramatic, but nothing Judah wouldn't expect from the man who attached a fifteen-foot salmon replica to his roof, then lost it a week later during Addy.

"It might blow over." Judah patted Bert's arm. "I thought you should know. Stay safe, my friend." He opened the door and dashed out into the rain. The exchange cost him three minutes.

"What about the alarm?" Bert yelled after him, his voice almost lost in the winds already blowing in from the ocean.

Judah stopped running, glanced back. "We'll sound the alarm if it comes to that. We don't want a panic."

"Yeah, yeah, thanks." Bert waved, then shut the door to his diner.

Judah sprinted to the parking lot, jumped in his two-door pickup, and gunned it toward the main road leading to the north side of town. As he sped past Basalt Bay Peninsula, the higher than usual sea spray catapulted over the point in explosive white bursts. Good thing Paisley wasn't sitting out there with such rough waves today. Was she at her dad's? When Judah knew more about the weather threat, that stirred up too quickly for his comfort, he'd call Paul's and make sure Paisley was safe. As soon as possible, he was going to buy her a cell phone so they could communicate with each other easier.

Almost to C-MER, he mentally checked off the tasks awaiting him. He'd probably have to go out in the skiff for a pre-storm check of the coastline. During Addy, he nearly didn't make it back to the dock. Talk about an adrenaline rush. Even so, if that's what had to be done, he was one of the most experienced boatmen at C-MER. He was prepared to do his job.

No doubt, his workplace would be a chaotic hub of employees seeking up-to-the-minute weather updates and answering frantic calls from concerned citizens. If the storm worsened, Craig would release a preliminary statement to radio stations and marine outlets. In the case of imminent danger to the town, he'd send out a wireless emergency alert. Once initial warnings were issued, if winds increased to upper hurricane levels, or dunes were found to be deteriorating, or if severe flooding caused road closures out of the city, they'd sound the evacuation sirens.

It might be a long day. And night.

Judah entered the parking lot where sand swirled across the pavement, looking almost like snow flurries. A couple of branches tumbled by. The wind was picking up.

He pulled into a parking space as several other workers exited their vehicles. Some held onto their hats and ran toward the building. Judah turned off the engine, said a prayer for wisdom and safety, secured the hood of his raincoat, then jumped out of his truck. Rain and sand pelted him. He leaned forward and braced into the wind.

Inside the C-MER building, coworkers scurried around, carrying stacks of printed pages from the copy room into their work zone at the back. Others spoke loudly into their cell phones. Shouting came from the conference room. Someone was obviously upset. Several guys hovered over blueprints, not making eye contact. He didn't see Craig.

"Judah!" Mia waved him over with both hands.

"Where's Craig? What's my assignment?"

She flipped through post-it notes on her dry-erase board.

"He's in there." She jabbed her thumb in the direction of the conference room. She cringed as several voices rose. Sounded like a shouting match.

Judah nodded toward the ruckus. "What's going on?"

She shook her head as if to say, "*Don't ask.*" "You know Craig's brainchild?" She leaned closer, her voice a whisper. "That amazing state-of-the-art early warning system?"

"The answer to all our problems?" He attended enough lectures about it with Craig leading the charge.

"Right. Doesn't work."

"What?"

"Tech hasn't been able to activate the test. Mike Linfield tore in here a few minutes ago, screaming at everyone." She winced. "He's threatening pink slips."

"Not good." No doubt, Craig's job would be on the chopping block if his crew didn't get the system running, especially with the whole town counting on the alarm. "What am I supposed to do? Normal storm routine?" Judah knew the drill, but did Craig have any other tasks for him?

Mia sorted through her notes, flinging several of the colorful squares on the floor. "Here it is." She held up a bright orange one. "Judah"—she read—"check the rock on the peninsula and the dunes south of town. Get anyone off the beach who's stupid enough to be taking pictures there."

"Right." There was always someone who wanted to capture a photograph or a video of a tempest despite signage warning them to stay off the beach during a storm. "Will do." He hustled into the locker room.

Knowing he was going into a potentially dangerous situation on the water, he wanted to be prepared. He grabbed a bomber-style float coat with an insulated hood, rain bib overalls, rubber boots, and warm gloves, then headed to the equipment checkout station. Once he located the clipboard and signed out his skiff, leaving a notation of his checkpoints, he exited through the back door.

As he strode down the ramp to the dock, the increasing winds and rain battered him. Nothing like facing strong gusts and curling waves in an open skiff to make him feel alive, and at the same time, cause his insides to quake. He'd done it before and survived. With God's help, he could do it again. The thought of Paisley made him hesitate. Hadn't he promised to put her first? Yet, he didn't even call to check on her. He groaned. No time for that now.

But always time for a short prayer. *Lord, please be with Paisley. Keep her safe at her dad's until we find out how bad this squall will be. Be with me in the bay. In Jesus's name.*

By the time he returned, Craig and his team would surely have the warning system figured out—preferably without anyone losing their job. C-MER was tasked with monitoring the coastal region and alerting towns to potential danger. If they couldn't accomplish their basic mission, they'd have a crisis. No wonder Mike Linfield was outraged.

However, despite the whitecaps bubbling around the docks, Judah felt optimistic the winds might still change direction or die down. Too early to tell. Other than the prediction that hurricane winds were on a possible trajectory of making landfall by midnight.

Please, God, stifle the storm as You've done so many times.

Before untying the sixteen-foot skiff from the dock, Judah made sure he had oars and a bailing bucket. Check, check. He patted his coat pocket; cell phone in place. He sat down in the driver's seat, turned the key to start the engine, then checked the fuel gauge. He had a moment's hesitation as he thought of his boat ride the other day when the engine stalled and he jumped into the waves. He didn't want that happening again today.

Following the no-wake rule, he steered slowly through the docking area, the skiff bobbing and dipping up and down and side to side with the waves. He brought the boat around the protective bar of rocks a C-MER crew built about a decade ago, and then slowly moved into open waters. The sea rolled in swells.

His hood flew off his head and bounced against his back. Good thing it was secured to the coat or he would have lost it. He pulled the covering onto his head and tied the knot beneath his chin. About a hundred yards out, sheets of rain fell like nails, pelting him and the boat. Winds building in velocity forced him to slow down and take the next waves carefully, or he'd be swamped. Following orders, but anticipating possible danger in the waters ahead, he pointed the bow toward the peninsula, repeating his prayer for safety.

Lord, help us all.

Fifteen

As Paisley reached the southern end of Front Street, her car coughed and rattled, nearly stalling. She gunned the gas and kept it running, but the engine's hesitancy alarmed her. She quickly pulled into a parking space next to where she thought Judah was volunteering, then turned off the motor. For a few minutes, she sat there staring at the damaged, sad-looking building on the ocean side of the street where plywood had been nailed over the front windows. So this was Paige's art gallery, huh?

Despite Paisley's reluctance to see her sister, she got out of the car, slammed the door, and dashed through the rain until she reached the alcove near the entrance. The wind billowed against her as if it were trying to stop her from taking shelter under the torn awning. A sign hanging sideways read *Paige's Art Gallery and Coffee Shop*. She brushed raindrops from her coat, then pulled on the door handle. It didn't give. Wasn't there supposed to be a work party here? She tugged on the doorknob again. Nothing. If Judah was finished helping Paige, where did he go?

She banged her knuckles against the plywood in case someone was inside.

"Why, if it isn't Paisley Cedars." The artificially sweetened voice that came from behind her had to be Lucy Carmichael's.

Paisley wanted to disappear into a crack in the sidewalk. She slowly faced the friend-turned-nemesis she antagonistically called "Red" in high school.

"When did *you* get back in town?" Lucy's acidic tone made Paisley's stomach churn.

Old feelings resurfaced like a piece of cork let loose from a sunken ship. She forced herself to breathe normally. Hard to do with her heart hammering against her ribs.

"Hello, Lucy." Paisley plastered on a fake smile that had to be as convincing as the one on Lucy's lips. "So, you still live in Basalt Bay?"

"Always have. Always will." A gust of wind blew off the redhead's knit cap. She chased it down the sidewalk, then jogged back. In a move that surprised Paisley, her old classmate scooted into the alcove beside her, too close for comfort in the confined space.

"Can you believe this weather? You hear about the storm?" Lucy's freckles were less noticeable now than in high school. Apparently, she outgrew her teenage awkwardness and, hopefully, her meanness.

Paisley remembered their last fight on graduation night—a terrible row in the middle of the street over Brian Corbin, who turned out to be unworthy of anyone fighting over him. Paisley had shouted and called Red a "freckled face warthog." Thinking of the unkind words she hadn't thought of in ten years made her cheeks heat up. A heaviness filled her chest and softened her response. "Sure, it looks like the storm is already here." She'd be a fool not to be able to read the signs after living next to the ocean for most of her life, but she didn't say so. She leaned out of the nook where she'd taken refuge, trying to get a glimpse of the sea and distract herself from her guilty thoughts over things she said to Red years ago.

"I wonder what they'll call this one." Lucy shrugged. "Betty? Beatrice?"

"I hope it won't come to that."

"Bet it will." Lucy's eyes glimmered.

Paisley had never been in a storm with strong enough winds to deserve a name. Other than the ones locals dubbed "Storm of the Century" or "Storm of '02" or "Basalt Bay's Fury."

At the end of the street, just beyond the Fish Shack, waves exploded against Bert's broken dock. It would be exciting to get close enough to see farther into the cove during such strong winds. Plus, she would jump at any excuse to get away from the woman who invaded her personal space.

"I'm heading over to City Hall." Lucy rocked her thumb toward the town's governing offices across the street. "You should find somewhere safe to wait out the storm."

Not at City Hall, that was for sure.

"Nice seeing you." Paisley said the obligatory words.

"You too." Lucy nodded toward the building behind them that used to be O'Reilly's Fine Dining when Paisley was young. "Your sister's place took a beating during Addy."

"Yeah, I can see that." Paisley maintained her aloof tone, but in truth she felt badly for Paige's loss now that she saw the extent of damage. Unfortunately, she didn't feel any empathy about it this morning. She'd have to apologize to Judah about that, too.

"You want to get some coffee and see what the mayor has to

say about Bertie or Belinda?" Lucy pointed to the two-story town centerpiece.

"Nah, think I'll head down to Bert's and have a look."

"You and your daredevil ways, Paisley Cedars." Lucy scoffed.

"Grant." She corrected even though she previously imagined herself reverting to Cedars.

"Just for now, right?" Lucy's gaze pierced Paisley's. "All of us single girls know Judah Grant's about to become the hottest bachelor in Basalt Bay."

Mia, Red, and how many others waited in line to chase after Judah once he was officially free? Pain arched up Paisley's middle. But why should she feel jealous? Hadn't she relinquished him three years ago? *Yeah, but my ex-friend going after my ex-husband?* The notion riled her.

"Find shelter." Lucy leaned closer and shouted above the howling wind. "I don't want Judah risking his life out there hunting for you." She winked as if she told a joke, then she jogged into the street with the wind whipping her long red hair like a rope.

So Lucy thought she had a chance with Judah? Did they ever go out? Paisley glowered, contemplating Lucy's assessment of Judah being the "hottest bachelor in Basalt Bay." But then, heat crept up her neck. Other than the bachelor bit, she had to concede with Red's sentiment. He *was* handsome. But Lucy and him? *Come on.* Was her taunt more about revenge, since Brian Corbin took Paisley to prom all those years ago? If so, why didn't Lucy pursue the police deputy now that he was more reputable in the community?

Suddenly, rain fell like buckets of water were being poured from the clouds, but the wind seemed to have let up a little. Should she make a run for the peninsula? She imagined the waves pounding the beach, foaming and frothing over the rocks. She'd love to sit on her favorite boulder and experience nature's fury again. Did she dare?

As she stepped out of the alcove, raindrops pelted her raincoat. The sky was dark, the sun obliterated by dense, low-hanging clouds. An eerie feeling overcame her. A rise in barometric pressure, or some premonition of disaster?

Maybe they were in for a storm unlike any she'd experienced. Would it be as destructive as the one that rammed logs through Paige's building and broke the windows at the cottage? Should she heed Lucy's warning to find shelter? She could head over to Bert's and get some coffee, but the Fish Shack seemed even more in line with a storm surge from open waters. Besides, the diner looked dark. No cars in front. Had it already closed?

What if the town's emergency alarm sounded? Judah had probably been called in to work. No help there. What would she do without a reliable vehicle?

Harsh winds shoved her back into the recesses of the building's entrance. Boards above her creaked as if they might give way. Her shelter of sorts didn't feel very safe. Where should she go? Too far to hike to the cottage. Dad's? She hated the thought of him weathering the storm alone. Of course, he lived here his whole life. He'd know what to do.

Another blast of wind careened past her, whirling trash and papers. The storm seemed to be worsening before her eyes. The gallery sign crashed to the cement. Paisley screamed. Another board came loose and fell on top of the sign. Enough of this. She dashed into the rain, cinching the hood of her raincoat until she peeked out of a two-inch circle, the better for no one to recognize her. A powerful gust pressed her against the outer wall of the gallery. She clung to a piece of decorative metal, waiting for the wind surge to cease.

When a lull finally came, she lunged for the next alcove near the entrance to Nautical Sal's Souvenirs. She cupped her hands to the glass and peered inside. The lights were off. The big windows in front were boarded up. Had the owners done that today?

What about Dad? Did he board up any windows? Thinking of the neglect she saw earlier, in the overgrown yard and the house's peeling paint, she doubted he did anything to preserve the old place.

Just then, a howling siren pierced the air with one short blast. Did that mean they had to evacuate? But, wait. Only one tone? Wouldn't a real evacuation siren go on and on, or else have a rhythm of long and short blasts? Something wasn't right. Where could she find out the town's emergency plan?

City Hall.

Ugh.

At that moment, the most overstated building in Basalt was being overrun by citizens charging up the sidewalk and disappearing inside the wide doors. Did she want to join them?

Uh, no.

But if they had to evacuate, she needed to know what to do.

The wind blew her back against the wall of the souvenir shop just as a "No Parking" sign flew at her. She raised her arm to deflect the metal from hitting her face. The sign clattered to the cement, and she leaped onto the sidewalk. She had to find somewhere safer. Bracing into the wind, she faced the structure housing the city departments and a community gathering place. Someone had probably prepared coffee and snacks. She wouldn't mind a giant-sized cup of coffee and a place to get out of the rain.

Running in spurts, then holding on to signs, she made her way across the street. At the last sign—a tsunami warning—the rain fell harder than ever, rolling down her slicker onto her pants, puddling on her shoes. Two inches of rain had accumulated on the street. Too bad she didn't wear rubber boots today.

Everything within her resisted going inside the government building. She remembered the last time she saw Edward— his ugly words and his condemnation of her. But she couldn't stay outside, gripping a sign for dear life.

With her heart pounding like it might pummel through her chest wall, she dashed for the front door. She didn't know what she'd say to Judah's father, if she saw him.

But the odds of her *not* seeing Mayor Grant inside City Hall were highly unlikely.

Sixteen

Judah steered the skiff through a series of jarring waves, eyeing the turbulent seas ahead. He'd rarely seen a sky as pewter colored as this one, except at night. As in every other stormy weather event when he had to check the coastline, his thoughts turned prayerful. *God, be with me. Wherever Paisley is, be with her. Protect the citizens of Basalt Bay.*

He needed to stay focused on the emergency, but his concern over his wife's whereabouts hadn't let up. He pictured her the way he saw her on the peninsula three days ago: limp, unresponsive, and with waves crashing over her. The memory made his heart thunder in his chest. Surely, she wouldn't go back there today. Not in such terrible conditions. Yet, she was exactly the sort of person who'd want to see the effects of the storm on the ocean—he knew that much about her.

Fortunately, he was headed in the direction of the public beach. If she, or anyone else, were on the rocks there, it would be his duty to get them to move to safety.

With his hand on the throttle, ready to increase speed, his

phone chirped the emergency alert that ramped up his fight-or-flight response. He snagged his phone out of his coat pocket.

"Judah, here." He adjusted the throttle, keeping the skiff moving slowly.

"Return to base now!" Mia commanded.

He bristled at her tone. "On whose orders?"

"Craig's," she snapped.

He swallowed back a curt response. "He said I was supposed to—"

"Things have changed." She sounded riled. Maybe the alert and all the franticness around the office were taking their toll on her. "The storm is becoming a monster. We just received updated satellite reports. Hurricane winds combined with up to thirty inches of rain, on top of an already high tide, are expected to lash the coast within hours. And the emergency—" Her next words were garbled.

"What was that last part?" The wind's roar and the rumble of the engine made it difficult to hear.

"The preliminary alert failed," she shouted. "A pitiful blast, then nothing. Get back here immediately." She took a breath. "If the tech team can't fix the system in the next few minutes, we'll have to go door to door alerting everyone."

You've got to be kidding me. Texting would work better than knocking on every door in Basalt Bay. Of course, some folks didn't have mobile devices, especially the elderly. "Okay. Thanks, Mia." He ended the call and made a wide one-eighty. Now he wouldn't be able to check the peninsula and make sure Paisley wasn't there. Hopefully, she was at her dad's.

As he steered the skiff back toward C-MER, he recalled his father telling him about a time when the sheriff banged on his parents' door in the middle of the night, warning of flooding conditions. Dad's family escaped to higher ground, despite Grandma not wanting to go. The way Dad told it, Grandpa scooped up his wife and carried her over his shoulder to their car, Grandma kicking at him the whole way. Judah would have enjoyed seeing such fiery passion in his family. It made him wonder what he'd do if Paisley dug in her heels about leaving.

In every storm, there were those who didn't want to leave their homes. But if a life-threatening wave approached, and folks refused to budge at C-MER's urging, law enforcement would step in.

Terrible news about the new warning system's glitch. Mayor Grant would be enraged, along with the city council and dozens of citizens who contributed financially. What a mess.

Back at the berth, Judah took extra precautions securing the skiff. As he walked toward the ramp, a blast of wind knocked him to the other side of the dock, almost to the water's edge. *Whoa.* His arms shot outward, flailing as he fought for balance. He gasped at the near miss, then regaining his footing, leaned his head down and forced his legs to move forward up the ramp. The feeling of helplessness in such strong winds made him remember how he was caught off guard in the storm a month ago. That was one freaky boat ride back to C-MER.

Maybe that's why Mia seemed upset today. She'd probably been out of her mind with worry for the guys caught in boats during Addy. He recalled her hugging him when he returned, saying she was glad he was alive. Nothing personal. It was just how she acted with all the guys, right?

Now, as he entered through the back door at his job site, Mia stood there ready to hand him a plastic sleeve with a stack of papers in it, all businesslike. "Here's your information packet. You've got midtown. Notify every house on your list about a potential evacuation." She rattled off her spiel as if she weren't nervous about the approaching storm, although her voice on the phone a few minutes ago told him otherwise. "Mark off addresses on the sheet. Tell residents to check this phone number for a recording"—she tapped the top of the first page—"or online at this website for emergency updates and shelter information." She patted his arm, her palm lingering on his forearm a tad longer than necessary. "Judah, I'm glad you don't have to be out on the ocean during this one."

"Uh, thanks. Me too." He put two steps between them.

As she walked away, he didn't watch. Had he ever? He didn't think so. Still, Paisley's question about what was going on between him and Mia bothered him. His answer of "nothing" had been true for him. It still was.

Scanning the sixty addresses Mia gave him, he recognized Paul Cedars's place about midway down the list. Good. That meant Judah would have the chance to check on him and make sure Paisley was safe.

If an evacuation happened, they could leave in his truck together. His vehicle would be more efficient in flooding conditions than Paisley's low-riding car.

He made a beeline for Craig's office. Five guys lined the small room, leaving a couple of workers standing outside, their heads bent down as if listening but avoiding eye contact. Judah joined them and watched the interaction between Mike Linfield and Craig through the open door.

"This is an outrage!" Mike's face was tomato red. "We purchased an expensive high-tech system and your knuckleheads can't figure out how to make it work?" Mike jabbed his finger at Craig's chest. "Heads will roll over this mistake!" The manager slapped his palm against the desk and leaned down, glaring around the room, person by person.

Judah gulped. He could almost see fumes blasting out of the room that wasn't much larger than his cubicle.

"Equipment malfunctions, sir, nothing more." Craig's tone sounded edgy, lacking any hint of contriteness. Might not be such a great approach, but he was probably catching all the flak for the problem. "We'll get it fixed, I promise."

"You better. Too many things have 'malfunctioned' on your watch, Masters." Mike's icy tone could have formed crystals on the window.

Judah thought of a few things that went wrong recently: his skiff engine dying, Sample D moving, the busted gazebo at Baker's Point. Not that Craig's work performance had anything to do with those foul-ups.

"Can we get back to the plan? Time is essential." Craig nodded at the circular wall clock.

"Your plan failed." Mike sneered. "If I didn't need you to fix this embarrassment today, I'd fire you on the spot."

Craig's shoulders jerked. Every person in the area probably gasped like Judah did. If Craig could get fired that easily, what about the rest of them?

"Do we have approval to knock on doors and reach out to the community? You know, *attempt* to save lives?" Craig's voice held barely controlled anger—Judah recognized it by all the times he heard him get riled at some of the other employees in the past. "Or shall we continue rehashing this debacle over failed electronics that will soon be fixed and forgotten?"

In the ensuing silence, Judah kept his gaze averted.

"Why are you morons still standing here?" Mike yelled at the cluster of workers. "Get out there and reach as many homes and businesses as you can before five."

Five? Judah checked his watch. Thirty minutes? Not possible. Even so, he scurried from the office door with the others.

"Wait!" Craig's voice bellowed.

Judah's footstep paused mid-stride.

"We don't want a panic." Craig sounded more in control, less volatile. "Use the term 'possible' evacuation. The same warning is being released by text, social media, radio, and TV. Most folks will know what to do. Our main concern is for those who don't." He sounded like an orator encouraging the troops before battle.

"Go!" Mike bellowed and pointed toward the door. "What are you waiting for?"

Judah, still wearing his raingear and boots, sprinted through the building and out to his truck, the same as his coworkers were doing. Hopefully, an evacuation wouldn't be necessary. With any luck, the high winds blasting sand and tree limbs across the parking lot would veer back to sea. If it hit Basalt Bay head-on, his hometown might never be the same again.

He had to find Paisley.

Seventeen

Paisley sneaked into the back of the cramped community room at City Hall, trying to reach the coffee table on the other side of the room without anyone noticing her. She kept her raincoat hood pulled snugly around her face. Maybe Mayor Grant wouldn't see her. *Please, please.*

Right then, Edward seemed preoccupied with questions citizens were hurling at him. Was an evacuation imminent? How would they evacuate the elderly? What about pets? Why did the emergency system blare once, then stop? What was really going on? By the sounds of their voices, the townspeople were blaming him for all problems relating to the storm. *He's more powerful than I imagined*, she thought sarcastically.

The mayor kept repeating his mantra that Basalt Bay's Coastal Management and Emergency Responders were doing their best. He admonished everyone to have patience with the process. "We'll get through this storm in fine shape as we have all the others."

Paisley rolled her eyes.

Several residents groaned like they weren't pleased with his contrived answer, either.

She stole a peek at her father-in-law. He looked grayer than he had three years ago when he yelled at her and told her she wasn't worthy of his son. Considering what he said to her, his caring tone now sounded like hogwash. Under the best of circumstances, he wasn't a thoughtful person. Why should she expect him to be one now?

"That you, Paisley?" Lucy leaned near her face.

Not again.

"Twice in the same day. I can hardly contain my happiness." The redhead spoke in a monotone that exaggerated her displeasure in running into Paisley again.

"Yeah, me too." Paisley was sipping bland coffee from a Styrofoam cup, mostly staring at the floor. How did Lucy spot her so easily?

"Guess you'll be glad *he*"—Lucy jerked her head toward Mayor Grant—"won't be your father-in-law much longer." She had the audacity to grin. "What a pain in the neck, huh?"

Paisley ignored the comment. She wouldn't give the woman who claimed to be in line for Judah's affections any ammo.

"How will we know if we have to leave town?" Someone in the front asked.

Edward ran his right hand through his wavy hair. "We're waiting to hear from C-MER. Hopefully, a full evacuation won't become necessary."

"Why wait? It's obvious their system isn't working," Lucy called out.

Paisley wished she weren't standing by the outspoken woman. What if Mayor Grant glanced this way? She kept her gaze lowered, still sipping the bad tasting coffee.

A rumble of voices erupted.

"People, we haven't received any official word that the system isn't working." The mayor's voice got louder.

"Judah Grant said the town is on high alert." When did Lucy speak with him? "He said everyone should be prepared to evacuate."

Paisley glanced up. At the mention of his son's name, Edward flinched.

The voices of worried homeowners broke out again.

"The second I hear from C-MER, I promise I'll let you know!" Edward shouted, his hands cupped around his mouth. "For now, go home and treat this like any other storm until you hear differently from me or someone in an official capacity." He turned on his heels and stomped down the hallway, probably to call Mike Linfield or Craig Masters.

Paisley cringed at the thought of Craig coming down here. That man wasn't trustworthy. A scum. The unfortunate way she discovered his true personality was another secret stacked against her. Had Craig ever hinted to Judah about what he tried to do? Did Edward tell his son what he observed the night she left? She'd rather Judah didn't hear about that from either of those two losers.

She inhaled deeply, but the air seemed void of oxygen. She coughed. Felt her heart palpitate. She shouldn't have been thinking about Craig. Or Edward. She gulped down another swallow of coffee. Her face turned hot, her neck itchy. She needed more air. She bent over, one hand on her chest, hoping no one saw her distress.

"What's wrong with you?" Lucy leaned down next to her. "You okay? Need a doctor?"

Paisley shook her head, biting back another cough. "I-I'm fine."

"You don't look so good." Lucy peered at her as if seeing through her facade.

Paisley stepped back, uncomfortable with the woman's scrutiny. "I think I'll head out." Outdoors she could get fresh air and move farther from emotional triggers. Maybe then, she could stop contemplating the things she had to tell Judah but didn't want to. Yet if she didn't explain, how would she ever be free of this internal chokehold?

Almost through the crowd and nearing the front doors, she was overcome by dry coughing and the feeling of intense pressure on her chest. *Please don't let me pass out.*

"You okay, dear?" An older woman patted her shoulder, surprising Paisley with her grandmotherly tone. "Heavy atmosphere makes me cough too."

Paisley faced the white-haired woman she didn't recognize—strange, since she knew most everyone in the small town—staring at her with navy-hued eyes.

"I have peppermint oil in my bag. I carry it all the time. Might help you breathe better. Would you like some?" The lady who was dressed in purple outerwear smiled, her face dissolving into a million beautiful lines. It had been ages since anyone, other than Judah, treated Paisley with such kindness. Was she an angel in disguise?

"Okay, thank you." Paisley had used essential oils before. Sometimes they helped. Right now, she'd try anything to not have an attack at City Hall. All she needed was for Edward to see her at her weakest.

"I'm Kathleen Baker, by the way." The white-haired woman dug around in her bag that resembled a beach tote more than a purse. Several items clinked like the kitchen sink might actually be in there. Her hand stilled, then she thrust her clenched fist toward Paisley. "Here you go, dear."

Paisley had always hated it when people in Basalt called her "dear"—like it was a judgmental term. Something about the gentle way Kathleen said the word removed any sting. She opened her palm and a small dark brown bottle lay on its side. She grabbed the jar, untwisted the top, and breathed deeply of the strong scent. Coughed.

"Try again." Kathleen patted Paisley's arm.

She sniffed the peppermint aroma, then coughed again, but her airways felt clearer. She secured the bottle and handed it back to Kathleen. "Thank you so much."

"Keep it." The older woman closed Paisley's hand around the jar. "You need it more than I do."

Normally, she would argue that she was independent and didn't need anyone's help. This time, she slid the jar into her raincoat pocket. "Thanks."

Kathleen moved through the crowd toward the front of the room. Paisley continued toward the exit, a difficult task now that the room's capacity was maxed out.

Just then, Mia Till shoved through the doorway, almost colliding with Paisley. Her eyes were wide, her face wet. She smoothed her hand across her mascara-smeared cheeks and stared at Paisley before barging into the middle of the group, shouting, "Hold up, everyone! I have news."

Shushing sounds spread across the room.

Someone must have notified Mayor Grant. He bolted out of his office and pushed through the sardine-packed room toward Mia. "You have an update for us, Miss Till?"

Apparently, in this tension-filled room, Mia was the official C-MER rep. Why was she here instead of Judah or Craig? Although, Paisley was extremely thankful not to see Craig. Being in the same room with Edward created enough tension.

"Are we evacuating?" Mr. Carnegie, postmaster and local historian, blurted the question that had to be on the forefront of everyone's thoughts.

"Not yet." Mia waved and giggled at someone across the room.

Paisley groaned at the worker's flirtatious ways even in the face of a crisis.

"When will we know?" someone in the back asked. Other questions followed. "Why did the siren sound for ten seconds then stop?" "Is the storm worsening?" "Isn't it safer to leave now than to wait until the last minute?" "What about sandbags?" "Why isn't C-MER answering their phone?"

"Citizens of Basalt Bay!" Mayor Grant shouted above the clatter. He raised his hands. "Please, listen to what Miss Till has to say."

"Thank you, Mayor Grant." Mia gave the man a wide smile before she ran her fingers through her rain-soaked blond tresses. How could she look such a mess, yet still resemble a magazine model? "As you can see, the storm has worsened. The latest news from the C-MER weather station is that wind gusts may *possibly* reach seventy-five miles per hour or more tonight."

Huffs. Groans. A few people pushed toward the door.

"The same as last time!" The feminine voice was Maggie Thomas's.

Paisley put her hand over the opening of her hood to keep the woman from spotting her.

"Yes, it appears to be rushing up the coastline much like Addy." Mia palmed the air as if to quiet everyone down.

A couple near Paisley argued over whether they should leave town immediately.

"Why don't we evacuate now for safety?" Pastor Sagle waved his hand. "We know what happened last month."

"Because the winds may still shift directions like previous storms." Mia smiled confidently, like she was the voice of authority.

"We know what happened all right. The road washed out. Folks were stuck." Mrs. Thomas's voice carried blame. "Wasn't it *your* responsibility to get the roads fixed before another storm, Mayor Grant? That's the reason folks voted for you—so you'd work for them." Her chin rose. "Not me. I never voted for you."

Gasps. A round of applause.

"We didn't expect another storm to hit so soon." Edward cleared his throat. "I'm doing my best, Maggie."

"Your best?" Mrs. Thomas cackled. She rocked her thumb toward the windows. "You got your new windows in. What about our roads?"

"Yeah." "That's right." A clattering of voices. "What about the roads you promised?" "We need a new mayor." The attitude of the crowd became agitated. Angry glints filled the eyes of some closest to Paisley. Three burly fishermen she recognized as the Keifer brothers moved forward, fists clenched, as if to do Edward harm.

Paisley felt emboldened by their action. Not that she wished her father-in-law ill. But she wouldn't mind if some tough weathered-looking guys with snarls on their faces took him to task.

"South Road is still passable." Edward tightened his tie as if that made him look taller or braver. The opposite effect happened.

"Single lane," Mr. Carnegie called out. "It's been difficult for mail delivery all month."

"Maybe that's why the Mayor hasn't called for an evacuation." Maggie shouted. "Because we can't all make it out of town alive."

A thunder of voices blasted off the walls. Some people shoved their way toward the door. Others yelled threats. The three fishermen moved forward like a gang out to claim their turf.

"Wait, you guys!" Mia climbed on top of a receptionist's desk and stomped on the wooden surface with her now soaking wet *So Kates*. Didn't the woman own boots? "Listen to me!"

Some townspeople stopped pressing toward the door, but they didn't give up their floor space.

Mia clapped her hands. "Waiting is hard, but right now, it's just a storm out there like we've experienced time and time again. It's coming in at about forty miles per hour with only the *possibility* of increased speeds and only a chance of it hitting landfall."

"Does it have a name yet?" Lucy's voice.

Mia frowned like she didn't want to answer. Then, "A short time ago, when it reached thirty-nine miles per hour, we started calling it Storm Blaine." She shrugged. "Our team is going door to door giving preliminary warnings. But I repeat, the wind may change directions or die down entirely. You all know that is true."

A mumble of agreement crossed the room.

"And if it doesn't?" Mrs. Thomas's demanding voice rose above other grumblings. "Stay home and twiddle our thumbs until 'Storm Blaine' is too horrific to escape? No, thank you!" She pushed through the crowd, making her own aisleway. "I'm getting out of town."

The mob pressed toward the door in a frenzy of shoving and yelling. It appeared there would be a race for the single-lane South Road exit from the city after all.

"We don't want a panic." Mia stomped her foot. "Please, come back!"

Too late.

Kathleen clasped Paisley's hand. "Why isn't the town alarm working, dear?"

"Good question." She patted the woman's hand, hoping to return some of the comfort Kathleen offered her earlier.

"What about the public warning system?" Paisley yelled toward Mia. "When will it sound?"

The C-MER receptionist glared at Paisley and shook her head as if telling her to be quiet.

What? This gathering didn't deserve the truth? That Mia might be following protocol but not giving them vital information was unacceptable. Lives were at stake. The residents of Basalt Bay trusted C-MER to be the eyes and ears in the weather world. Paisley let go of Kathleen's hand and pushed through the cluster of people. Regardless of her aversion to Mayor Grant, she undid the tie on her hood, exposing her face.

"What aren't you telling us, Mia?" She moved to stand next to the receptionist as Mia descended the desk with Mayor Grant's assistance.

"You." Edward's eyes were as wide as snowballs.

"Yes, it's me." Filled with semi-false bravado, she turned from her father-in-law and addressed Mia again. "What gives? We have the right to know the truth."

"That's right," Kathleen agreed from beside her.

"Yeah, tell us what's going on." Brad Kiefer, one of the fishermen Paisley recognized as a classmate of Peter's from high school, stood on her other side.

Standing between the two of them, she felt momentarily protected.

"Everyone should go home and stay safe for the duration of the storm. We'll be fine as rain come morning." Mia's tight smile said she wasn't saying anything else. She rushed toward the exit as if to escape Paisley's questioning.

"I don't think that saying works in this squall." Paisley followed her. "Look, if C-MER even suspects an evacuation, tell me now. I have to get my father out of town."

"Like I said, you'll have plenty of warning." Mia sashayed into the crowd.

Mayor Grant blocked Paisley's exit. "I'm sorry to see you back in town." His eyes glinted.

"Yeah, me too." She tried sidestepping him.

"Stay away from my son." He hissed in her ear.

She wouldn't give him the satisfaction of knowing he irritated her. "Well, Edward, that's hard to do since I'm staying in his house."

He didn't react or look surprised. Had Judah already told him?

She resumed her stride, putting distance between her and her father-in-law, as she joined the group fleeing City Hall.

Outside, the rain and winds hadn't let up. Would Storm Blaine become Hurricane Blaine tonight? A garbage bag and a lawn ornament blasted across the street in front of her. Walking even two feet in a straight line was difficult. She wouldn't make it to Dad's on foot. She'd have to drive her car.

As she leaned into the wind, her thoughts turned to Judah. Where was he? Hopefully not in his skiff in this wretched weather.

Eighteen

Judah thought he heard a low rumble of thunder as he stomped through several inches of standing water on the street near Paul Cedars's house. That the storm hadn't veered away from land yet worried him. The possibility of another high-powered wind strike kept him sloshing through water to the next house and the next. He'd already knocked on thirty doors, and he was only halfway down his list.

What if the townspeople couldn't evacuate fast enough once an official alert came—if one came? He felt the weight of that possibility as he issued his preliminary warnings. He learned from Addy that Pacific storms moved a bit differently than the simulations they practiced and planned for in their C-MER training. They had to be ready for anything.

Most people were home and acted appreciative that he stopped by with the emergency information. Some had boarded up their windows—something he wished he had time to do to his cottage. Others were packing up their cars, just in case. A few told him a family member was at the public beach stacking sandbags for a levee. He knew the team from C-MER assigned to that task would be grateful for the help.

Preparing for the possibility of a severe storm in an area recently hit by one was difficult. At least, Judah and others from C-MER were doing their due diligence. Everyone's safety was foremost in their minds.

When he strode up the soggy path to Paul's, and Paisley's car wasn't in the driveway, he groaned. She didn't go to their beach house, did she? With its sea-level flood position, that was one of the worst places to be during a high-water storm. The most dangerous of all would be the peninsula. She wouldn't go out there. Of course, she wouldn't. Still, his chest constricted. If Paul said she went to the cove, Judah wouldn't have a choice. He'd do anything to keep her safe. But what about his commitment to helping all the others in Basalt Bay? He would be facing a moral dilemma, but wasn't his first responsibility to his wife?

He reached the Cedars's porch and rapped firmly on the door. "Coastal Management and Emergency Responders!" He beat on the door again.

So far, his flotation coat kept him mostly protected from the elements. However, the rain and wind pummeled his face and hands. Water had been trickling down his neckline, soaking his shirt, and causing discomfort. But, no matter how wet and cold he was, he wouldn't stop until he got through his list—unless he heard that Paisley was at the peninsula.

The door opened slowly. Paul Cedars's eyes widened. "Judah."

"Hello, Paul." He didn't have time for chitchat or to feel nervous in front of the father-in-law he hadn't seen much of in the last three years. "Is Paisley here?"

"Not since earlier." Paul pushed his black-rimmed glasses up the bridge of his nose and peered at Judah. "Everything all right?"

"Do you know where she is?"

Paul shrugged. "Probably where she spent most of her life."

A shudder coursed through Judah. "You mean at the beach?"

Paul nodded and closed the screen, probably to keep the wind out, not to stop Judah from entering.

Despite his apprehension for his wife's safety, he issued the warning he came here to give. "Hurricane winds may possibly hit tonight. And the new warning system isn't running yet." He pulled on the screen handle and passed Paul a damp copy of the printout he'd been distributing over the last hour and a half. Even though the papers were in a protective sleeve, each time he opened it, a little rainwater got inside. "Read this. Check the website or call this number for updates. That way you'll know if you have to evacuate and where to—"

"I'm not leaving." Paul lifted his chin as if anticipating an argument.

"That's not wise, sir. If only you'd—"

"My choice. Nothing you can do about that."

Judah could see where Paisley got her stubbornness.

"Your house isn't beachside, sir, but it sits low. Please reconsider, for Paisley's safety, if not your own." Judah edged toward the steps. He'd used up his time allotment for this property. He had to move on.

"Like I said, she isn't here." Paul shut the door.

"Yeah, but she'll head here as soon as she hears you aren't leaving!" Judah shouted toward the closed door, not knowing whether Paul heard him. Paisley's dad probably wasn't thinking clearly. Ever since his wife died and Paisley left, he didn't act like the man Judah knew him to be in the early days of his acquaintance with the Cedars family.

Judah said a prayer for him, then stomped toward the

Andersons next door. His urgency to get through the row of addresses, and find his wife, made him press on, despite the wind and pouring rain. Was Paisley at the beach? If they had to evacuate, would she go with him? Even if her dad refused?

After he checked off twenty more homes from his list, his phone buzzed. His hands were so cold he could hardly move them. However, he answered, thinking it might be Paisley.

"Hello." He swept rainwater off his face.

"How many houses left?" Craig's voice.

"Nine."

"Hurry up and finish." His supervisor spoke tersely.

"I'm trying. Conditions are bad."

"Same as everywhere. Other team members are wrapping up. So should you." Now that Craig's job was on the line, he seemed more uptight than ever.

Judah kept walking. "What's the verdict on the storm?" He charged up another set of stairs to a porch without a light.

"Category 1, if it hits at all." Craig spoke quickly. "We've seen this pattern before. It will probably head out to sea."

Too much guesswork in his assessment for Judah's peace of mind. He rapped on the door knocker. A child opened the door a couple of inches. "Get your mom or dad, please." The kid trotted away, and Judah returned his attention to the call. "Get that warning system running, will you?"

"That's the plan." Craig spit out a word Judah chose not to decipher. "Or else I'll lose my job."

Judah figured.

"You too." Click.

What? Why would he lose his job?

An older man, maybe the child's grandfather, came to the door, stopping Judah from further pondering. He went through his memorized warning, explaining the possible severity of the approaching storm and what to do in case of evacuation.

No one answered at six of the remaining houses. At each of those, Judah curled up the printout and stuck it inside the screen door.

When the last of his assignment was done, he sighed in relief. By then, the rain was blowing sideways. Maybe he should sprint down to the beach and see for himself if Paisley was there. But what if they had to evacuate suddenly? They'd need his four-wheel-drive truck in a washout.

Powerful gusts shoved him as he trudged in the direction of where he left his pickup on the other side of midtown. Had anyone informed Mom about the possible evacuation? With all of Dad's responsibilities concerning the town, had he even thought to update his wife?

Judah kept splashing through the water en route to his truck, but he pulled out his cell phone. He searched the contact list and tapped "Mom."

As soon as she answered, he spoke, "Hey, Mom, you probably know this, but the storm is worsening. Possible evacuation. I wanted to make sure you knew."

"Thank you, Son."

At her endearment, a knot formed in his chest. He felt badly about ignoring her because of his frustrations with his father. Although, it was hard not to do when Mom and Dad lived in the same house.

"What will you do?" she asked.

"If we evacuate, I'll head to a shelter. You?" He spoke as he trudged down the street, slightly out of breath.

"Oh, you know, we live on the hill. Our fortress."

Did that mean she was staying put? "Alone, you mean?"

"Dad will get here when he can." She sighed like it was an old argument she didn't want to discuss.

"Mom—" Maybe he should drive up and get her. She could ride in the truck with him and Paisley. Of course, she had her own four-wheel-drive vehicle for getting up to their cliff-side home.

"I know it's your job to tell everyone to leave"—she chuckled—"but I'll be fine."

"Why don't you drive down and stay at the shelter with me and Paisley?" What would she say about his wife being back in town?

"Oh, Judah. She's back?"

So she didn't know?

"Yeah, she's staying with me."

"That's wonderful news."

"I think so too." Unfortunately, he didn't have time for visiting. "I gotta go. I just knocked on sixty doors, alerting people about the storm."

"My son, the hero." Sounded like she smiled.

"Just doing my job." He coughed.

"A good one, too. Love you, Son."

Her words warmed a chilled part of his heart. "You too, Mom." He ended the call, and his truck came into view. As soon as he got inside, he made his numb fingers start the engine and crank up the heater. He undid his hood and slid it off so he could see better.

His phone buzzed. His hands shook, and he fumbled the phone, almost dropping it.

"Yeah?"

"Mom again." He heard her swallow as if tugging back emotion. "If you . . . and Paisley . . . want to come up higher, you're welcome here, okay?"

He didn't know what to say.

"The view of the ocean is fantastic."

He wouldn't mind waiting out the storm with Mom. But Dad? How would he respond to Paisley's presence? Judah couldn't put his wife through that kind of ordeal, especially since she'd probably feel uncomfortable around his dad. So would he, for that matter. "Thanks, Mom. Nice of you to offer."

"I know you're busy, but I wanted to invite you."

"Okay. Talk to you later." He clicked off, then sighed. Mom meant well. She'd do everything she could to make Paisley feel welcome. But no one, and he meant no one, could stop Edward Grant's verbal attacks once he got started.

Judah drove toward the beach, the truck tires rolling over downed tree limbs and debris on the street. At the beach parking lot, with blowing rain and the wind churning an already high tide, water poured across the pavement. He was surprised to see just how much seawater and rain had accumulated. After the wave receded, he maneuvered the truck through what looked to be about six inches of standing water, maybe more. He stopped at the northwest corner of the lot where he had a clearer view of the peninsula and the beach below.

So far, the sandbag levee the crew built was standing, although it looked kind of narrow for enduring strong waves. Had they rushed the job? He hoped it could hold through the night. At least, no one appeared to be on the beach. That was a relief.

He turned around and drove slowly out of the parking lot. Then he took a pass through downtown, searching for any sign of Paisley's car.

A few people rushed out of City Hall. Of course, citizens would gather there to question his father. Craig probably sent someone to issue current weather updates.

He saw a lady in a mini-skirt—hard not to notice someone

dressed up like that in a torrential storm—rushing down the sidewalk. At least she wore a rain jacket, although it looked too short to do much good. Wait. Mia? Craig sent Mia to City Hall to represent C-MER? What was he thinking?

Judah pulled over to the curb and lowered the window. "Mia!" he shouted to his coworker. "Need a ride?"

She scurried toward him in spiked heels. Her feet had to be soaked. "Oh, Judah, you're a lifesaver." Giggling, she climbed into his truck. "Thanks so much. I parked up the street, that way." She pointed toward the west side of town. "Cars were parked all along Front when I arrived."

"Why were so many people here?"

As soon as she buckled her seatbelt, he drove in the direction she pointed.

"Oh, you know, worried locals demanding answers." She thumbed her chest. "Good thing I showed up. Your dad appreciated my knowledge too." She laughed like it was a pay raise.

"Hmm." He didn't appreciate the familiar way she talked about his dad, as if she were on close terms with him. Judah clenched his jaw. Maybe Mia just acted flirty with every man in town. He remembered Paisley commenting in the past about Mia's male-crazed behavior. Not that his wife had ever had anything to worry about in that corner.

"I also stopped by Hardy's Gill and Grill to let people know." She shivered, then giggled.

Inwardly, he groaned. Had she been drinking on the job? "You okay to drive?"

She laughed again. "You're sweet, Judah. I only had coffee."

"Okay." He pulled in next to Mia's red sports car, hoping she was telling him the truth. "Be safe out there."

"You too." She laid her palm over his hand on the steering

wheel. He pulled back. She grinned like she didn't notice his cool response. "If you need a place to stay, you know, a safe distance from the water, you can join me. My apartment is on the second floor."

"That right?" Was she just being friendly or offering something more than a safe place?

"We could watch old movies—or something." She winked.

She *was* being flirtatious.

"You should go." He nodded toward the door. He didn't want to be rude, but he didn't want her thinking he was fishing for a romantic interlude.

"I'm serious about a place if you—"

"Thanks, but I'm looking for Paisley. She'd be welcome to join all the people you're providing shelter for, right?" *Good thinking, Grant.*

Mia's mouth closed and opened a few times. "Oh, uh, sure. Why not?"

If the rain wasn't thrashing his truck's roof, he'd laugh at how fast she climbed out. At the last second, she glanced back. "She was there."

"Where?" His heart skipped a beat.

"City Hall."

"Paisley was at City Hall . . . with my father?"

Mia nodded and leaned forward into the truck.

"Did she say anything?" If his dad was impolite—

"She said she needed to get her father out of town. Maybe she left with him." Mia rocked her eyebrows. "Nothing for you to worry about then, huh?"

Even if he didn't plan on doing everything a husband could do to regain his wife's love, he wouldn't take Mia up on her suggestion. Not only was she not his type, he still had strong feelings for Paisley. One second with her in his arms three days ago proved that.

He put the engine in gear. "Thanks, Mia."

Wearing her pouty expression, she slammed the door. Then she wobbled in her heels to her car with gusty wind blowing against her. Once he was sure she made it into her vehicle, he pulled into the street and plowed through the water flowing across the pavement.

There was an eeriness about the steely gray, almost black sky. The silence following the next blast of wind made the hair on his neck stand on end. He heard about pre-wave conditions when the air went graveyard-still just before the worst slammed into a town. Were they almost to that point?

He hoped not. A severe storm with hurricane winds might undercut the fragile sand structure that had been deteriorating around Basalt Bay since Addy. Like Sample D sliding on the peninsula. If that kind of a squall happened tonight, what buildings would suffer damage? What flooded roads would become impassable?

He had difficulty seeing through the downpour, the condensation on the windows, and the rapidly moving windshield wipers. Leaning forward, he gnawed on his lower lip and stared straight ahead. A stress headache pounded between his temples, but he ignored it. He had to find Paisley.

Maybe he should drive back to Paul's and check again. His father-in-law said he wouldn't leave. Paisley might be there by now.

Judah's truck splattered a wave of water over the sidewalk as he zoomed west on Front Street. He came to a fast stop in front of the Cedars's paint-chipped house. Stepping out of the truck, he faced away from the onslaught of rain. No cars were in the driveway. So his wife wasn't here. What about Paul? Had he changed his mind about leaving? None of the windows on the house were boarded up.

Judah tromped over the wet walkway and up the porch steps. He pounded three times on the wooden door, even though he doubted anyone was home. No sounds came from inside. He rapped three more times, just in case.

Before he got back to his truck, the warning system blasted a wail loud and long enough to hurt his eardrums. His boots froze midstream. Another siren sounded three short blasts, then that hair-raising long one again. The muscles in his gut clenched.

Basalt Bay was officially under evacuation.

Nineteen

Before Paisley went to check on Dad, she wanted to drive by the peninsula, just for a minute, so she could store the memory of waves bursting over the point in her mind forever. What if a tidal surge destroyed the coastline and it was never the same again?

At the public beach, seawater rushed across the parking lot—something she'd never seen before. Slowly, she drove through standing water to reach the far side of the lot, then parked as close as she could get to the peninsula. She didn't turn off the engine or her headlights.

On the beach, a long pile of sandbags resembled a short castle wall. White water burst over the entire peninsula in great spurts and explosions. The water receded. Then bam! A wave tumbled over the beach, crashing into the pile of sandbags, and cresting onto the parking lot. Her car jerked and swayed with the water's rush. *Whoa.* Staying here might be too dangerous. She put the car in gear. Time to go to Dad's and get out of this storm.

The engine hiccupped and sputtered. Then died.

"No, no, no." She turned the key and pumped the gas pedal several times. "Come on." When nothing happened, she tried again. Same result. She groaned. Did the car stall because a belt or something got wet? Driving through the water on the parking lot was probably a bad idea.

She pulled on the hood lever, hating the thought of stepping into the swirling water that looked about six or seven inches high, strong enough to knock a person over. But she couldn't sit here and do nothing. No one knew where she was. She didn't have a phone to call anyone to come get her.

As soon as she got out of the car, water rushed forcefully against her ankles, chilling her, and nearly knocking her over. To keep herself upright, she ran her hands along the side of the slippery, wet vehicle—not much help, but some—as she waded toward the hood with harsh winds slamming against her.

Something banged into her thigh, and she gritted her teeth. When she glanced down, a beach chair was wedged between her and the car. She shoved it away, and it half floated, half flew, across the parking lot, then was gobbled up by waves. An image flashed through her mind of her being stuck in the Accord and it being swept out to sea just like that chair.

A shudder raced through her.

She was foolish to have come here in such extreme conditions—her impetuous nature was getting her into trouble again. Her desire to see the peninsula didn't seem important now.

Fighting the next blast of wind, she lifted the hood of her car and secured it so she could check inside the engine. She could barely see anything through the darkness. Still, she felt around but didn't find any loose wires. It had gas. Electrical failure? Maybe.

So much for using this car to escape if they were forced to evacuate. She slammed the hood, then made her way back to the door, wading through cold water. When she grabbed hold of the handle, she froze. She didn't want to get inside—not if there was any chance her car might be dragged into the sea with her in it. What should she do?

Out on the peninsula, white water burst against the boulders, then sea spray shot high into the air so beautifully, almost majestically, in its display of power and fury. A breath caught in her throat as she watched. But then, waves crashed up onto the parking lot, ramming against her, nearly taking her down as she clutched the door. She felt trapped, like she was in the middle of a disaster movie, or in a nightmare, and she fought the impulse to scream.

As soon as the wave abated, she ran, splashing through the water on the pavement. The wind buffeted her back, shoving her upper body forward. She almost tripped, caught herself, then kept sloshing toward town. Could she make it the few blocks to Dad's?

As she reached Front Street, the public warning system blasted a loud spine-tingling alarm. So they were going to evacuate, after all?

What about Dad? Would he leave his home? If so, maybe she could catch a ride with him. Help him somehow. This could be her chance to make amends. She walked faster.

A truck zipped past, splashing a four-foot wave of water, drenching her. "Hey!" She yelped and wiped wetness off her face. She groaned but kept sludging through the water.

If Dad decided to weather the storm, she'd stay with him. The old house where she grew up wasn't much higher than sea level, but it had a second story. Was it strong enough to withstand a massive wave? She thought of how Paige's business looked battered and broken. How the upended dock at Bert's Fish Shack must have been rammed with a gigantic wave. Was that what would happen to her childhood home tonight? To her hometown? Anxiety rippled through her.

A vehicle stopped beside her, splashing her with more water. She groaned and turned to yell at whoever it was. When she saw Reverend Sagle peering out the window at her, her anger melted.

"Need a lift, Paisley?" His voice sounded kind.

His SUV was already loaded down with household belongings. Where did he expect her to sit?

"That's okay. Thanks for asking." She kept walking, fighting the wind blowing against her.

The pastor drove his vehicle alongside her. "Aren't you leaving town?" His wrinkled face showed concern.

"Maybe." The wind knocked her against a lamp post. She held on for a moment, glad for something stationary. She remembered the day she and Judah asked Pastor Sagle to marry them on the sly. He refused and said he wouldn't perform a wedding without their parents knowing, even though they were both of age. She held a grudge about that ever since.

"Where's your car?"

"Stalled at the beach. I'm on my way to Dad's."

"He's not home." The older man shook his head.

"How do you know?" She wiped more moisture off her face and stared at him.

"I saw him at your sister's." He waved his hand in a westerly direction. "They were loading up her car."

Dad was leaving town with Paige? Disappointment hit her. She wanted to be the one to help him, for him to need her during this storm. However, his escaping with his youngest daughter was probably a good thing. At least, he was safe. They were safe.

Where did that leave Paisley? Would the second floor of Dad's house be high enough and hold together while she waited out the storm—alone? It had an attic, although small and terrifying.

"Let me drive you somewhere. You need to get out of the rain before you catch your death of cold." The pastor smiled in a grandfatherly way. "Where's Judah?"

"I'm not sure." She took a shallow breath. "Okay, um, would you take me to my dad's?"

"Sure. Sure." He shoved some stuff off the front passenger seat. "Get in."

Paisley rounded the SUV and opened the passenger door, thankful for the pastor's offer. Maybe he hadn't meant any harm in not hearing their wedding vows. Besides, that was seven years ago. Water under the bridge, and all that.

The items he removed from the seat were on the floor now.

"Sorry. Not much room for your feet."

"That's o-okay." Her teeth chattered as she sat down and shuffled her soaked tennies in the limited space. She extended her hands to the warmth blowing from the heater. "I appreciate the ride. Thank you."

"Of course."

The siren sounded again, a weird, horrific wail, reminding her of a dying animal. Three short blasts reached them as Pastor Sagle drove down the watery street, his car creating a wave of its own.

"I could drive you east, if you don't mind close quarters." He nodded toward the backseat piled with stuff. A gust of wind blasted against the vehicle, shoving it slightly sideways. "Whoa." He gripped the steering wheel. "It's getting worse."

She didn't want to consider how bad the storm might get when the idea of staying at Dad's by herself had her rattled. "Why didn't you leave town earlier?"

He clicked the windshield wipers to a higher speed. "I had to make sure some elderly folks were safely on the bus or heading out of town with family."

So he was a considerate, helpful guy, after all. Like Judah. She sighed.

"I hate to think what will happen if the winds increase." Pastor Sagle shook his head.

Her thoughts exactly.

The swish-swish of the blades kept time with her heartbeat. Would she be stuck in this dreadful storm with everyone gone from Basalt but her? Panic as intense as the wind outside clambered through her veins. She pictured herself huddled upstairs in the old house, maybe hiding under her bed. No way would she climb into the attic. She went up there to look for Christmas ornaments, years ago, and felt suffocated in the tiny space.

They rode the rest of the way without speaking. The loaded vehicle came to a stop on the deserted street in front of Dad's. It was weird not seeing a single parked car in the neighborhood. She glanced up at the dark two-story house and wondered how the frail-looking building would manage in hurricane winds. It had weathered decades of storms, hopefully it was tougher than it appeared.

"Thank you for the ride." She nodded at the pastor but didn't attempt to open the door. A minute longer and the wind might settle down enough for her to run to the porch. A cardboard box bounced down the sidewalk, zipping past the vehicle.

Pastor Sagle watched her intently. "I'd feel better if you came with me. I have friends in Eugene where you could stay."

"Thanks, but Judah's probably looking for me." She said it more for the pastor's peace of mind than her own. Had Judah already left town thinking she'd done the same thing? If only she had a cell phone.

"Probably?"

"You know how busy C-MER is during a storm." She thrust open the door.

"He'll be along shortly, then?"

She doubted it. "Thanks for the ride." She stepped into winds strong enough to hurl her down the street like the cardboard box she saw a minute ago. She slammed the door, then bracing her knees, leaned forward into the gusts and trudged through the yard and around the house to where she knew the back door would be unlocked.

The wailing of the sirens came again, sending tingles up her spine. How many times would she have to endure that noise before the storm ended its rampage?

As she pulled open the screen door at the back of Dad's, the porch light shut off—like a "Vacancy" sign turning off. She remembered how Dad didn't invite her inside earlier. How he told her to come back tomorrow. *Well, I'm here now.*

All the neighbors' houses seemed dark too. The whole town must have lost power.

She couldn't see the door handle she was so sure would open, but when she grabbed hold, it didn't budge. When did Dad start locking this door? She shook the doorknob. It didn't give. Had he hidden a key? If so, where? This was never a problem when she was a kid. She came through the unlocked door a million times before.

Had Dad secured the door against looters? Or because he didn't plan on coming back for a while? Both thoughts hit her hard. If burglars showed up, how would she protect herself? And in her father's exodus with Paige, did he even consider his other daughter's safety, or her need for a place to stay?

A blast of wind shoved her against the screen door. She had to find a way inside quickly.

She leaned over the porch railing, peering through the dark for anything that would make a good hiding place for a key. Where Mom's petunia garden used to be, Paisley spotted a pet rock Paige painted ages ago to resemble a salmon. She dashed down the steps, clinging to the loose handrail so the wind wouldn't capsize her. She scooped up the oval-shaped rock and checked underneath. No key. She looked under a couple of other items, but when another wind surge pressed her into a bush, she grabbed the salmon-shaped rock and gripped it firmly.

She stomped back up the steps, fighting the gusts, and yanked open the screen. Then, protecting her face with one arm, she pulled her other hand back, and flung the seven-inch rock like a football through the door window. Glass exploded into tiny pieces all over the porch. Some must have scattered on the floor inside also.

Carefully, she picked glass shards off the window frame and dropped them onto the porch. Her hands were stiff and shaking from cold, so she didn't want to make the mistake of ramming her knuckles against any sharp glass. When the lower edge of the frame seemed clear, she reached her hand in and unlocked the door.

She pulled her arm away just as a loud crash made her jump. Did a tree fall? She couldn't risk going around to the front yard to see. She had to get out of the pounding rain and wind. Grabbing the knob, she pushed the door open, being careful not to step on broken glass. She'd clean up the mess later.

Inside, she shoved the door closed, then rushed up the darkened stairway between the kitchen and the living room in search of a change of clothes. With the electricity off, the furnace wouldn't work, so she had to hunt for something warm to wear.

Teeth chattering, chills skittering across her body, she opened Dad's bedroom door and rushed to his oak dresser. Yanking drawers open, her fingers fumbled around for something thick that might fit. Dad wasn't a large man, but he was taller than her. She found one of his flannel shirts. Sweatpants? There.

She shed her wet clothes as quickly as she could with numb fingers and pulled on the dry things. She explored in the closet and found a weathered wool coat that smelled of Old Spice. It might be a bit scratchy but should help her get warm. She sniffed as she plunged her arms into the jacket, enjoying the scent as memories of her dad when she was a kid floated through her thoughts. Sadly, no time for a trip down Memory Lane. She had a possible hurricane to prepare for. She dug in the drawer again and clasped a pair of thick boot socks. Perfect. She sighed just thinking of getting her feet toasty.

She grabbed the essential oil bottle out of her pocket that Kathleen gave her earlier and tucked it in Dad's coat pocket. Now to locate supplies, mainly a flashlight and water for drinking.

A loud crash shook the house.

She stood still, afraid to move. Then, knowing she had to face whatever it was, she tread slowly down the steps, her heart pounding in her ears. Through the darkness bathing the living room, she saw the apple tree protruded through the broken front window by about five feet. Its limbs fluttered like ragged flags. *Poor thing.* A blast of wind barreled through the gaping window, knocking several paintings off the walls. Knickknacks dropped from Mom's whatnot shelf, bursting into pieces. What a mess.

How was she going to get the tree out of the window? The wind bombarding the interior might devastate Dad's belongings, but she didn't want to go back out into the rain and yank on the tree. She didn't have the strength to move the heavy trunk, anyway.

If only Judah were here to help her get through this miserable night. But he wasn't. She was alone—like she had been for the last three years. Come what may, she would have to take care of whatever tasks befell her.

Twenty

Judah decided to check the beach one last time in case he and Paisley somehow missed each other earlier. He drove his truck slowly into the parking lot. His headlights cut a beam of light straight across a parked car on the far side. *Oh, no.* Paisley's Accord? Dread slammed through his middle. Had she gone to the point where he found her the other day? The image that played through his mind ever since the moment he found her collapsed on the rocks made him feel sick to his stomach now. What if she lost consciousness and—?

"Oh, God, please no."

He leaped out of his truck and splashed through the water rolling across the parking lot in waves, wading toward his wife's purple car. Seawater poured into his boots, and he grimaced. The wind blasted him with a pounding force, but he leaned into it and kept moving forward. He had to find her.

When he reached the vehicle, he held his breath, warring with himself, both wishing he'd find her there, and afraid he would not. He leaned down and shone his cell light on the inside. The car was empty. A wave of thankfulness came over him, then an equal wave of dread and fearful thoughts assaulted his mind. Had she come here to see the waves? What if she was hurt? Where was she?

He tromped through the water, easing his way closer to the peninsula, wishing he brought a spotlight. His truck headlights allowed him to see the ocean water breaking through the levee his crew and city volunteers built. The narrow barricade wasn't holding the avalanche of waves this storm was bringing. But, at least, no one was on the beach or on the peninsula, as far as he could tell. Yet how could he know for certain Paisley wasn't here somewhere?

A wind surge shoved him four feet backwards. He nearly toppled over. *Play it safe, Grant.* But he didn't have time to play it safe. Not when his wife's life might be in danger.

They should have evacuated with the rest of Basalt Bay's citizens by now. They might have thirty minutes or so to get out of town. Any longer and the junction of South Road and Highway 101 could be under water, blocking their escape route.

"Paisley!" He yelled toward the whitecaps breaking over the rocks. Another wave hit the boulders, sending a spray of water twenty feet into the air.

"Oh, my goodness." So much power existed in the sea tonight. He peered into the darkness and called her name in each direction. If she were out in this tempest, maybe hiding in the cleft of a rock somewhere, the shrieking wind and crashing waves would override the sound of his voice. He shouted louder.

Maybe she didn't even walk onto the peninsula. But, if not, why was her car here?

"Paisley!"

A nearly overpowering gust of wind hit him just as a wave pounded his knees and splashed seawater up his thighs. He wouldn't be able to remain standing if the surge got any stronger.

He waded toward his truck. A loud crash made him glance back. A churning, violent-looking geyser of water cascaded over the peninsula. As the wave receded, a gaping hole remained where Sample D used to sit. Whoa. The rock fell into the sea?

Forget seventy-five miles per hour. This wind had to be closer to eighty-five or ninety.

He yanked open his truck door, fighting wind pressure, and climbed in, dripping water all over his seat. He needed a plan. And he had to stay positive or go crazy. Paisley's car was here. Why?

A police siren sounded in the distance. Deputy Brian and other officers were probably helping people in distress. Some who were determined to stay in their homes, despite the storm, may have changed their minds now. Was the entrance to South Road still passable?

Help me know what to do. Judah prayed. *Show me how to find her. Stop the storm if it's Your will, but please keep Paisley safe either way.* Immediately following his plea, he felt a measure of calmness seep into his spirit. A verse came to mind, a gentle reminder of God's continual help. *God is our refuge and strength, an ever-present help in trouble.* He repeated the words twice, needing the comfort. God was with him. *He* was present to help both Judah and Paisley get through the storm.

Feeling more confidence than he had a few minutes ago, he gazed back at Paisley's car being beaten by wind and water. Sometime between when he checked the peninsula earlier and now, she was here. What if she caught a ride with someone? Her dad? Paige? That made sense, until he remembered Paul said he wasn't leaving town. Had he changed his mind?

With a groan, and one last prayer that Paisley wasn't anywhere near the sea, Judah sped out of the parking lot, skidding the truck tires through eight or more inches of water. He drove down the empty, blackened Front Street that went through the middle of town. Most of the businesses were boarded up. He passed by City Hall. No movement there. Dad must have gone home.

A garbage can careened in front of Judah's pickup. He stomped on the brakes. Debris peppered his truck with sounds of metal hitting metal. Soggy newspaper pages clung to the windshield. A clattering noise came from the wiper mechanism. The duo blades skimmed across the windshield with a thud, thud, thud, then quit working.

He groaned, then stopped the truck in the middle of the road. Out of habit, he looked both ways, not that any other cars were on the street. He slid out of the vehicle and made his way to the front with blasts of wind shoving him backward. Pressing himself against the hood, he yanked wet papers off the front window. A few chunks wouldn't budge from the linkage. Hopefully, it wasn't down in the windshield wiper motor. Otherwise, he'd have a hard time driving.

Back in the cab, he found only one windshield wiper worked—on the passenger side. He grumbled and put the truck in gear. His lights made blurry shadows ahead, like someone was walking. But when he lowered his window, hoping to find Paisley, no one was there.

Would he be able to see through the rain well enough to get to Mom's? And what if Paisley was still in Basalt Bay? Had anyone stayed behind? He hadn't heard any more police sirens. The piercing sound of the public alarm was painful enough to send the most resilient people fleeing town. No wonder Craig fought to have the new system installed. Too bad it failed in its preliminary attempts. But the tech team prevailed. Thank God. Lives would be saved because of it.

Paisley must have left with her family. Judah had to believe she was okay. That she found somewhere safe to wait out the storm. He turned onto South Road, heading toward Mom's—until a gnawing question ate at him. How could he leave and find safety for himself without knowing for sure that his wife was okay? He pulled over to the side of the road. He had to think and pray.

"Lord, You know where Paisley is. If she's in any kind of trouble, send help. Rescue her. Let us have a chance for our love to be restored. Your will be done."

The wind slamming against the truck made a howling sound through the slight opening at the top of the passenger-side window that never fully closed. Good thing his truck was a solid vehicle. Lighter automobiles might have been blown over by now.

An image of Paisley's stranded car came to mind. The other day he heard a slight ticking in the engine. His heart beat faster. Was it possible her car stalled? That, maybe, she drove onto the watery parking lot near the peninsula and the timing belt got wet? That would explain—

He put the truck in gear.

If that happened, where was she now?

Paul wasn't home. Paisley and Paige hadn't reconnected. What if she went to the cottage? His blood froze. Their beach house was too close to tonight's turbulent seas. And too far for her to have walked in such strong winds.

He made a quick U-turn. He'd start at her dad's. Then Paige's. And he'd keep looking until he found her.

Twenty-one

Strong gusts barreled through the open living room window, but Paisley tried to push the apple tree out. It wouldn't budge. A chainsaw would solve the problem, if she could find one—and if she knew how to operate one. Finally, she gave up and went in search of something to cover the whole window. In the morning, she'd figure out a better solution.

With the flashlight in hand that she found earlier, she scrounged around in the kitchen drawers until she located a small plastic container with nails. Beneath the sink she unearthed a rusty hammer she used more than a decade ago to build a tree fort. Good thing she knew her way around the place. Next, she hunted for a blanket. In the cupboard above the washing machine, where guest linens were stored when she was a kid, she found a queen-sized quilt someone in the family must have sewn. She and Peter used that same thin blanket for a rainy-day fort, ages ago. Too bad it might get ruined now.

She set the flashlight on the coffee table, propping it toward her work area. After she nailed the green quilt to the left side of the window frame, and with powerful winds still blowing through the open space, she stepped onto the tree trunk with one foot and placed her other foot on the recliner in the corner. Balancing herself, she lifted the edge of the blanket and pulled the fabric taut across the gaping window. The town siren wailed again just as a blast of wind hit her, knocking her off the unsteady perch. Impatiently, she jumped up again.

She lifted the hammer, ready to drive the nail through the blanket and into the wall at the right, when a loud rumble like a truck engine made her pause. She listened closely. Had a car door slammed? Suddenly, someone banged hard on the front door. Paisley dropped the hammer.

"Just a sec—"

She stepped back, her foot in midair and the quilt clutched in her hand, as a man-sized person lunged through the open window and dove into the blanket. She screamed as whoever he was took her down with him, both of them thudding against the tree, groaning, then tumbling onto the carpeted floor.

Paisley shoved against the person and stood. "What do you think you're doing?"

The marauder jumped to his feet and the blanket fell from his face. "It's me, Pais."

Judah?

Shock and relief dueled inside of her. "What are you doing here?"

"Paisley, I'm so glad to see you."

Then she was in his arms, and they were hugging, him clinging to her, or maybe she was desperately clinging to him. Whatever spitting-mad rage she felt toward an intruder moments ago disintegrated into a gut-deep appreciation that Judah was here, and that he'd come looking for her. "I'm so glad to see you, too."

She stepped back a little, but they still held onto each other's arms. The wind raged all about them, yet the fierce conditions didn't seem as scary now.

"Oh, Pais. I'm s-so"—he seemed choked up—"happy you're alive."

"Well, me too." She pointed at the floor, then rubbed her hip. "Did you have to do that?"

"I did." He grabbed the flashlight off the table and pulled her across the living room toward the staircase. "C'mon. Hurry."

"Wait. What are you doing?" Fear scrambled up her chest. "I have to cover the window. The tree's—"

"Too late for that." He kept pulling her up the stairs.

"Why? What's going on? Judah, wait."

"I think a tidal surge is coming." He didn't let go of her.

"Now?" She followed him up the stairs, past the pictures of her and her siblings that remained on the staircase wall, with dread filling her. "How big?"

"Big enough. Water's pouring across the street as we speak."

"Oh, no." What should they do? Grab food? Water? She jerked her hand free and turned back.

"Paisley, no!"

"I have to get something." She ran back down the stairs, and rushing to the fridge, flung open the door. Dad had some water bottles. She grabbed several.

Judah was right behind her and scooped up a foil-covered bowl out of the fridge. "Get upstairs. Now!"

Outside, either the booming of thunder or the sounds of heavy objects crashing and falling made her pause. "Judah, listen. What is it?"

By his shocked expression, he heard the loud roar too.

"Ruuuuun!" He pushed her with his free hand toward the stairway. "Don't stop for anything."

They sprinted up the steps, Judah fast on her heels, as something smashed against the house. The whole place thudded like a semitruck rammed into it. Judah shoved her into her old bedroom and slammed the door. He breathed hard, his eyes wide.

"Will the house hold?" Shivers raced over her skin as she stared at him leaning against the door as if his sheer strength might keep out the storm. "Otherwise, what are we doing in here?"

"Where else can we go?" He met her gaze with such tenderness, she didn't want to look away.

"There's an attic," she whispered. She wouldn't go up there alone, but with him, maybe. She set the water bottles on the end table next to her old twin bed.

He shook his head. "Just stay here by me. And keep away from the window." Finally, he seemed to relax a little—even though the howling winds still sounded threatening—and stepped away from the door. He set the bowl and the flashlight next to the water bottles. With a rusty-sounding sigh, he dropped onto the bed, then tugged on his rubber boots. He pulled hard like they were stuck. After a few attempts, he managed to get them off, then slid out of his coat and rain pants and wet socks. The pile of outerwear made a water stain on the wooden floor. Not that she cared.

Something screeched loudly across the floor downstairs. She dropped down beside Judah on the bed, closer than she would have if it didn't feel like the world was crashing down around them. When he laid his arm over her shoulder and tugged her against his side, she didn't pull away. She might have even leaned into his chest a tad, and wrapped her arms around his waist, just for comfort.

"It'll be okay." He was trying to reassure her, she could tell, but he couldn't know for sure they'd be safe. He ran his palm over her arm. "God is with us."

She wanted to believe that, but when the house shuddered again, she held her breath, waiting for something horrible to happen. The flashlight created weird shadows on the steep ceiling overhead that exaggerated the eeriness of them hiding out in her childhood bedroom while a tempest raged. She scooted back a little to see his eyes. "Why didn't you leave town with the others? I mean, I'm glad you're here"—if only he knew how glad she was to not be alone—"but why didn't you go?"

"I couldn't." His face puckered like he was about to cry, but she knew better. The Judah Grant she knew before didn't cry. "I, um, found your car down by the peninsula, and I thought—" He winced.

"Oh. You thought I was sitting on the point?" That's what he meant earlier about being glad to find her alive.

"Yeah." His blue eyes filled with some undefinable emotion. She couldn't break free of the warmth in his gaze. Had a wretched storm not been threatening them, she probably wouldn't have done it, but when a tree or something large scraped the window like it might bust through at any moment, she clasped his hands and held on tightly. He clutched her hands, too.

The rain fell hard, then, as if rocks pounded the roof above them. Listening, yet trying not to listen, she resisted the urge to fall into Judah's arms for more of his comforting assurances. Because, if she did, that would be unfair to him, since she didn't mean anything by it, right? Still, she didn't move away. Although, when the pounding overhead let up, she released his fingers, embarrassed by her clinginess.

Thankfully, he didn't mention her reaction. "I almost went out on the peninsula to look for you."

"That would have been terrible." A picture of him being swept into the sea while hunting for her flashed through her imagination. She shivered. That he nearly risked his life to find her made her want to scoot closer to him again. "What happened?"

"I couldn't get out there." He bit his lower lip. "The whole thing was covered in water. I didn't want to think of the possibility you might be hurt . . . or lost."

Like she'd just been thinking about him.

He stood and walked to the window facing the backyard—the one where Paisley sat on the windowsill daydreaming of their wedding seven years ago. He peeled back the faded blue calico curtains. A flash of lightning lit up the window. "The wind and waves almost took me out."

She drew in a sharp breath. "Then I would have hated myself worse than I already do." And another person might have passed away without her having the chance to make things right.

He scrunched the thin curtains together, then swiveled around quickly, his eyes wide. What did he see that caused such a startled expression? "Don't ever hate yourself, Pais. God made you beautiful, inside and out. You're full of adventure and life and goodness. I love those qualities about you."

Goodness? No one ever said that about her before.

"God loves you. And so do I. We're going to be okay."

Where did so much confidence in him come from? Especially in the middle of a storm that was shaking her family's house, and her, to the core?

He grabbed an afghan off the end of the bed and wrapped it around her shoulders. He rubbed his hands over her arms as if to warm her, when he had to be freezing too.

"Thanks, but you need this m-more than m-me." Teeth

chattering, she clutched the blanket her mother crocheted a life-time ago.

"Don't worry. I'll find another." After he grabbed the flash-light, he opened the closet door and pulled out an extra blanket and pillow. "These will come in handy." He tossed them on the foot of the bed.

The window rattled. Paisley jumped, her nerves on edge. Something clattered on the roof, then scraped down the side of the house.

"Loose shingles." Judah opened a drawer where her socks used to be kept. "The storm's bound to get worse before it gets better. In my experience, most do." Was he talking about the weather outside or about them? "Since we're situated beneath the steepest point of the roof, we should be fine right where we are."

She swallowed, wishing she had his positive outlook.

He pulled off his soaking wet shirt, his shimmering chest glowing in the flashlight's beam. She closed her eyes, not wanting to be caught staring at his bare, sleek upper body. Good thing he didn't know what she was thinking—that she loved the way he used to hold her close in his arms, like he thought she was precious. Ugh. Too much time, and too many hurts, had passed since those days. They cared about each other as friends now, just waiting out a storm in the same room. That's all.

Then why did her heart pound so hard?

She glanced up. He put a throw around his shoulders. Good. She sighed.

When he sat down on the bed next to her, a little too close, she stood, anxiety twisting her nerves. "What do we do now?" She took a step toward the window, but he clasped her hand and drew her back.

"Stay away from the window."

"Why?" She wanted to see whatever he had. How bad was it out there? Wind and rain pelted the glass, a duo assault on the old panes.

"The glass might give any second."

She stepped back. "Think the wave made it this far?"

"Sounded like it." He cleared his throat. "And looked like it." He let out a sigh. "Why don't you try to rest. It'll be a long night, and all we can do is wait it out."

"What if the roof collapses?" She sat down next to the head of the bed and shivered as she glanced up at the arched, white painted ceiling illuminated by the flashlight.

"I'm praying it doesn't."

That he was praying and trusting God, even though he lost so much, too, was inspiring. Maybe God was listening to Judah's prayers. In fact, maybe He listened to hers by sending Judah here. She was thankful she wasn't alone right now, hiding under the bed and scared out of her wits.

"Hungry?" Judah grabbed the bowl off the dresser.

"Kind of." Mostly, she needed a distraction. She snuggled into the afghan surrounding her shoulders. If the elements outside weren't throwing such a tantrum, sitting next to Judah and chatting as if nothing was wrong between them would have been like a dream.

"Let's see what we have." He pulled the foil off the bowl, then pointed the light at the pottery dish. "Ah, mystery meat."

His lighthearted comment eased some of the tension in the room.

She chuckled at the memory of how they used to call the meat in fast foods and casseroles "mystery meat." "Sloppy Joe sauce, perhaps?"

He stuck his index finger in the red sauce and lifted it to his tongue. "You're right."

"Cold tomato sauce *and* no silverware?" Didn't sound appealing.

A loud, booming crash made her clutch Judah's arm.

"The stairs, I think." He leaned his head against hers for a moment.

"Gone?" She whispered.

He nodded tensely, but then seemed to visibly relax, maybe for her benefit. "So, we'll have to be creative without a fork." He shuffled back to the closet. A trail of wetness followed him across the floor. His jeans had to be soaked.

"Your pants are dripping."

"Sorry."

"I didn't mean that. You should just take them off." Heat blazed up her neck. "Oh, I didn't mean anything—" Ugh. That was the second verbal blunder she made about removing their clothing in the last couple of days.

Judah leaned out of the closet and looked at her with a raised eyebrow. Then he smiled. "I know what you mean, Pais. Thanks for being concerned about me." He ducked back into the closet, nearly out of sight.

She heard some shuffling. Then he tossed his jeans out onto the floor with the other wet clothes.

What was he going to wear now? He wouldn't find anything that fit him in her old closet. A moment later, he shuffled out with the throw that was previously around his shoulders wrapped snugly around his waist like a skirt—which meant his chest was bare again.

She averted her gaze. "I can take the flashlight into Dad's room and see what he has that might fit you."

"Your dad's shorter than me."

"I know."

"See what I found?" He waved something in the air as he sat down beside her.

"What is it?"

"A ruler." He wiped it across the blanket. Then he handed her the grade-school measuring tool and the bowl. "You first."

"A ruler for a fork?"

"Uh-huh. Use what's at hand, that's my motto." He grinned.

"Yeah, since when?"

"Since I've been caught in a few storms." He picked up the other blanket off the bed and wrapped it around his shoulders like a shawl.

She remembered what he told her the day she arrived back in town about his jumping into the ocean and fighting the current to get his skiff to shore. He was resourceful. Maybe, with his ingenuity and her gritty determination, they'd be okay waiting out the storm in her old room. "After we eat, I'm finding you some dry clothes." It would be a relief for her when he covered his skin that smelled too spicy for her senses with them sitting so close.

"Fine." His eyes twinkled in the dim light. Did he sense her discomfort? "These, um, batteries might not last long."

"I put in new ones this afternoon." She shrugged. "But who knows how long they've been in Dad's drawer?"

As if in answer, the light flickered. What would they do if it went out? For now she needed to see the mystery meat. She grabbed the flashlight and aimed it into the bowl.

"How about if I hold it while you eat?" He took the flashlight and redirected the light.

She ate a bite. "Not bad." Although, his watching her was disconcerting. She let the meat roll over her tongue. "Turkey burger. Mystery solved." She ate a few bites then handed him the bowl. "Your turn."

He passed her the flashlight. Their fingers touched, and a familiar zing raced up her spine. Why was she feeling butterflies around a man she lived with for four years and avoided for three? No excuse, but some part of her was tempted to lean in to his strong arms again.

The storm was at fault. It forced them into a situation of closeness she wouldn't have chosen or thought she wanted a week ago. Not that anything would happen romantically. Goodness, no. And yet, what if it did? What if deep inside she still harbored feelings for Judah?

Maybe . . . even . . . loved him.

Ugh. She scooted against the creaky headboard, putting space between them. Love and marriage weren't in her plans anymore.

She kept the light shining on the bowl but saw his beautiful blue eyes in the peripheral beam. With a certain intrigue, she watched him eating. Every time the ruler grazed his moist lips, she swallowed. A slight glob of red sauce was stuck in the crease of his lips, but she rejected the impulse to bring attention to his mouth. His soft lips that she—

Enough! She leapt off the bed and yanked open the door. "Um. I'll be right back." She needed a room's length to keep herself from doing something foolish—like touching his lips or, heaven forbid, kissing him! Her wayward thinking was due to fatigue and fear over their possible imminent death because of the storm. Nothing else. Still, even with that reasoning, she trembled from her reaction to him. She was romance starved, that had to be it.

In Dad's room, she scrounged through his drawers, then tossed a flannel shirt and some pajama bottoms that would probably fit Judah into a pile on the bed. The window panes rattled and crackled and seemed on the verge of breaking. She didn't want to be in here if that happened.

Just then, a huge crash rocked the house. She fell against the dresser. Groaned.

A cry or a loud moan came from her old bedroom.

"Judah? What's wrong?" She ran out of her dad's room and down the hall.

Twenty-two

Something crashed against the window, and an explosion of glass shrapnel hurtled across the bedroom. Judah yanked the blanket over his head and dove under the pillows near the headboard. A searing pain shot up his leg. He tried to muffle the cry that tore from his mouth. Every muscle in his body tensed. He gritted his teeth as the blast pummeled the room with tiny fragments. Objects fell from shelves to the floor. Pictures dropped from the walls, and the wind continued its rampage in the small space. Holding his breath, he waited for the surge to abate, praying for the house to hold and begging God to keep Paisley safe. He tried to ignore the agony in his calf.

"Judah!" Paisley burst through the bedroom door.

He jerked upright. Grimaced. "Don't come in here! Stay back."

Her light beam swept across the floor which was strewn with tree branches and glass fragments and childhood memorabilia, ending at the gaping window and darkness beyond. The whole room looked devastated.

"Oh, no." She stepped toward him.

"Stay back, Paisley. I mean it. There's glass everywhere. We have to get out of here." Although, he wouldn't be able to step on the floor in bare feet. The boots he dropped earlier were probably filled with glass. How could he get off the bed without slicing his foot?

Paisley gasped. "Judah! Don't move."

"Why not?" Adrenaline shot through him.

She pointed the flashlight at the bed. "L-look." She whimpered.

His gaze followed the light. A crimson stain spread across the quilt. Then he saw why. A three-inch jagged glass shard was embedded in the outer, lower portion of his left calf. "Oh, man." He moved his leg slightly, then clenched his jaw to hide the pain. Inwardly, he groaned. If he'd kept his wet jeans on, this might not have happened. Or not as badly. What should he do?

The light shifted as Paisley came closer. "What can I get? Tell me what you need. Does it hurt? Of course, it hurts." Her face crumpled like she was about to cry.

"I'll be okay. I, um, need a clean cloth to wrap around my shin." He held out his palm to her. "Stay back, though."

She fidgeted like she didn't want to do what he said.

With the wind still blasting things off the shelves, one of them could get hit with something else. For both of their protection, they had to get out of this room. With the glass impaled in his leg, he would be useless. If Paisley needed him, he wouldn't be able to do anything. So despite his C-MER first aid training that it was better not to remove an embedded item, he was going to have to do just that. He grabbed the edge of the blanket to use like a glove, then he clutched the three-inch piece of glass between his index finger and thumb. He gritted his teeth, wishing for something to bite down on.

"What are you doing?" She shrieked.

He met her gaze—she shook her head as if begging him not to do it, but her gaze never left his. He stayed focused on her. The woman he loved. The woman he wanted to protect. Then he pulled out the impalement in one anguish-filled movement. He moaned loudly. Blood squirted. He fought the urge to yell again. Then he pressed his fingers hard against the wound, his teeth chattering. *God, help me.*

"Oh, Judah." Paisley was crying now.

He grabbed another dry edge of the blanket and held it against the cut, sopping blood, fighting dizziness. "I-I need something to wrap my l-leg. Maybe s-some scissors to c-cut up this blanket."

"Wait." She clomped out of sight, taking the light with her. The door crashed closed.

He needed a second to collect himself, anyway. Leaning back in the darkness, he heard loud crashing and rushing water outdoors, maybe downstairs. He groaned, then his thoughts turned to prayer. *Lord, please keep us through the night. Help this roof to hold.*

In a few seconds, the room lit up again. Paisley tossed him a thin but long towel. "It's clean."

Stopping the blood flow was his main concern, especially since he didn't know how soon he could get to a medical facility. He wrapped the towel snugly around his calf, cinching it, knowing it probably wouldn't do the job effectively. He'd need stitches, come morning. Once the oversized bandage was secured, he carefully stood. He yanked the bloodstained blanket from the bed and tossed it over the glass on the floor. He grabbed a water bottle, then gingerly limped into the hallway, grimacing with every step. The wind slammed the door shut behind them.

Paisley got under the crook of his arm, supporting him. A moment later, lightheadedness hit him. He sank against the wall, bumping a picture of Paisley as a kid to the floor. All they needed was more glass beneath their feet.

"Don't worry. I never cared for that picture." She wrapped her arms around his waist.

He liked her being close, and the way she was trying to take care of him was comforting, but he wouldn't play on her sympathy. He was supposed to be the one protecting her.

"You okay?" She glanced up at him. "I can't believe you pulled the glass out yourself."

"I had to." Still in a lot of pain, his thoughts seemed muddled. "Um." He cleared his throat. "Which room?"

"You need to clean the wound, right?" Her gaze met his over the light coming from the flashlight. He read fear in her eyes.

"Not right now." He wanted to reassure her somehow. "We're going to be okay, Pais."

She nodded but looked doubtful.

He loved how soft she felt, her arms around him, and how caring she was being. Maybe she did still love him. He swayed slightly, clenching his jaw at the burning sensation in his leg. "Does your dad have a first aid kit?"

"I don't know." She let go of him. "I'll go look."

"No." Pain shot up his calf, and he didn't hide his facial reaction quick enough.

"You're hurting. I'm so sorry, Judah." She gripped his hand. "C'mon. Let's get you settled in Dad's room. Then I'll hunt for a kit or some bandages."

"I don't want you wandering around the house. Stay close to me, okay?" As soon as they entered the bedroom, he saw the bank of large windows was being battered by wind gusts and hammering rain. "These windows might break too. Any windowless rooms?"

"Not up here." She shook her head. "Even the bathroom has a small one."

He sat on the bed, unsure what to do next.

Paisley grabbed the water bottle, undid the lid, and handed it back to him. He took a sip, then she set the bottle on the dresser.

"Let me help you get this shirt on." She directed his arms into a flannel shirt, then did up the buttons for him. "Here's some pajama bottoms, but I don't know how to get them on over your injured leg." She held up black checkered pjs.

"I'm okay for now." He'd put them on later, when his injury felt more stable. He still had the blanket wrapped around his waist.

She fluffed a couple of pillows behind his back. Maybe he'd close his eyes for a minute. "I don't want to bleed on your dad's blankets."

"Don't worry about it." She grabbed a smaller pillow and gently propped it under his leg.

He moaned but stifled it with a yawn.

She smoothed her hand down his arm. Stroked his forehead. Her being his nurse wasn't so bad. Although, he wished the injury hadn't happened. He sighed.

"You okay until I get back?"

He'd rather she stayed by him, but he probably needed a better bandage. He linked their fingers and drew her closer to him. "Sure. You be careful." He looked up at her, saw her shining dark eyes gazing back at him sweetly. Her soft expression made him want to span the distance between them. Just one brief kiss. Would she allow them a moment of tender affection in the middle of this terrible storm?

They stared at each other for a good thirty seconds, their faces, maybe, a foot apart. She blinked slowly, her gaze meshed with his.

He gulped, his heart kicking up a rapid beat. He licked his lips, anticipating what their first kiss might be like after their three-year absence.

She glanced at his mouth, then her gaze skittered back to his, then she was glancing at his mouth again. *Oh, Paisley.* He let go of her hand and stroked the backs of his fingers down the side of her cheek, felt the softness of her skin. She closed her eyes and sighed. Was she looking forward to something romantic happening between them as much as he was? Sure, he needed a distraction from the pain in his leg. But kissing her? Them breaching the harrowing gulf that existed in their marriage for so long had to mean more than a mere distraction in the middle of a hurricane. It had to mean she wanted the same thing, that she wanted them to still be together—husband and wife—like he did. Did she?

A moment later, she opened her eyes and gazed at him, and that warm, amazingly gentle look he couldn't resist was still there. An invitation, it seemed. Even if she wasn't in the same place as him emotionally, he wanted to draw her closer and feel her in his arms. He smiled at her, hoping she could see he was giving her an invitation too. She smiled back, with an almost shy look.

Then, somehow, the distance between them was gone. Her lips were pressing against his, soft, pliable, caressing, needy, yet gentle, and oh, so sweet. He kissed her with all the love he'd stored up in his heart. He pulled her to him, his arms going around her back. Her feet stayed on the floor, like she was bracing herself so as not to lean against his leg, but she was kissing him too. Or maybe, she was the one who kissed him first.

Several unbelievable moments later, she drew back and gazed at him beneath lowered eyelids that seemed filled with deep emotion. She smiled, and he grinned back at her.

"That was one amazing first kiss." He met her lips again.

"Mmhmm." She stroked her hand down the side of his face this time, gazing into his eyes. He leaned his mouth into her palm and kissed her skin.

He sighed and closed his eyes, wondering if he possibly imagined the whole thing. But then, he must have dozed off. Or lost track of time. Surely, only a second passed. The next thing he knew, the house rumbled and groaned as if it were in the throes of collapse. What was happening?

From somewhere, Paisley screamed.

Judah shot off the bed faster than he would have thought possible, given the condition of his leg. "Paisley?" He limped down the hallway in the dark, wishing for his cell phone light. "Where are you?"

The structural shudder came again. A thundering crash. Then he froze, waiting for the ceiling to cave in on him. "God, help us. You are our strength in time of trouble. Nothing can happen to us that You don't know about. I'm trusting You for favor and safety and peace." He continued limping through the darkness. Where had he left his phone? "Paisley?"

"Judah!" She banged on a door down the hall. "Judah!"

"I'm coming." Letting his fingers trail along the wall, he followed the indents and doorways until he got to the bathroom. Light from her flashlight splayed beneath the door. "You okay, Pais?"

"Oh, Judah, you're here." She whimpered. "I'm so s-sorry." She seemed to be talking through the crack.

"I'm here, sweetheart. What's wrong?" He rapped softly on the wood. "Open the door."

"I can't. It's s-stuck." She shook the knob again. "I h-hate it in h-here. I don't w-want to be l-locked in this t-tiny space." She sounded panicky.

He had to get her out of there. He knew about her claustrophobia, although he didn't know why she suffered from it. "Stand back. Let me try shoving against it."

"No, I don't w-want you h-hurting yourself even more." She sniffled.

"I'm okay." He wanted to reassure her, although he cringed at the pain to come. "I'm going to shove against the door."

"D-didn't you hear that crash?" She banged against the door like she was ramming into it.

"Hold up, in there. Yeah, I heard. Did something happen?" He positioned his shoulder against the door.

"I think a tree crashed onto the roof." Her answer sounded tinny and distant.

"Oh, man." He automatically looked up but didn't see anything in the dark. Was the roof unstable? Near collapsing? It sounded that way a few minutes ago. "Are you safe where you are?" He'd break down the door if he could, but might that be worse for the structure if a tree was on the roof above them?

"The r-roof caved in. That's why the d-door's jammed." She shook the handle. "The window broke too. And—" A moaning sound made his heart rate accelerate.

"And what?" He shoved his shoulder firmly against the door. Nothing gave. He'd have to back up and ram his weight against it.

"There's a lot of w-water out there, Judah."

So, she saw what he had earlier—the whole area was flooded. "It'll be okay." He remembered her panic attack on the peninsula, then again outside the Beachside Inn. He didn't want that happening to her while she was alone. "I'm going to try to get you out of there."

"Okay."

"Stand in the tub." He knew the tub was the farthest spot from the door.

"Too much glass in it."

He hadn't thought about that. "Stand wherever you feel safest."

He heard her shuffling back.

"How's your leg?" Her concern for him in the middle of her own nightmare was endearing.

"I'll be fine." For now, he had to ignore the discomfort. He stepped back about five feet—hard to tell in the dark.

"Judah?"

"Yeah?"

"Thank you for coming here. For finding me." She was quiet for a moment. "I would have been terrified going through this alone."

"You're welcome." Tears filled his eyes. He came so close to going to Mom's. What if he left without searching for Paisley? Thank God, he hadn't.

For a second, he imagined himself back in his high school glory days playing football, then he shoulder-rammed the door powerfully at close range. Intense pain tore through his injured leg. He groaned and fell backward.

"Judah?" Paisley's flashlight danced light around the door's edges.

"Yeah." He gritted his teeth. "I think you're right. The roof caved in. The door's stuck." He smoothed his hands over the doorframe, searching for whatever might be hindering it from opening. He found a bulge at the top. What if he got the door open, but the roof fell on them? *Lord, help us.*

He slid to the floor, adjusting the blanket around his legs, and tapped on the edge of the bathroom tiling beneath the door. "Paisley?"

"Uh-huh?" Her voice came softly. The light shone on the floor. He heard her drop down on the other side of the door.

"I can't get you out tonight. I'm so sorry. We'll have to wait until morning." He tried to keep his voice calmer than he felt.

A few moments passed. "Thanks for trying." It sounded like she slumped against the door and groaned.

He wished he'd done more to keep them safe. "Are you all right in there?"

"Kind of freaked out." Something rustled on the other side of the door. She was probably clearing glass away from where she sat. "How's your cut?"

"Hurts." Understatement. "At least, I can't see it." He touched the makeshift bandage and found it damp. Not a good sign.

"Why don't you go back into my dad's room, or use Peter's old room across the hall, and rest. I'll be okay." He could tell she was anything but okay, yet trying to be brave.

All he wanted to do was protect her and hold her. "I'm not leaving you, Pais." Now or ever.

He felt her little finger brush against his hand beneath the door. Adjusting his position, he leaned against the doorframe and moved his finger to touch hers. He sighed and closed his eyes.

"Think it'll get w-worse?" The worry in her tone was obvious.

"Hard to say. Hopefully, the worst has passed."

"And the tree over me?" A shuffling noise sounded like she curled up on the floor. "Think the house will hold?"

He stretched out on the linoleum, grimacing as he propped his throbbing leg on his other ankle. Their little fingers still touched.

"I hope so. Think you c-can sleep like this?" He heard the groggy sound in his voice. He shivered—from cold or possible shock. He tried to suppress his teeth from chattering, so Paisley wouldn't hear and be even more concerned.

They lost contact for a moment. Then she was back. "Can you talk to me for a few minutes?"

"Sure." He blinked to stay awake. "What do you want to talk about?" Did she mean talk about deeper things? Like why she left? About hurts in their past? Or something light?

"Tell me what you've been up to for the last few years." She sighed.

Ah, platonic things. But then he remembered the kiss they'd shared—he didn't only imagine that, right? Because there wasn't anything platonic about that romantic moment that was engrained in his thoughts forever. Even if it was caused by charged emotions after his injury, Paisley's tenderness toward him made him think she still had warm feelings for him. That made him smile, despite his pain and the uncomfortable position he was laying in.

Then, with their pinkies touching, he talked to her about things he'd seen on his skiff rides with C-MER—gray whales, leaping salmon, and overly-curious sea lions. He told her about his ideas for restoring their beach house, including making the veranda bigger. He wanted to share about that first year she was gone. About how angry he was until God finally got ahold of his heart. He wished he could confess about the day he bought a plane ticket to Chicago on the spur of the moment. But the soft sound of her snoring reached him, so he'd wait for another time to share that story.

He closed his eyes and thanked God for Paisley being close to him. A small miracle. If only that door weren't stuck, him on one side and her on the other. But then his thoughts skimmed through other things that stood between them—the past, the secrets, the rumors—and that door seemed to represent a whole lot of things he didn't want to contemplate right now.

Maybe he'd spend a few minutes praying. He winced as he moved his leg, trying to get comfortable. Before long, he felt himself relaxing too.

The last thought as he drifted to sleep was of Paisley's and his kiss.

Twenty-three

Paisley stretched, and her feet bumped into something. The toilet? What was she doing on the bathroom floor? She peeled her eyelids open and stared at the cracked, bulging ceiling above her. The storm's madness came rushing back to her, followed by thoughts of Judah's injury, and then the ... kiss. *Oh, my.* She bolted upright and took a deep breath.

Through the broken window, she saw early morning haze hung low in the sky.

They'd survived.

The flashlight still rested in the same place she set it on the floor last night, but without any light coming from it. She clicked the off switch, although the battery was obviously dead.

She glanced beneath the door. Judah's pinkie still rested slightly on her side. Had they slept close enough to touch each other's fingertips all night? Sweet, sweet man. *Sigh.*

A warmth spread through her at the remembrance of that moment in Dad's room when she leaned down and touched her lips to Judah's. How she acted every bit the wife she told herself she wasn't, so many times. Yet in that crazy instant of fearing for their lives, something within her longed to be his wife, his sweetheart. He'd been in so much pain, and she thought they might die. And when he kissed her back, *deep blue sea in the morning,* everything she ever loved about Judah Grant came rushing back to her.

Now, glancing up at the damaged ceiling hanging low and tilted, an image flashed through her mind of what could have happened if the tree crashed through the roof. She could have been crushed—both of them badly injured. Perhaps God protected them through the night. *If that was You, God, thank You. I mean it. I really am thankful.*

She heard rustling on the other side of the door. A groan. Judah's finger disappeared.

"Judah?" She got on her hands and knees. "You awake?"

"Uh-huh."

"How are you?"

"Hurting all over." He groaned again.

"I'm sorry. Just move slowly, okay?" It was strange how comfortable she felt talking with him, when just a couple of days ago she thought she never wanted to see him again, let alone sleep next to him. Now she'd give anything to be on the other side of this door, helping him, being close to him—at least until they got through the aftermath of the storm. Her stomach growled loudly. "I'm hungry. How about you?"

He chuckled, then moaned.

"I hate that you're hurting, and we can't do anything about it." She leaned her back against the door. Even though she couldn't see him, knowing he stayed in Basalt to be with her comforted her and made her feel calmer than she had in a long time. She pictured herself curling up next to him without the door between them—

his arm around her, her cheek resting against his chest—if only he didn't have the injury. "How's the leg?"

"I'll live." She heard movement. "I'm going to take a look around, find my phone, and try to put on those pajamas."

"Judah?" Her voice sounded too needy, so she cleared her throat to hide it.

"Yeah, Pais?"

The soft way he said his nickname for her made her sigh. "Don't go far, okay?"

A pause. "I won't." His bare feet shuffled away.

"You might find some shoes in Dad's closet." Oh, right, her dad's shoe size was smaller than his. "Uh, never mind." She shoved her back against the door, wishing it would spontaneously open.

Judah's footfall got fainter, like he went in the direction of the stairs. What if he fell or hurt himself and she couldn't get to him?

Ugh. No dwelling on negative what-ifs.

She stood and tiptoed around a pile of glass. Then, leaning over the edge of the tub, she peeked out the broken window. Water was still everywhere. Junk floated inside the backyard fence. The dilapidated shed that was in the corner of the property her whole life now lay on its side. The spruce tree she'd loved to climb when she needed solitude straddled the corner of the house— apparently overhead. Were all the shingles from the roof floating in the backyard? Such devastation! How long would it take for the water level to go down?

Judah tapped on the door.

"Yeah?" She scuttled back to her spot on the floor.

"The stairs are gone, as I suspected."

"Oh, no."

"Water must have come in through the living room window and beneath the door."

Her father's home was terribly damaged. Was it even fixable? Had any of Mom's paintings survived? Not that she cared. However, Dad might mourn their loss.

"I called Craig."

"What?" Her heart rate ramped up to hyperdrive. "Craig Masters? Why would you do that?" She never wanted to see that cad again.

"We need help getting you out of there." His calm and steady voice made her think he didn't know anything about Craig's offenses.

She'd rather tie washcloths together like a rope and risk climbing out the bathroom window than to ask the man who caused so much trouble between her and her father-in-law three years ago for help. "Can't you c-contact the p-police or someone else?" Her voice cracked, and she didn't attempt to hide her reaction.

"Police are preoccupied. Craig said he'll try to get here in an hour." He bumped the door as he sat down on the floor. "What's wrong with Craig helping us?"

Now wasn't the time to explain. Things were still tentative and unsettled between her and Judah, even with that kiss. Or maybe, more complicated because of it. She didn't know what the next step for them would be. But discussing Craig's wrongdoings this morning? No, thanks. "I'd prefer it was someone else, that's all." She swallowed hard, hoping he didn't read too much into her hesitancy.

After a pause he asked, "Did something happen between you and him?"

Why was he pursuing this subject? She didn't want to talk about that. Whenever she had to tell Judah about her deepest struggles, she'd rather be gazing into his shining blues, seeing his understanding, maybe even his compassion. Not sitting like this with a door between them.

Although, was it possible that a solid wooden door blocking her from seeing the disappointment in his eyes might be for the best?

She groaned.

"Pais, you can tell me."

If she did, would the tenderness in his tone disappear? Would he hate her? She grabbed a washcloth off the edge of the sink and twisted it in her hands, wringing out some of her fear and frustration. She could refuse to explain. But he deserved to hear the truth from her. They had an hour. She glanced at the door, imaging him sitting on the other side.

She took a deep breath. If only she could talk to him *and* keep herself from having a panic attack. "Okay, there's something I need to tell you about the night I left."

Twenty-four

Judah adjusted his pajama-covered leg, waiting for Paisley to continue. Apprehension crept up his spine. Whatever she was going to tell him might threaten the tenuous ties between them as devastatingly as the storm endangered this house last night. Why did she react so strongly to Craig's name? What if the rumors about Paisley and a guy were true? Were the two connected? His wife and his friend? Talk about a brutal betrayal.

But there he was jumping to conclusions. Hadn't he determined that no matter what transpired in the past, he was going to offer her forgiveness and grace like Jesus offered him? Like Hosea in the Old Testament did with his bride? Although, right now, Judah didn't want to contemplate any similarities between Hosea and himself. Just the thought of the story, or of something going on between Paisley and Craig, made his insides quake. Her continued silence added to his suspicions.

Mercy and grace. But sometimes, mercy and grace were easier in theory than in action. *Lord, help me.*

"Pais?" He forced his tone to sound calm, contrary to his

inner turmoil. He tapped the floor under the door with his little finger, silently inviting her to come closer.

A few moments passed before her little finger touched his. He sighed and thanked God. He was grateful for how close he felt with Paisley during the storm. He wouldn't let that go easily.

"You can tell me anything." He needed to hear his wife's heart regardless of the pain in his chest over any possible unfaithfulness. "About Craig . . ." he coaxed her.

"He, um, he was the one who . . ." Her voice trailed off.

Tension tightened every muscle in his shoulders. "The one who what?"

"H-he did s-something he shouldn't h-have." Her voice shook.

Oh, man. If his supervisor hurt her in any way, he'd— What? Punch his lights out? Have him fired? That might already be happening. It would be difficult not to want revenge. "What did he do?" He ground out the words.

"Well, uh." She blew out a long breath. "The night before I left, I got really angry with you."

"I know." He relived their argument many times. "We both said things we shouldn't have." He knew he had.

"Afterward, I went out drinking."

He figured that was the case, since she went out on her own more often after they lost the baby.

"I had too much to drink, and at the bar I said some things I didn't mean. I may have been flirtatious with a few of the guys around me." She drew in a raspy breath. "C-Craig was there, drinking too."

Judah clenched his other hand, knowing she couldn't see his reaction.

"We were at Hardy's Gill and Grill. Not together, of course."

"No?"

"No." She huffed. "He happened to be there when I was there. However, I was probably making a fool of myself." She took a breath. "When I left, he did too. Then he, uh, offered to take me home."

"He knew who you were, right?"

"That I was married to you?" She cleared her throat. "Yes."

Judah muffled a groan as his irritation escalated. Still, he kept his pinkie next to hers. "Then what happened?" The Lord had to be helping him stay calmer on the outside than he felt on the inside.

"I didn't think I should drive, so I accepted. I thought he was just being nice." A pause. "But when we got to his car—" She stopped talking and it drove Judah crazy.

"Please, just say it. I need to know what happened." He felt his arms shaking with suppressed tension.

"It'll make you m-mad." She gulped like she was subduing a sob.

"Maybe, but I want you to tell me so I can understand." Even though frustration raced through him, he had to find a way to reassure her that whatever she said, he was here for her. That he loved her unconditionally. "Take your time, Paisley. It's okay. I'm not mad." Well, not mad at her.

"O-okay." She groaned. "It's just hard to tell you this stuff."

"I know." He waited, although it was a test of his patience. He needed to hear everything—he'd waited three years for this conversation—but it wasn't easy to listen and do nothing.

"He, um, he grabbed my shoulders roughly"—she inhaled loudly—"and pressed me back against his c-car."

Rage sizzled through Judah.

"Then he kissed me h-hard. H-he acted as if he were going

to—" She pulled her hand away from his. A moan or a subdued cry came from the other side of the door.

That his supposed friend dared to push himself on Judah's wife, against her wishes, was more than he could handle. He slapped his other hand against the floor.

"Ju-u-dah?" He heard her fear. The regret.

Oh, man. "Sorry, Pais." He clenched his fist against his front teeth, trying to control his anger. He sighed. "Go ahead. I want to hear it all, really I do." *Grace and mercy. Grace and mercy.*

"Okay." She paused. "So, um, due to the quantity of liquor I consumed, I wasn't in my right mind. He probably wasn't either, although there's no excuse for his a-actions." Her voice shook. "Or maybe, I don't know, I may have kissed him back at first. Or gave him the wrong idea."

So hard to hear. "No, whatever he did was not your fault. He can be an overbearing clod." Judah thought of the callous way Craig told him he'd probably be out of job and the rough way he spoke to some of the other employees at work. Besides, the guy should have treated Paisley honorably, no matter what.

"I didn't want anything to happen with him, so, so I pushed him and tried to get away." She sobbed. "I told him 'no!' He wouldn't listen."

Judah growled, then tried to cover it with a cough. He was struggling to stay calm and not overreact.

"I kicked him in the shins. Slapped his face." Her voice rose. "Oh, Judah, you have to believe me."

"Of course, I do." Although, rage pummeled through him toward the man who dared to act aggressively toward his wife. Even so, he made sure his pinkie was under the door for when she was ready to let their fingers touch again. "Did he, did he hurt you?" The moment of truth.

She groaned. "H-he would have."

He expelled his breath, but any relief was short-lived. All this time Judah considered Craig his friend. Yet, in three years, that man never had the guts or the decency to come clean about what he attempted. Judah's anger intensified. He had to know the whole story. "What stopped him?"

She let out a tremulous sigh. "Your dad."

"My dad?" Judah sat up straighter.

She inhaled and exhaled loudly. Then coughed.

"Pais, it's okay." He slowly released his clenched fist and kept his voice gentle. "I'm so sorry for whatever happened that night. Just tell me, okay? How was my dad involved?"

"I will explain, promise, b-but I don't want to have a p-panic attack."

Her breathing sounded even more ragged. His heart filled with compassion for her. "I don't want that either. Just take your time. Relax for a minute." He pushed his little finger under the door. "Sweetheart, you can stop talking for a while if it will help." If he could knock down this door, he'd sit beside her, hold her, and try to comfort her

He heard a noise, then he thought he smelled peppermint candy.

She breathed deeply. Coughed.

"You okay? What is that scent?"

"Peppermint oil. Someone gave it to me." She cleared her throat and the sound came from below the edge of the door. Was she laying down now?

He stretched out, wincing as he adjusted his leg. He craned his neck until he could see under the door with his right eye. She was there, as if trying to be closer to talk with him. Unless resting like that helped her breathe easier.

"I love you." He needed to say the words. "Whatever happened between you and Craig, I want you to know I love you. I still want you to be my wife." He determined months ago to tell her that. But right now, he knew every word was true. "That kiss we shared last night? It meant everything to me."

Her one eye that he could see filled with unshed tears. She nodded. "That n-night, other than what Craig tried to do at first, n-nothing else happened between him and me."

"Really?"

"But your d-dad—" She made a wheezing sound.

He waited, wishing he could do something to help her. Some, but not all, of the mystery of that night was clearer now. He and Paisley argued, then she left and didn't come home until sometime after he went to bed. The next morning he found the note saying she was leaving and that she loved someone else.

"Your dad came around the corner. Saw us. Craig and me." Her little finger moved next to his. "By then, I was fighting and scratching and kicking mad."

He tried to picture the scene, her struggling against Craig's advances, and Dad observing the attack. "Dad never said a word about that to me." Why didn't he explain what he witnessed? Why would he allow his son to suffer in silence for three years?

"I'm not surprised." She stared at him through the crack under the door. "He hates me. Always has."

While that frustrated him to no end, he didn't disagree. His judgmental father had said too many negative things about Paisley. Judah gritted his teeth as a powerful surge of anger over past issues with his dad meshed with his current fury. "So what did Dad do?"

"He grabbed Craig by the shirt collar, shook him hard, then threw him to the sidewalk." Her eye blinked. "I didn't know Edward had that in him."

"Me, neither." His estimation of his father went up a notch.

She shifted on the floor. "He *kicked* Craig and told him he better not touch me again or he'd call the cops."

"Wow. Good for Dad." Yet, why didn't he tell Judah the truth?

"But then, he turned on me." She made a low growl.

"Turned on you how?" Surely, his dad hadn't harmed her.

A long silence.

"Pais?" Anxiety rippled up his neck.

"He grabbed my arm and yanked me down the street. Called me a"—she gulped—"a prostitute."

Judah groaned. Hadn't his father said similar things about her to him? Every time Judah shut him down, but the man was so spiteful.

"He said I wasn't worthy of a man like you. Never had been. Never would be." She drew in a stuttered breath. "J-Judah, he was r-right."

"No, he wasn't. I'm sorry he said such terrible things to you." His heart broke for her and what she'd been through without him. "I wish I'd been there."

"What would you have done?" Her voice softened.

"Slugged Craig to Timbuktu. Chewed out my dad." He inwardly groaned. "I would have brought you home. Loved you like the husband I wish I'd been."

"Oh, Judah." She sighed. "I never deserved you."

"Of course, you did." He tapped her little finger. "We were in love."

"Past tense."

"Present, for me." Then it was his turn to sigh as he wondered what that earth-shaking kiss meant to her. And he had another question. "When you left, did you go because of me? Or Craig? Or Dad?"

"Not Craig. But there were problems between you and me. Between me and this town." She moved farther away from him, their fingers losing connection.

"Did that have something to do with my dad?" He still tried to see her beneath the inch-and-a-quarter space under the door.

She groaned like she didn't want to say anything else. She was sitting up now, her legs crossed.

"You might as well tell me. I'll find out." He'd confront his dad. If he asked about that night, would Dad tell him the truth?

"He told me to leave and never come back." She paused. "Or he'd smear my name and our relationship by telling everyone he caught me having an affair . . . until you'd gladly leave me."

"You're kidding." That's how the rumor spread? By his own father? Acid churned in his gut.

"I-I'm not kidding." She inhaled loudly, sounding asthmatic. "But I was looking for an escape. So many bad things happened. The miscarriages. Misty Gale. Mom. Our . . . difficulties."

"I know." Sadness replaced his angst.

"Edward drove me home that night and said awful things to me." She sniffed. "Then he handed me a wad of money. And I . . . I did his bidding. I left you." She sounded wounded. "I've regretted that decision for a long time."

He couldn't believe the extent of pain his dad caused them. He tapped the floor with his finger. "C'mere, Pais."

After a minute, she leaned down beside him as she had before. He heard her huff a little like she was tired. Same as him. But tired or not, this was his moment to share something vital with her.

"I still want to be your husband." How could he make her see into his heart? "I'm in this marriage for the long haul. Isn't that what I promised you on our wedding day? You and me forever. I meant it that day. I still do." He felt so much vulnerability in those words. He held his breath, waiting to hear what she'd say.

"How can you still want that?"

"I do, that's all that matters." He stroked her finger. "Please, give *us* a second chance."

"I don't know if there even is an us."

How could she say that after their kiss? "Oh, Pais, there's definitely an us."

She sighed. "I haven't told you all the things I've done."

"Well, I haven't told you all the things I've done, either." He smiled at his own drama, although there were things he needed to tell her. "Whatever we have to say to each other, I want you, Paisley Rose Grant, to be my wife . . . from this day forward. To have and to *hold*." He emphasized the last word and hoped she got his message. "We're going to be okay, you and me."

"How can you be so sure?" She watched him too, both of them gazing at each other beneath the door.

"We're surviving this storm, aren't we?"

"I hope so. But I don't like being in this tiny space."

"I wish I was in there with you." He prayed she saw the sincerity in his gaze.

She blinked a couple of times. "Me too."

Her answer encouraged him, but would she still feel the same way after their rescuer arrived?

Twenty-five

A vehicle door slammed outside. Craig, no doubt. Paisley cringed. How would Judah deal with seeing his coworker now that he knew the truth about the scoundrel? And even if Judah's response to her telling him all that stuff hadn't been as terrible as she feared, the thought of interacting with Craig made her stomach churn.

"He's here." Judah tapped the floor. "I just got his text."

"I know." She hated that she needed Craig's help at all.

"Pais? I'm right here."

She appreciated the kindness she still detected in his voice. Not that his being on the other side of the door remedied the tightening in her chest when a ladder scraped the house below the broken bathroom window. The top rung swayed just beyond the gaping glass, and a bitter taste filled her mouth.

Breathe.

Craig was here to help her get out of the second story, then she never had to see him again. Although, this was a small town, and it was hard not to run into someone.

"Hey!" Craig's voice. "I'm coming up."

She didn't answer.

"It'll be okay," Judah said softly. How he managed to remain positive in the face of everything she told him, and what happened, she had no idea.

Suddenly, the villainous face in her nightmares filled the window. Craig nodded and smiled at her, a greasy look. She kept one arm crossed over her ribs like a shield. Didn't say anything. She wouldn't speak to him at all, if she could help it.

"Judah asked me to come get you." He broke a couple of chunks of glass out of the window frame.

She still didn't move from where her finger touched Judah's.

"Hey, Masters!" Judah yelled, and his voice had a steely quality she never heard before.

"Yeah?" One of Craig's eyebrows quirked at Paisley. Could he tell by Judah's tone that she told him about his behavior that night?

"Help my wife out, then come around to the other side of the house for me." His vocal intensity didn't soften.

She was surprised he didn't add some warning about Craig keeping his dirty hands off her. But then, he wouldn't want to risk her safety by riling their rescuer.

"Be around in a minute. Water's about a foot high. Worse at the crossing." Craig glared at her. "Are you coming out, or not?"

If there was a second option, she'd take it.

"Pais?" Judah spoke quietly, probably so Craig wouldn't hear.

She leaned down. "Yeah?"

"If he even touches you once, he'll answer to me."

She smoothed her index finger along his pinkie. Then she stood but didn't clasp Craig's outstretched hand. She wouldn't have contact with him, physical or otherwise, if there was any way to avoid it.

"I can do this myself." She stared into his dark eyes she once found attractive. Too bad she ever entertained such fickle notions. Judah's blue eyes were more beautiful, and truer.

"You sure?"

"Positive—about a lot of things." It felt good to return the glare he gave her a moment ago.

Craig scowled. "Fine by me." He disappeared from the window, grumbling. "Too bad I came all this way, at my own peril. A lot of thanks I get."

She wasn't thankful to him at all, other than Judah getting the medical help he needed.

When she was certain enough time passed for Craig to be off the ladder, she leaned out the window. "I'm going now." She wanted Judah to know what was going on, even though she was sure he heard her exchange with Craig.

"I'll have my arms around you in a minute, sweetheart." Judah's voice sounded husky.

She smiled. Then she double-checked for glass on the window frame before climbing out. The ladder wobbled, and her gaze darted to Craig's. He stood at the bottom of the ladder, in shin-deep gray water, smirking. Had he let the ladder sway on purpose? *Rat!* She didn't want him here. Didn't want to step off the ladder and have him standing too close, but she required his holding the ladder steady.

When she reached the last rung, which was submerged in brackish water, Craig had already stepped back. At least he had the courtesy to do that.

She put her stockinged feet into the cool water, then waded carefully over uneven ground, not wanting to misstep and fall on her face in front of him. She shuffled toward the front of the house, easing around floating trash and roofing shingles, leaving Judah's coworker to retrieve the ladder. When she rounded the corner, the damage around the flooded neighborhood shocked her. Downed trees. Branches. Garbage everywhere. Across the street, the Weston's camping trailer was on its side. Judah's truck had butted up to the porch where the steps used to be. The scene was surreal. Weird.

She tried to glimpse the ocean between two of the neighbors' houses across from her, but it was hidden by low fog. With all this water, how much damage happened in town? Had Dad found sanctuary somewhere? He'd be discouraged to see his family home and land now.

Craig waded around the house, his boots swirling the water. The ladder clattered in his arms and scraped the corner of the house. No use telling him to be careful with all the other damage. "Which window?"

She glanced up to the second floor.

"Over here." Judah lifted his hand from Dad's open bedroom window. At least those panes didn't break last night like she feared they might.

Craig made a muffled sound of agreement.

"Did you see your truck?" She gazed up at Judah.

"Can't believe it moved that far."

"Must have been some wave." Craig settled the ladder against the house. "Come on down when you're ready."

Craig glanced at her, and she averted her gaze.

But, a moment later, Judah groaned, and she glanced up. He clutched the top rung, his pajama-clad injured leg dangling free. Did he almost fall?

"Judah, you okay?"

He stayed still for a few seconds, gripping the sides of the ladder. Then slowly he lowered his foot covered in one of Dad's wool socks onto the rung. "Give me a minute. I'll get there."

"No hurry, man." Craig gazed upward, his face contorted. Was he worried for Judah after seeing the bloodstained cloth on his leg? Or anxious to get out of the flood zone?

Paisley shuffled through the water to grab Judah's arm and help him reach the ground. Craig got under the other arm, and together they led Judah away from the ladder and toward Craig's monster truck. Good thing he drove a tall vehicle to get through all this standing water.

"Guess we got the wave we didn't think would hit, after all." Craig nodded his dark hair in the direction of the ocean. "What possessed you to disobey orders and stay in town? You could have been killed."

"I had my reasons." Judah glanced at her and winked.

She smiled back at him. Her hero.

"Why don't you sit in my truck? I'll have a look at your leg." Craig opened the truck door.

After Judah pulled himself up onto the seat, Paisley stepped back and watched as Craig retrieved a first aid kit from the backseat. He seemed to know what he was doing as he rolled up the pajama fabric and untied the bloodstained faux bandage from Judah's leg. Judah groaned, and Paisley wished she were close enough to hold his hand. He looked pale. It seemed he'd lost a lot of blood.

"It's inflamed." Did the C-MER employee have medical training? Was that why Judah called him?

Paisley cringed at how red the gash was.

Craig washed the injury with antiseptic, and Judah groaned again.

"You need stitches," Craig said gruffly.

"Yeah, yeah." Judah gritted his teeth.

"I mean it." Craig secured a square gauze over the cut with white tape. "An antibiotic, probably."

"But he'll be okay, right?" That was all that mattered.

"Sure, he will." Craig nodded.

Could she trust anything he said?

As soon as Craig finished taping the wound, Judah slid down from the truck, landing back in the water.

"Hey, that cut needs to stay dry." Craig pulsed his thumb toward the interior of the truck. "Get back in there. I'm taking you to the ER in Florence."

"No, that's all right." Judah shook his head. "Thanks for rescuing us, though."

Why was he refusing to see a doctor? Because of her? His flushed cheeks made her think he might have a fever. Was the cut infected?

"Craig's right." She nudged Judah's arm. "You should go get stitches." Even if that meant she'd be alone, he required medical attention. "And you probably need that medicine."

"Come with me?" His warm blues met her gaze.

Before she could answer, he pulled her against his chest, holding her close. She rested her cheek near his heart and sighed, thankful to be standing next to him without a door in the way.

"I told you I'd be doing this in a few minutes," he whispered near her ear. He ran his palm down the back of her hair.

She breathed in the masculine scent of him. If home was where the heart was, she was home in his arms. But what if this feeling of closeness with him was due to the storm and the harrowing experiences they went through together? When the crisis was over, would she feel the same way toward him as she did right now? She glanced up and met his gaze. Sighed.

Craig cleared his throat like he felt awkward standing there watching them, which was fine with her. Let him feel uncomfortable all day long.

But then, Judah eased his hold on her. He ran both of his palms up and down her upper arms. "You okay?"

"I am. You?"

"I'll live." He smiled, and the way he gazed into her eyes, even though her villain was nearby, spoke volumes to her heart.

Judah was a kind and trustworthy man, she knew that more now than ever. He said he still wanted her for his wife, and that they'd work together on the things they hadn't done so well at before. Did she want him for her husband? Could they, perhaps, try again and see what happened?

She clasped his hands, her gaze still fixed on his.

Was she willing to trade all her preconceived ideas for a chance at happiness, maybe love? And if so, how could she let him know her heart was changing without saying so in front of Craig? She leaned up on tiptoe and kissed Judah's rough, unshaven cheek.

His eyes lit up.

She grinned, feeling a little amazed by her new, tender feelings toward him, even if she had some doubts. "What now?"

"Marriage?" He laughed.

"I didn't mean—"

"You coming or not?" Craig asked gruffly and climbed into his truck.

Judah watched her intently. "You too. I won't go without you."

"I'm sorry, but I can't." No matter how her heart felt stirred toward Judah, she wouldn't ride in Craig's truck. "You go." She unclasped their hands. "I'll stay and work. The water should start going down soon, right?"

"Might not for a few days. Come with me, Pais. We'll spend time talking." He kissed her cheek, his lips lingering close to her mouth. If she moved her lips half an inch . . . but no, Craig was watching. "Please?"

Her heart kicked up a beat. Judah's gaze held so many promises.

"I'll be here when you get back." After what she told him, he had to understand she didn't want to be in close proximity to Craig. "Besides, I want to clean up before Dad sees any of this."

"But—" Then he sighed as if accepting his inability to convince her otherwise. "I need to tell you something." He rubbed his forehead like it hurt. "I should have mentioned it last night, but I didn't want you worrying even more."

"What is it?"

"Judah!" Craig barked from the truck. "I gotta go, man."

"Hang on a sec." Judah frowned at Craig, then turned back to Paisley. "Your dad told me he wasn't leaving Basalt Bay."

"When was that?"

"When I first stopped by his house to give the pre-alert." He clasped her hand. "Sorry. I should have said something."

"I would have gone looking for him if I thought he might be alone."

"I know."

She recalled what the minister told her last night. "Pastor Sagle saw Dad loading Paige's car. Most likely, he left with her."

"Well, then, that's good."

"Yeah, but he'll be sad when he sees all this damage."

"It'll need a restoration." He stroked a few strands of hair away from her cheek. "Like us."

This time she didn't get angry over his marriage-makeover talk. He was right, if they were even going to consider starting over, they'd need a complete redo. But first his leg needed stitches.

"Go and get fixed up." She tugged on his hand. "That gash looks bad."

"I can't stand the thought of leaving you." He glanced in the direction of the house. "Only work outside, okay? The place is unstable."

"I will. I just have to go in for—"

"No." He grabbed her arms and pulled her against him again. "Promise me you won't go in the house until I get back. And stay away from power lines."

"Okay. Promise."

Craig blasted his horn.

Judah pulled his cell phone out of his pocket. "Here. Keep this."

"But you need it."

He clasped his hands around hers and gave her the phone. "I'll use Craig's, or I'll call you from the hospital."

"All right. Thanks. Hurry back."

"I will." He touched her cheek, and she thought by the gentle look in his gaze he might kiss her. Instead, he limped a few steps, then glanced back. "You know I have to talk with him, right?"

"Please, don't make waves." Tears stuck in her throat. "I needed you to understand, that's all."

"And I do." Did that mean he wouldn't talk with Craig? "Stay safe."

"You too."

He stepped up into the vehicle and closed the door. The monster truck pulled into the flooded street, and Paisley lifted her hand, wondering how long she might be here by herself. Had any neighbors weathered the storm too? Or would she be the only person left in Basalt?

As the truck rumbled down Front Street, Craig stared back at her through the side-view mirror with a dark glint in his eyes. What did such a brooding expression mean?

Twenty-six

The ride back to Highway 101 was one of the worst overland trips Judah ever endured. With each bump and jarring motion of the giant truck, he clenched his teeth and fought the urge to bellow out in pain. The junction of South Road and the highway was completely flooded and impassable. Large chunks of pavement had broken off the road due to water damage and soil erosion, and some pieces had fallen down the cliff. But thanks to Craig's ability to maneuver an off-road four-wheel-drive vehicle, they kept moving.

So far, Judah hadn't confronted Craig with Paisley's accusation. He was praying about it. How would God have him address the grievance? Paisley's unwillingness to ride in Craig's truck showed him just how much she was still affected by his supervisor's misdeeds. He couldn't keep silent much longer. While he was thankful Craig rescued them, part of him wondered why. Because of their friendship? Or his guilty conscience?

After they traveled several miles down the coastal highway, the ride became smoother, and Judah, not able to keep his eyes open, nodded off to sleep. But each time the truck hit a pothole or drove over a branch, he awakened with a start, grimacing at his leg burning like it was on fire. Then his thoughts roiled with snippets of Paisley's confession and his fists clenched. He imagined himself planting them in the driver's face—the opposite of offering grace, he knew. And not only was he dealing with his anger toward Craig, he was furious at Dad also.

And yet, what if Dad hadn't intervened that night? The story could have ended far worse. Had God sent him there to protect Paisley? It was hard for Judah to imagine his father listening to any heavenly direction. He groaned, not caring if Craig heard.

"Hurting?" Craig glanced his way.

"Hmm." He didn't trust himself to say more than that.

"Want me to call your parents?"

"Why?" Judah felt instantly defensive. "Since when are you chummy with my parents?"

Craig's mouth dropped open, he squinted at Judah, then faced the front windshield again. "I wouldn't say 'chummy.'"

"Enemies, perhaps?" Judah muttered under his breath.

The truck nearly leaped over a tree limb. Judah grabbed hold of the door bar to steady himself.

"Your folks are probably worried with your staying in Basalt Bay during a hurricane, that's all." Craig made a "tsk" sound. "I still say it was a stupid move."

Judah didn't have to explain anything outside of work to him. When the vehicle swayed again, he moaned. "Can't you drive straighter?"

Craig smirked. "There's your fighting spirit."

"Oh, I've got plenty of fight left." Judah glared at Craig. He didn't have any reason to show respect to the other man, now that he knew he didn't deserve admiration. However, he was failing at the attitude of grace he was striving for.

"What's gotten into you?" Craig's eyebrow quirked. "Delirious with pain, or something?"

Judah gnawed on the inside of his cheek, irritation knotting up in his chest until he couldn't remain quiet another second. "If I am delirious, it's with rage," he spit out. "Truth is, I'm furious over something I heard—about you." Forgiveness would have to come later. Right now, standing up for his wife burned in his gut like a wildfire.

"What did I do?" Craig shrugged and acted guiltless.

"As if you don't know." Judah clenched his fists.

Craig coughed. "If Paisley told you some garbage about me, don't believe a word, man. We've been pals for too long."

So, he automatically assumed it was Paisley who told him? *Guilty!*

"Pals?" Judah almost yelled. "Were you my 'pal' when you kissed my wife? When you tried forcing her to do something she didn't want to do?"

"Is that what she told you?" Craig smacked the steering wheel with his right palm. "Look, she's been gone all this time, and now she comes back, spouting half-packed bologna? Get real, man. Would I kiss your woman?"

"I would never have thought it of you." Judah glared at him again, looking for culpability.

"See there."

"So, you deny making an advance on her?" Even if he denied it, Judah wouldn't believe him.

"Advance? C'mon. You're out of your mind, Grant." Craig turned on the blinkers for his approach to Peace Harbor Medical Center in Florence. The parking lot was already packed with vehicles. "Since I've never been alone with her, how could I have kissed her?"

Something didn't add up. Pain and lack of sleep might be making Judah's thinking fuzzy, but Paisley wouldn't concoct that kind of story. Last night she cried when she explained Craig's aggressive actions toward her. She was broken up about it, even after all this time. Was Craig bald-faced lying to cover his tracks? Or, since he'd been intoxicated, was it possible he didn't remember what happened?

When the truck came to a stop, Judah opened the door and slid out before his coworker ran around the vehicle. He winced at the ripping sensation in his calf, but he kept limping forward, aggravation churning in him. At the front of the truck, he pointed his index finger at Craig. "Look, Paisley is my wife, and I believe what she told me. Stay away from her. You hear me?"

"Yeah, sure. Of course." Craig shrugged again, like it was a nonissue.

Judah gritted his teeth, doubting he could work with this guy again. Unless he forgave him. But that might take time, especially if Craig continued denying the offense.

As he moved toward the ER entrance, an idea came to mind. "All I have to do is call my dad."

"About what?"

"About that night." Judah held out his palm to stop Craig. "He was there. He can tell me what he saw."

"Ask him then." A tic twitched in his supervisor's jaw. Maybe he was more nervous about Mayor Grant becoming involved than he let on.

Judah wasn't going to get into a scuffle in the hospital parking lot, and besides, he still needed Craig to drive him back to Paisley. So, this matter would have to be tabled. He switched topics, but he couldn't turn off his annoyance with Craig as easily. "Why did you say I might lose my job?"

"Positions are in jeopardy over the system malfunction." Craig scowled. "Mike Linfield wants to blame someone."

"I didn't have anything to do with the alarm." That wasn't part of his job description.

"No?" One of Craig's bushy black eyebrows rose.

"No."

"The mayor pushed for the upgrade, didn't he?" Craig rubbed his hands like he was cold, or else plotting something. "Even the town helped back the investment."

"So?"

"So"—Craig snorted—"didn't you discuss the new technology with Daddy?"

Judah could almost smell the blame being thrown at him. "Years ago, maybe." He and his dad hadn't been on friendly terms in seven years.

"Mike wants a scapegoat. So will the mayor." Craig nodded his head toward Judah as if the answer were obvious.

He was tempted to knock the sneer off Craig's face, even though they were standing in the hospital parking lot. "It's not going to be me, I can tell you that." Wanting to put distance between them, Judah resumed his limp toward the entrance where others were already lined up outside the ER. Two offenses were piled up like a broken levee against his previous friend—how he treated Paisley and his lies. What Judah did about them remained to be seen.

"You could make a deal." Craig caught up to him. "Get the mayor to pull some strings." He swayed his thumb back and forth. "For both of us."

"You've got to be kidding." A sinking feeling twisted in Judah's gut. "What do you have to do with my dad?"

"Nothing," Craig said quickly. "You're implicated because of his involvement."

"And you."

Craig scoffed. "No idea what you're talking about."

Your dad came around the corner. Saw us. Craig and me. By then, I was fighting and scratching and kicking mad. Paisley's description of that night pulsed through Judah's thoughts.

He was going to speak to Dad, all right. Then he'd find Craig and tell him just what he thought of him—even if it got him fired.

But first he needed stitches. And a ride back to Basalt Bay.

Twenty-seven

For the last four hours, Paisley had been working outside, sloshing through shin-deep water, gathering and stacking tree limbs, broken boards, and shingles into a huge pile in the front yard. She collected sopping wet garbage and more boards from the backyard too. Her most difficult task was making herself follow Judah's instructions to stay out of the house. Once, she ignored his warning and climbed over the apple tree and went through the front window to get inside so she could unlock and open the door. Thirty seconds, that's all—long enough to be saddened by the standing water covering the floors of the home she grew up in. What a cleaning job this was going to be.

If Judah didn't return soon, she wouldn't have a choice about going inside. She had to find somewhere to dry off and get warm. She'd already been working in the cold, wet conditions for too long. What if he didn't make it back before nightfall? She shivered at the thought of staying in the swamped, dark house alone. It was weird enough working outside in silence without seeing anyone else in the neighborhood. A ghost town, for sure.

Fortunately, there was fresh drinking water—for now. Thanks to the spigot on the side of the house still working, and after making sure the liquid ran clear, she guzzled enough to satisfy her several times. But she was ravenously hungry. Another reason to go inside.

Was anyone else left in Basalt? Front Street was flooded. She could wade a few blocks, shouting out greetings to see if anyone answered. However, Judah warned her to stay away from downed power lines. To get around safely, she needed a rowboat, which Dad didn't have.

Judah's phone buzzed in her back pocket. She yanked it out, her cold fingers fumbling with the screen. "Hello?" She hadn't checked caller ID.

"Who's this?" A woman's voice.

"Paisley. Who's this?"

Click.

Wait. Who was that? She climbed up on a pile of wood to get out of the water, although the large boots she found floating in the backyard earlier were filled with liquid anyway. She thumbed through the menu to recent calls. Mia's name came up last. A work-related call? Or personal? Why did she disconnect? Paisley groaned. Then pressed redial.

"Yes?" Mia's voice again.

"Why'd you hang up?" No pleasantries were needed.

"Just checking on Judah." Mia sounded defensive. "I'm calling all the workers."

And hanging up if a female answered the phone, hmm? Paisley swallowed back her spiteful assessment. "He isn't here."

"He's required to have his work phone with him at all times." Mia's bossy tone irked Paisley more than her hanging up did.

Not wanting Judah to get in trouble because he lent her his

phone, she had to explain. "There was an emergency. Craig drove Judah to the hospital. He gave me his cell."

"Oh, no. Judah's hurt?"

Mia's gushing tone grated on Paisley's nerves. Still, they were in a disaster, so the truth seemed necessary. "Yes, he was. We stayed at my dad's house last night."

"In Basalt Bay?" Mia screeched.

"Uh-huh."

"You could have been killed!"

One, two, three. "You think I don't know that?" Paisley suppressed a groan. "At least, we're alive."

"Thank God."

"Yes." *Thank You, Lord, for letting us live*—she sincerely meant that. However, two seconds of humility didn't absolve her frustration. "Was there something you wanted? I have work to do."

"You say Craig took Judah to the hospital?"

"Yeah. In Florence." Maybe she shouldn't have given her those details.

"Thanks, Pais." Mia ended the call abruptly.

Paisley groaned. She didn't allow anyone to call her "Pais" other than Judah.

Her stomach growled. She craved comfort food, especially after that phone call. Maybe a frosting-covered donut and a twenty-ounce cup of heavily creamed coffee from a barista. Impossibilities today.

To get her mind off her hunger pains, and her angst toward Mia, she returned to her work. An hour later, she had to figure out how to climb inside the kitchen safely. The large spruce still leaned against the roof. Hopefully, it wouldn't cave in the structure any more. Peering around the watery backyard, she spotted a lawn chair that might work to support her while she peeked in the kitchen window.

She waded through the flooded yard and grabbed the patio furniture. One leg wobbled in her hand. Would it hold her weight? Near the back porch, she leaned the chair against the wall. She stepped up on the seat, then propping her right foot on the top edge, heaved herself upward. Grabbing the framework around the window, she held on and peered inside.

From this angle, she saw all the way into the living room, with the apple tree its uninvited centerpiece. The water may have gone down a little since she pried open the front door earlier. Everything that previously decorated the walls, including Mom's garish paintings, were floating in the water, some face down. She should have felt relieved. Never again would she have to stare at the distorted images and wonder what Mom had been thinking when she painted them. But for some reason, she didn't feel relief. A deep sadness filled her chest. Maybe because they were Mom's, and she was gone, and Paisley didn't have any chance of making amends with her now.

Sigh.

She made herself refocus on the scene before her. The couch cushion on the kitchen table was evidence of how high the water had been or how strong the winds blew through the open window. The chairs by the table were knocked over, and whatever kitchen-ware had rested on the countertop was gone, swept away by the watery intruder.

The frame around the back door, beneath the bathroom she slept in, was crushed. She wouldn't be able to open that door. When the stairs fell, they apparently exploded. Broken wood was piled up in front of the back door and the washer and dryer like a beaver made a dam there. Maybe she could break out the kitchen window and climb in. Judah's warning to not go inside rang through her mind. But he wasn't here and might not make it back until tomorrow. Terrible thought.

The phone buzzed. Judah? She leaned back to retrieve the device from her pocket, and the chair wobbled precariously. Then she was falling backwards, gasping as she landed with a splash. Water cascaded over her head and shoulders, but somehow, she managed to keep the phone extended in the air.

She stood quickly, dripping as if she'd been swimming in the ocean. She tapped the screen. "Hello."

"Paisley?"

Hearing his voice, she almost cried. She took a breath. "Hey, Judah."

"You okay?"

"Mmhmm. You?" She shivered, clenching her teeth to keep them from chattering. She had to find dry clothes soon.

"I'm all s-stitched up." He sounded groggy. "P-pain meds m-made me a l-little woozy."

"I can imagine. Glad you're feeling better." She rubbed a sore place on her hip from the fall. "How soon can Craig drive you back?"

A gulp, then silence. "Thing is, he, uh, left."

"What?"

"He isn't answering his phone. I don't know w-what to d-do. Or how to get b-back to you." He groaned, and she wondered about his slurred speech. "Everything's k-kind of f-fuzzy right now. I'm sitting in the hospital l-lobby, using the public phone." He laughed oddly.

Did that mean he wouldn't be coming back tonight? Even though he had a genuine medical emergency, the thought of her solitary evening ahead, in the dark, incited instant fear in her. "Did you, um, talk with Craig about what I told you?" Was that why he abandoned Judah?

"Maybe. Can't r-remember." He cleared his throat. "I'll find s-someone who can drive m-me back."

He probably meant that, but he was in pain and dependent on others. Not many would chance driving in such flooded conditions. Florence was on the coast, too, and had probably been hit as badly as Basalt. Travel between the two towns would be almost impossible. Maybe she should have endured Craig's presence long enough to ride to the hospital with Judah. At least, then, they would be together. She wouldn't be here alone.

Too late for second thoughts.

"I'm going to break into the kitchen to get some food." She might as well confess her plan to him since he'd hear about it later. Besides, he wouldn't expect her to sleep outside.

He made a disgruntled sound. "I didn't want you going in the house by yourself. I remember that."

"I know, but I have to sleep somewhere." Without electricity. With gaping windows and howling winds rushing through the house.

"I'll g-get to you some—" Then, deep, nasally breathing. Did he just fall asleep?

"Judah?"

"Oh, what?" He snorted. Yawned loudly.

"Are you okay?"

"Uh, yeah, sure. D-drowsy. C-can't—"

"Judah! There you are." A feminine voice in the background sounded familiar. "I've looked everywhere for you."

"Mia?" Judah sounded surprised.

Mia was at the hospital? *Oh, no.*

"I'm so glad you're here and alive." Her tone was all sugar and honey.

A muffled sound like Judah's hand shuffling over the hospital phone reached Paisley. Or else Mia hugged him.

That wasn't an image Paisley wanted in her thoughts.

"Mia's here," he explained as if she didn't hear the woman's voice. "I think I've found my ride back to Basalt Bay." He suddenly sounded stronger. Why was that?

"I don't think that's such a good idea." What kind of car did Mia own? Was it high enough off the ground to drive through flooded waters? Paisley bit her lip and shook her head to keep back what she wanted to say—*stay away from Mia*. Instead, she whispered, "Be safe, Judah."

"I will." He let out a soft breath. "Pais?"

"Yeah?" She wished he were here now, linking pinkies, saying he loved her. Instead, she felt like she was the only person left on the planet.

"I'll be w-with you s-soon." His garbled words were barely understandable.

"Judah, come with me. You need rest. Let me help you." Mia's wooing tone was the last thing Paisley heard before the connection ended.

Judah didn't even say goodbye.

Paisley stared at the cell phone, feeling abandoned. All too aware of her soaking wet, miserable condition.

So Mia was saving the day for Judah? How did the town flirt plan to help him find rest? And what about Craig? Had he and Judah exchanged words?

Paisley gazed around her dad's property that looked more like a shallow lake in the waning afternoon light than the yard she and her brother and sister used to play in. Dark gray clouds overhead appeared ominous. Another storm? That's all she needed.

She trembled, dreading the night ahead, and wished for morning to come quickly.

Twenty-eight

Instead of climbing in the kitchen window, Paisley waded around to the front of the house. She pulled herself up to the porch, using Judah's truck for leverage. Once she was inside the living room, every creak and crackle of the ceiling above made her skittish as she treaded through six inches of water on her way to the kitchen. Feeling numb and barely aware of the chilly wetness on her skin, she yanked open cupboards, ready to eat anything in sight. She nearly burst into tears of joy when she discovered peanut butter, strawberry jam, and bread that wasn't stale.

She grabbed a knife out of the drawer where they always stored silverware and made two sandwiches. She tried opening the refrigerator, but it wouldn't budge. Too much water remained in front.

She took her sandwiches out to the porch and dropped onto the rocker Aunt Callie sat in the other day. She propped her boots on the railing, and water poured out from them. While working, she adjusted to being wet and miserable, but with night coming, cooler temperatures were settling in and chills raced through her body. She needed a hot bath. Or an electric blanket. Dry clothes and a warm bed would do. But all the clothes were upstairs. And where would she sleep? The second story was off limits. Everything in the living room was drenched.

As she gobbled up her first sandwich, the one room in the house she hadn't looked in yet came to mind. The pantry. The dark, dreadful place. She remembered its long shelves where she might be able to climb up and get out of the water. No, she wouldn't sleep in there. Even if she was exhausted and in need of warmth.

What would she use for a light after dusk? She had Judah's cell phone, but the battery power was nearly gone. She needed to get settled before nightfall.

I can't sleep in the pantry.

She rocked back and forth in the rocker, water splashing with each movement, munching her food. Maybe she'd grab a blanket and sleep right here.

The unexpected rumble of a loud engine made her jump to her feet. She swallowed down the last chunk of peanut butter bread as a black truck barreled around a downed tree in the road and then skidded, plowing through water in the yard and shooting a ten-foot spray over the porch. Cold water hit Paisley, and she cried out.

Whoever was driving so recklessly needed to learn some manners. She didn't recognize the mud-speckled truck with its darkened glass. It looked like a high-end model. The window lowered slowly. She stared inside, curious to see if someone brought Judah back. As soon as she recognized the driver, panic as powerful as the wave that hit Basalt assailed her.

"Get in." Edward Grant rocked his thumb toward the other door.

Did the mayor think she'd go anywhere with him on

command? She stepped backwards, but her oversized boot caught on an uneven floorboard and she tripped, nearly falling into the water on the porch. What a sight that would have made in front of her overbearing father-in-law. "Why should I go with you?" She made herself stand still, her chin up. She had her pride.

Edward smirked. "If it were up to me, I'd leave you here." He messed with his phone like he was checking for texts.

"I'm fine here, anyway." Would she honestly prefer to stay in a dank, cold, and lightless house—even in the pantry—over going with Edward and spending the night in her in-law's luxurious mansion on the cliff? If that meant riding in the same vehicle and staying in the same house with the coldhearted man who paid her to leave Judah, then yes, a million times over.

He stared at her wet clothing. "Uh-huh. I see how fine you are." His eyes glinted, but he didn't make the slightest move to get out of his truck. Probably didn't want his expensive shoes getting wet. "Well, I don't want all that water and mud on my truck seat."

"No worries, then, since I'm not going with you." She lifted her hand in mock civility. "Thanks for checking on me." In all her thoughts about making amends, Judah's dad never crossed her mind as a recipient. Today wouldn't be an exception. Still, she asked, "How did you know I was here?"

He chewed on something black, maybe licorice, before answering. "Judah called. Asked his mom for someone to retrieve you. I drew the short straw."

So Judah was still looking out for her. "Is he okay?"

Edward's eyebrows lifted. "Like you care."

"I do, believe it or not. Where is he?" Concern for Judah's well-being was the only thing that made her risk asking Edward anything. The night Mayor Grant chased off Craig, the repulsive things he said to her, and her exodus from town raced through her thoughts now. No, she wouldn't get in his truck, even if he were her last good option.

"He's injured, but you know that." He bit off a chunk of black licorice—she was right about that—and chewed before continuing. "Overnighting in Florence with that sweet tart, what's her name? Mia Till." His eyes glistened like he enjoyed delivering the news.

Her heart hardened a notch.

"Get in, or I'm leaving without you." His voice turned gruff. "Bess wants you up at the house, so I'll bring you there. Once you've cleaned up, I'll drive you to the airport. Anywhere you want to go, I'll pay. As long as it's far away from my son."

Those were about the vilest words he could say to her—other than what he told her three years ago about her unborn child knowing she wouldn't be a good mother. Her gut clenched. She forced herself to turn her back to him and walk through the front door. Then, out of spite, or maybe because she was determined to stick to her guns and make amends with Judah, she leaned against the doorframe as if she didn't have a care in the world. "No, thanks, Eddie"—she knew he hated that nickname. "I think I'll stay. Basalt Bay is my home."

Edward made a guttural sound, spit a wad of chewed black candy in her direction, then gunned the truck. A wave of water and brown muck splattered her, covering the places that weren't already wet and muddy. She flicked grit off her face.

In the lonely silence, a question gnawed at her insides. Was Judah really staying with Mia?

Twenty-nine

Judah sat on the cot he was assigned to at the emergency shelter in Florence, his knees supporting his elbows, and his fists propping his pounding forehead. Over one hundred fifty cots were arranged around the high school gym, and the rumble of voices was nonstop. He needed quiet and a good night's sleep. He doubted he'd get either. At least the strong pain meds the nurse gave him were wearing off. He seemed to be thinking clearer now. And he was thankful for the large-sized jeans that fit loosely over his injured leg a volunteer distributing emergency clothing had given him.

He recognized quite a few people from Basalt Bay here. For most, it was their second night away from home. Judah was fortunate to find an empty bed at all. Although, Mia's proximity concerned him. She sat on the cot next to him wearing a pouty expression. The couple who slept in their spots last night found a room in a motel in Eugene, otherwise this shelter wouldn't have beds for Judah and Mia.

"I don't see why we came to this sardine-packed hostel."

She groaned like it was the worst place in the county. Apparently, thankfulness wasn't in her mindset. "Why didn't we check into a hotel?"

"They're all full, you know that." Besides, he would never have gone to one with her. He glanced around the populated room. In one corner kids were playing games. Adults sat on cots looking fatigued and discouraged—probably due to the update they received that they couldn't return to their homes yet, and might not be able to for a week. Bad news indeed. "I'm thankful for a place to sleep." Although he wished Mia had a bed on the opposite side of the room. Her whiny, demanding attitude was grating on his nerves. One thing kept his irritation manageable— she had a cell phone.

"Could I use your cell again?"

She didn't meet his gaze. "I don't know. I have to conserve battery power."

"It'll be a quick call. I need to check on Paisley." He extended his palm, hoping she'd set her phone on it.

"You sent the mayor after her." She huffed. "You've done your ex-husbandly duty."

He subdued his spike in irritation and clasped his hands together. "I'm not her *ex*-husband."

"Yet." She rolled her eyes. "Why you keep chasing a woman who doesn't want you when there are so many waiting for you to pull the marital plug, I have no idea." She plunged her hand into her bag, then pulled out a tube of lipstick and spread a thick red film over her lips.

He bit his tongue to hold back a rude response, then settled on an honest one. "She's my wife and the fact that I love her are reasons enough."

Mia's fingers clutching the tube of gloss came to a standstill. She met his gaze with a look of absurdity. "After all she's done to you?"

"For better or for worse." He held out his hand toward her again. "May I use your cell, or should I go ask one of my more compassionate neighbors?"

"Fine. Make it fast." Glaring, she tossed him her zebra-striped phone.

He caught it, then punched in his phone number. He turned away from Mia's gaze.

"Hello," Paisley answered.

"Hey." He closed his eyes, trying to shut out the noisy gym, and savoring the sound of her voice. "You okay?"

"Yeah." She spoke quietly. Was the connection bad?

"Did my dad find you?"

"He did." She sniffed.

Then silence.

Oh, man. What did Dad say to her? "Did he, um, explain that I can't get back tonight?"

"Uh-huh."

Her cryptic responses let him know something was wrong. "I'm sorry I can't make it back. The road's busted up and washed out. Craig had a terrible time getting through to take me to the hospital." His excuses sounded lame. Craig should have brought him back to Basalt Bay. Instead, he left without even telling Judah. "I'm sorry for sending my dad. I know you probably didn't want to go to his house, but I'm staying overnight at a storm shelter in Florence and can't get to you. I wanted you to be somewhere safe." She still hadn't said anything about going to his parents' place. Was she mad at him for calling Dad? Were things weird at their house? He imagined Dad asking Paisley all kinds of embarrassing questions, although Judah begged him to be polite. "My mom loves you. You know that, right?"

Still, silence.

"She'd do anything for you." He swallowed hard. "Maybe you can stay in one of the rooms in the loft, farther away from Dad. Just until morning, okay?"

A sigh, then, "I didn't go with him."

"What?" That may have come out harsher than he meant, but what she said shocked him. "Paisley, why not? What happened?"

Mia leaned in. "What's wrong?"

He shook his head at her, wishing she hadn't said anything. If Paisley heard her, she might jump to the wrong conclusion.

"I couldn't, that's all." Her breath came in a huff. "Was that Mia Till? Your dad said you were staying with her."

A sharp pain seared up his chest like a bad case of heartburn. "I never told my dad that." How did his father find out he was with Mia? He glanced at the C-MER receptionist. Did she call his dad?

Paisley cleared her throat. "So that wasn't Mia, then?"

"No, it was. But—"

"I've got to go." She sounded frustrated. "I have to find somewhere dry to sleep. Everything's wet. The water went down a couple of inches, but not much."

"Wait, Paisley, don't hang up." He stood and winced as pain splintered up his leg. "Craig left, and I couldn't find someone else to drive me back. The underside of Mia's car sits too low." He hated to tell her the next part, especially now that she was staying at her dad's alone. "Word is the National Guard is at both the South Road and North Road junctions, keeping residents from reentering Basalt Bay." He heard her gulp. "They're telling us those roads have to be fixed for public safety before they allow anyone to return. I'm so sorry you're there by yourself."

"Me too."

A lump filled his throat. "Are you inside the house now?"

"It's almost dark out, so I came in." She drew in a raspy-sounding breath. "No lights."

He felt helpless, and so far away from her. "I'm sorry I left you."

"Don't be. This isn't your fault." She paused. Sighed. "Your leg was in a bad way. You had to go."

Her words made him feel a little better.

"Are you in less pain now?"

"I am." He wished he was with her. "Please, be careful tonight."

She made a sound like she was shoving something. "Wish I could get this tree out, then I'd cover up the window."

He groaned. "I'm going to find a way to come to you tomorrow, even if I have to walk in. I promise." He didn't know how he'd get there—gimpy and limping, most likely—but he would find a way.

"The battery, Judah." Mia waved her hand in front of his face, making it hard to ignore her. "You think this is a fast phone call?"

"Wait a sec, is she sleeping next to you?" Paisley's tone turned sharp.

He wouldn't lie, even to ease her worry or his discomfort. "Yeah, that's how it worked out. I'm sorry. We didn't have any choice."

"I think there's always a choice. I—" Paisley exhaled. "Look, Judah, no judgment, okay? Just, um, sleep well."

"You too." He couldn't let their conversation end in frustration or suspicion. "Pais?"

"Yeah?"

He wished he were holding her safely in his arms, kissing away her worries, and staying close enough to comfort her through any panic attacks she might have. Instead, he was twenty miles away from her in an overcrowded gym, sitting on a cot next to Mia. "I'm praying for you."

"Thanks."

As soon as the call ended, Mia snatched the phone from his hand. She stared hard at the screen. "Battery's shot. Thanks a lot." She threw the device into her bag.

He never knew her to be so crabby and self-centered before. "Sorry." It seemed he was saying that a lot. He laid down on the cot and flung his arm over his eyes. If only he could shut out the noise in the gym as easily—and the haunting image of Paisley spending the night alone in a flooded house without electricity.

He should be with her. But what else could he have done? The medical team said his cut was infected. That it was a good thing he came in when he did. Twenty stitches proved his need for medical intervention. Still, he felt responsible for Paisley being on her own in Basalt Bay. He should have insisted she come with him. He thought of his grandfather hefting his grandmother over his shoulder. Maybe Judah should have tried that. He released a long sigh.

Mia laid down on her cot, less aggressively, it seemed. "It'll be okay, Judah." Her fingers brushed the bare part of his wrist.

He jerked his arm out of her reach, sat up. Paisley's words replayed in his mind. *Always a choice.* Even now, he had a choice to do the honorable thing. He stood on his bum leg, then snatched up the coat the volunteer gave him earlier.

"What are you doing?" Mia clasped his wrist.

He peeled her fingers from his skin, none too gently. "I'm going to find somewhere to sleep on the other side of the room."

"Why?" She made a flirty face. "Oh. Are you worried about us being so close?" She ran her index finger along the blanket on the cot he deserted.

"Not in the least."

She crossed her arms. "Then what?"

"I'm concerned with what my wife, the woman I love and want to spend the rest of my life with, might think of this arrangement, nothing more." He pushed his arms into the coat.

She harrumphed. "I don't see what the big deal is."

"Obviously, you don't." He walked away without a backward glance. Even if he sat on the floor all night, this was his decision. He'd spend the time praying for Paisley's health and safety, and for their reconciliation.

In the morning, he was going to find a way back to Basalt Bay and his wife, no matter what the officials guarding the road had to say about his plan.

Thirty

The apple tree wouldn't budge, so Paisley gave up trying to move it. The blanket she used to partially cover the window last night was sopping wet, which meant she couldn't secure the opening, either. One more night would pass with cold air filling the house. Fortunately, another storm didn't hit.

Earlier, she corralled wooden chunks from the collapsed stairs leading to the second story into a pile in front of the dryer. Broken boards, nails, handrails, and other debris still littered the kitchen and laundry area, but it had gotten too dark to continue working. By ten p.m., a little more floodwater drained from the house—something to be thankful for.

Throughout the evening, she used Judah's cell phone for light as needed, but its weak luminosity meant battery power was fading fast.

She'd put off the inevitable long enough. She had to find somewhere to sleep, or at least, to wait out the night. Everything in the living room was soaked, including the couch. Stretching out on the kitchen counter was a possibility, if she cleaned it first, except the wind blowing through the front window all night would be freaky. Even wild creatures could come in. She shivered and went in search of bedding.

In the cupboard above the washing machine, she found a twin-sized comforter and a beach towel. Then grumbling at her predicament, and the fact her arrival at Basalt Bay coincided so closely with hurricane winds, she trudged through the kitchen. At the closed pantry door, she stood there for about two minutes, staring through the darkness at the closet-sized entrance. She gulped and tugged on the knob. Now or never.

She stepped inside the narrow room and tapped the cell phone light—it flickered. The air that hit her smelled stagnant and musty, and not just because of the few inches of water on the floor. The small space seemed unused, and mostly empty. Hadn't Dad stored anything in this room since Mom died?

A harrowing picture of herself as a kid, huddled on the floor, skinny arms around knobby knees, waiting for her sentencing of an hour to think over her mistakes to end, pulsed through her thoughts. A couple of times, an hour turned into two because Mom forgot about her. Once when that happened, Paisley hurled two soup cans through the window, making enough space for her to squeeze through. Mom had been livid. After that, the escape route was boarded up, the way it appeared now. A shudder overtook her. How could she sleep in here?

Judah said he was praying for her. Did he sense she needed peace tonight?

The light flickered again. She aimed the dwindling glow on the three skinny shelves that resembled a miniature bunk bed. She pointed it at the wet floors. No moving creatures. A few boxes rested on the lower shelf, probably Mom's unfinished paintings. Mason jars and old canning equipment lined the upper shelf. The middle ledge appeared the most feasible for a makeshift bed.

I can do this. I'm an adult now.

Then why did she feel every insecurity she ever experienced rushing through her like a time bomb ready to implode? Her heart throbbed hard in her chest. Her arms shook.

The cell light shut off. Instant darkness engulfed her. She clenched her jaw and grabbed hold of the shelf in front of her. She counted to ten. Then taking a deep breath, she visualized the ocean, *her ocean*, the way she loved it when she sat on the peninsula and let sea-foam arc over her head. In her mind's eye, she felt the spray cascading over her hair and caressing her cheeks. Then she thought of Judah's blue eyes staring into hers so sweetly—and that moment last night when their lips touched, and he held her close. She'd never forget how bonded she felt with him through the storm.

She inhaled and exhaled. Panic averted.

Sigh.

At least this room had a door that closed and would keep the wind out, unlike sleeping on the kitchen counter or on the washer and dryer. The shelves were dry. She ran her hand over the middle board to get rid of any dust or dead spiders, even though she couldn't see what she was doing. She spread out the towel and blanket, her faux sheet and comforter, going through the motions of preparing for bed even though she doubted she could sleep.

Her clothes had to come off to dry. She hung Dad's sweatpants and socks on some wall pegs. Shivering, teeth chattering, she climbed up and huddled under the blanket in the dark, wishing for the warmth of a sleeping bag or two thick quilts. The shelf moaned but held.

She squeezed her eyes shut, blocking out shadows of yesterdays. She'd lay here and wait for morning, then before long, Judah would be here. No thinking of Mom's unfinished art pieces stored in this room. No contemplating the half-painted purple irises of a blurry child resembling Paige. Or the brightly-colored round face that might have been a portrait of Aunt Callie. Or the one Mom said was of Paisley falling off the rocks and into the ocean—was that her greatest fear? Although, Paisley had never recognized herself in the distorted paint-splotched canvas.

The house's creaking intensified. Every noise caused by the wind coming in the windows made her shrink into herself, her arms clutched about her ribs. Even though she couldn't see the board above her, it felt too close. Her whole body curled into a fetal position shook with cold. And fear.

She hated the pitch dark. Even when she and Judah were married, she kept a night-light on in the hallway. Something about blackest darkness made the air seem unbreathable. Poisonous.

Ohhh.

In her tiny Chicago apartment, where the panic attacks started, did she feel stifled and trapped? Unable to breathe in enough air?

Something crashed upstairs.

Paisley sat up, bumping her head on the upper shelf. She groaned. Something probably fell over, that's all. Even if a wild animal came inside, the pantry door was closed. Nothing could reach her. She blew out a breath and laid back down, listening, on edge.

If Judah were here beside her, his arm around her shoulders, she wouldn't be afraid. What a kindhearted man he'd become. Or was he always like that and she just didn't notice? No, something was different. Perhaps, his relationship with God? Judah mentioned Him more, as if he relied on Him in ways he hadn't before. She appreciated his promise to be praying for her.

She replayed their kiss in her mind again. Passion was obviously still there between them. What about marriage and commitment? Did she want to be married to him?

Last night, when she was locked in the bathroom, their fingers touching beneath the door, she imagined a life with them starting over as a married couple. Of course, that was before Edward taunted her with the news Judah was spending the night next to Mia.

She groaned, then stared into the dark at what she knew to be the solid shelf above her. Another time, she hid here when the three siblings were playing a game of hide-and-seek. Paige opened the door, took a quick look inside, then yelled that Paisley wasn't in the pantry. Afterward, Paisley gloated at having tricked her sister so easily. She won the game because Paige was too afraid to hunt for her in the creepy room—yet she'd never been locked inside. Unless she had, and Paisley never knew. *Oh.* She closed her eyes, pondering that.

Then she thought of their cottage. Had the storm destroyed the beach house they loved from the moment they saw it? She remembered how much she'd looked forward to bringing Misty Gale home. *Sweet baby, I miss you so much.* Tears filled her eyes. And her heart—was that possible? Yet her breathing didn't turn raspy. She actually thought of her daughter, even about missing her, without having an attack.

Thank God. Was the Lord healing her? Was He, perhaps, with her now in the scariest place of all? Last night, with Judah's and her pinkies touching, it seemed a layer of callousness broke free from her heart. And today she felt more alive. Not whole. But better.

She breathed in and out, relaxing. Maybe she could fall asleep, after all.

An engine roared to a stop outside.

Paisley sat up fast and slammed her head into the shelf again. She moaned, then froze. Who would be here after ten o'clock at night? Who was in Basalt besides her?

Looters? Edward again?

She tried to listen over the thundering of her heart.

The engine motor revved a few times. A warning?

The phone buzzed next to her. She silenced it. "Hello," she whispered. What if whoever was outside was calling her?

"Pais?"

"Judah." His name came out in a rush.

"I had to call you one more time." He spoke fast. "James Weston let me use his cell phone."

James was Dad's neighbor across the street, but she was only half listening. The rest of her was cued in to the sound of the truck shutting off outside. Then the silence.

"Pais, I wanted you to know, I moved to the opposite side of the gym, away from Mia."

"O-kay." She spoke softly, not wanting whoever was out there to hear her.

"I'll find a way to get to you as soon as—"

"Someone's here." She cut into his words.

"What? Who?"

"I . . . don't . . . know," she whispered.

A clatter at the front of the house jarred her insides. Fear prickled up her skin. She held her breath.

"Someone's there? Outside?" His voice rose.

"Yes." She had to get back into her wet clothes. She climbed down from the shelf.

"Do you have a stick or a tool to use if you have to?"

"For a weapon?"

"Yes."

If she could hurl Mason jars like mud balls, she'd be fine. "I have to go." How could she hit anyone with a glass jar? What if it was a National Guardsman? Or a FEMA worker? But why would they come so late?

"Paisley, wait. I'm praying for you." His caring words spoke to a need deep inside her.

"You're a wonderful man." Static came over the connection. The battery had to be nearly dead. "I'm sorry for hurting you."

When his voice came back talking about something else, she didn't think he heard her apology. "You should pray too, Pais. Trust God to keep you safe. He's with you. I'm going to keep praying and believing until the second you call me back."

She almost tapped the end button. His voice stopped her.

"I love you."

Then silence. The connection was lost.

She set the cell phone down on the shelf, then grabbed the soaked pants and forced her feet into the legs, struggling to put on the cold, wet fabric. She shoved her icy toes into the big boots. Forget socks.

As silently as possible, she crept to the door and opened it an inch. From previous experiences, she knew how to pull up on the handle so it wouldn't squeak.

A light that had to be coming from a flashlight splashed around the kitchen walls. Someone *was* looking for her.

Her heart pounded frantically. *Lord, help me. Protect me.* She didn't like desperate prayers, but she said the words internally anyway.

She closed the door, then returned to the shelf and picked up the phone. She shook it hard, hoping to coax the flashlight on even for a second. She pointed the faint glow toward the boxes, then she dug through them quietly, searching for something solid.

One box contained old broken picture frames. She grabbed two skinny boards. They wouldn't do any real damage, but she could hold them up and make a fierce expression, like she might be aggressive.

What if the other person had a weapon?

The cell light shut off.

God, please protect me. Stop whoever this is from doing harm. In the darkness, she thought of the way she shunned Him for the last several years. *I'm sorry for being angry at You and holding a grudge.*

She opened the door again and peered out with one eye.

"Paisley?" A deep male voice she recognized turned the blood in her veins to ice.

She shut the door and pressed her back against it. She needed more than a couple of chunks of wood to protect herself. Maybe she should get on her knees and beg God for mercy. No time. Instead, she opted for the words in her heart. *I know You've taken good care of my baby, Misty Gale. I've heard You're a good Father. Please rescue me. I would like the chance to make peace with my family.*

Heavy footsteps thudded through the house. "Paisley?" His gruff voice drew closer.

She didn't move. What if the cell worked and Judah called, giving away her hiding place?

A splash of light illuminated the watery space near her boots. She held her breath, her heart throbbing in her throat. She clutched the sticks. The Mason jars were within reach.

Instead of opening the pantry door, as she anticipated he might do, the man trudged toward the other side of the house. Did he think this room was a closet she couldn't fit into? An easy mistake, considering the narrow door. Or did God, somehow, make the handle invisible? She'd heard of miracles like that, although she never experienced one. With bated breath, she listened to the man's footfall as he scrounged through the lower floor, calling her name.

She had to act quickly. She tapped the cell phone screen. The slight flicker of light let her know she didn't have a chance of placing a call. She'd send a text.

She wanted Judah to know two things. Her fingers flew over the alphabet keypad.

I love you too.

She wished she could see his face when he read those words. Hadn't she been in love with him since the day he gazed into her eyes and called her beautiful over seven years ago?

She took a deep breath, trying to calm her frantic heartbeat. Then she tapped in words that would make her husband feel crazy since he couldn't reach her until tomorrow.

Craig's here.

Thank you for reading *Ocean of Regret*!

Ready to find out what happens next?

Sea of Rescue, Restored Part 2, is available now!

Here's a sneak preview from *Sea of Rescue*:

Ice-cold adrenaline raced through Paisley Grant's veins as she leaned against the pantry door, an empty quart-sized Mason jar clutched in her right hand. She ignored her shaky breaths, her throbbing heartbeat, and the heat rising in her flushed cheeks, because her nemesis, Craig Masters, was out there, somewhere, maybe just a few feet away.

Was he waiting to hurt her? Terrorize her? She couldn't put her finger on any other motive for his late-night arrival.

Swallowing past the bitter taste in the back of her mouth threatening to choke her, she clamped her mouth shut lest she make a sound and give away her hiding place. She gripped the jar tighter, mentally and physically preparing herself to hit the intruder, if it came to that. *Please, God, don't let it come to that.* In her left hand, she held two long skinny wooden frame pieces from Mom's old busted canvases. It was an odd collection of weapons, but she'd do what she had to do to survive.

She pressed her ear against the crack of the door, listening for the next sound that might alert her to Craig's location. Was he in the kitchen? Farther away in the living room? She didn't shuffle an inch, afraid her boots might make a ripple in the standing ankle-high water left by the flood following Hurricane Blaine. How long could she stand statue-still like this without him finding her?

A shiver raced along her nerves, imploding in her brain, or so it felt, as she thought of another time when Craig caused a terrible fear to rise in her. Her hand clutching the jar shook. Her heart hammered double-time against her ribs. Lightheaded, she blew out a breath. Had she locked her knees? She flexed her leg muscles. Inhaled silently.

Why was the man who worked with her husband, Judah, at C-MER, Basalt Bay's Coastal Management and Emergency Responders, being so quiet now? Moments ago, he yelled her name over and over. White fear had spasmed up her breastbone, leaving a spark of pain in her chest. Now, waiting in the pitch dark, with nothing but silence and her wild imagination, was nearly as terrifying.

If she could figure out how to run through the flooded house and escape without him seeing her, she would. But charging through the swamped kitchen, and dashing through the living room where Mom's paintings still floated in seawater, without Craig catching her? Impossible.

She swallowed hard. Kept the jar clutched to her chest.

Even if she could elude him, what then? It was late. Dark outside. The whole town was without power. No streetlights. And thanks to overcast skies, no moonlight. The neighbors had covered their windows with sheets of plywood, and probably locked their doors, before fleeing town prior to the hurricane. She'd have a hard time breaking into any houses.

Her thoughts rushed back to Craig and how she could get away from him. He was a solid man. Muscular. A football player in his high school days. Still, she was gritty and wily. She'd kick, swing her elbows, flail at him with her Mason jar and the broken frame.

Then run like crazy!

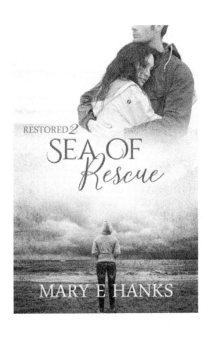

Order your copy of *Sea of Rescue* today!

About Basalt Bay

I took many creative liberties with my imaginary coastal town and its stormy weather and C-MER—and I loved doing it! To all those who live on the Oregon Coast, please forgive my embellishments. I enjoy the Pacific Ocean and the Oregon Coast so much that I wanted to create my own little world there.

For readers with a scientific inclination, if my meteorology or oceanography facts appear skewed, all I can say is, "That's the way it happened in Basalt Bay!"

If you would like to be one of the first to hear about Mary's new releases and upcoming projects, sign up for her newsletter—and receive the free pdf "Rekindle Your Romance! 50+ Date Night Ideas for Married Couples."

Check it out at …

www.maryehanks.com

A Special Thanks to all who helped make this book happen!

Paula McGrew . . . You have been such a blessing in my life. Thank you for tweaking my work, helping me dig deeper into my characters, and for cheering me on with affirming words. I hope we can meet in person someday!

Jason Hanks . . . Thanks for letting me ramble about my writing projects on our many walks. And thanks for being my go-to guy about car parts and boat operations. Love you forever!

Suzanne Williams . . . I love your cover designs! Thank you for another beautiful one. Your talent is a gifting, and I love the emotion and beauty in your artwork.

Michelle Storm, Mary Acuff, Kellie Wanke, Melissa Hammerstrom, and Jason Hanks . . . Thank you for being wonderful beta readers. Every story needs a testing audience, and I thank you so much for being willing to weather the storms in Basalt Bay with me. Thanks for your critique and your encouragement. I appreciate you all!

Daniel, Philip, Deborah, Shem, Traci, and the special people in their lives who smile and act interested when I *just have* to show them my latest cover before anyone else has seen it. Thanks for the cheers. I love you guys.

Papa God . . . I'm so thankful for the chance to write a story of redemption and reconciliation again. Thank *You* for putting these stories in my heart.

Books by Mary Hanks

Restored Series

Ocean of Regret

Sea of Rescue

Bay of Refuge

Tide of Resolve

Waves of Reason

Port of Return

Sound of Rejoicing

Shores of Resilience (June '22)

Second Chance Series

Winter's Past

April's Storm

Summer's Dream

Autumn's Break

Season's Flame

Marriage Encouragement

Thoughts of You (A Marriage Journal)

Mary Hanks loves stories about marriage restoration. She believes there's something inspiring about couples clinging to each other, working through their problems, and depending on God for a beautiful rest of their lives together—and those are the types of stories she likes to write. Mary and Jason have been married for forty-plus years, and they know firsthand what it means to get a second chance with each other, and with God. That has been her inspiration in writing the Second Chance series, and now, in the Restored series.

Besides writing, Mary likes to read, do artsy stuff, go on adventures with Jason, and meet her four adult kids for coffee.

Connect with Mary by signing up for her newsletter and "liking" her Facebook Author page:

www.maryehanks.com

www.facebook.com/MaryEHanksAuthor

Thank you for reading *Ocean of Regret*!